Natasha Farrant previously worked in publishing and now runs her own children's literary scouting agency. She grew up in the heart of the French community in London, and has therefore never considered herself as completely English, although certainly not completely French, which makes for a quite interesting view of the world. Natasha lives in west London with her husband and two children.

www.rbooks.co.uk

Also by Natasha Farrant

DIVING INTO LIGHT

and published by Black Swan

SOME OTHER EDEN

Natasha Farrant

BLACK SWAN

TRANSWORLD PUBLISHERS
61–63 Uxbridge Road, London W5 5SA
A Random House Group Company
www.rbooks.co.uk

SOME OTHER EDEN
A BLACK SWAN BOOK: 9780552774925

First publication in Great Britain
Black Swan edition published 2009

A CIP catalogue record for this book
is available from the British Library.

Addresses for Random House Group Ltd companies outside the UK
can be found at: www.randomhouse.co.uk
The Random House Group Ltd Reg. No. 954009

The Random House Group Limited supports The Forest Stewardship
Council (FSC), the leading international forest certification organisation.
All our titles that are printed on Greenpeace approved FSC certified
paper carry the FSC logo. Our paper procurement policy can be
found at www.rbooks.co.uk/environment

Typeset in 11/15pt Giovanni Book by
Kestrel Data, Exeter, Devon.
Printed in the UK by
CPI Cox & Wyman, Reading, RG1 8EX.

2 4 6 8 10 9 7 5 3 1

For Jeanne Moorsom, my grandmother,
who loves books.

And, as ever, for Steve.

Acknowledgements

A number of people have provided invaluable help in the writing of this book, but the following deserve particular thanks. Ron Haviv, for sharing his memories as a photographic reporter during the war in Bosnia. Jonathan Howe-Jones and Neil and Tracy Brooks for their vivid descriptions of their tours of duty during the same conflict. Robin Pearce, indefatigable local historian, for his valuable insights into Dorset during the Second World War (with special apologies for the liberties I have taken with the facts). Thanks also to Sophie Hicks and Amy Finegan for providing me with a special haven in which to write (and to Barney for being such good company while I was there). To both my editors, Lydia Newhouse and Katie Espiner, for all their work in making this book what it is. To my agent, Laura Longrigg, for her usual impeccable advice and soothing words. And last but not least, to my wonderful husband, for his patience, enthusiasm and continuing support.

And so we beat on, boats against the current,
borne back ceaselessly into the past.
—F. Scott Fitzgerald, *The Great Gatsby*

Oh! I have slipped the surly bonds of Earth
And danced the skies on laughter-silvered wings
—John Gillespie Magee, 'High Flight'

Southern Spain, August 1995

Why? Why? Why?

There is no respite today from the children's questions. Today they waver on the line between exhaustion and exuberance, buoyed by a nervous energy which gives a febrile quality to everything they do. They have been like this ever since they boarded the plane at Gatwick, throughout the flight to Malaga and the taxi ride to the bus station, where they now wriggle fretfully in a bus which shows no sign of departing. Their fluty voices, sloughed of meaning by their mother's tiredness, merge in her mind with all the other external irritations of the day – the loud diesel thrum of the idling engine, the smells of strong tobacco and supermarket cologne, the limp cotton of her dress clinging to her sweat-slicked skin, above all the dull throbbing of the angry bruise which spreads over her cheekbone from her left eye.

Why isn't Dad with us?

Why isn't the bus moving?

Why are we here? When are we leaving? What time is it?

'Please,' snaps Isla. 'No more questions.'

And now there is a definite wobble to her seven-year-old son's chin, his tears held in abeyance only by the small brown paw of his younger sister in his hand. The beam of four reproachful eyes turns upon her, lighting the path for a fresh onslaught of guilt.

'I'm tired,' she says, excusing herself.

A commotion outside distracts their attention. The bus, it appears, is about to leave. On the station forecourt cigarettes are being crushed underfoot, final embraces are being distributed along with sandwiches, thermos flasks and last-minute advice. The revolutions of the engine change and the bus shudders as straggling passengers drop into their seats.

'How long till we get there?' asks the little girl, Beth.

'Shh,' says her brother, Marcus. 'You heard. No more questions.' He turns shyly to his mother for approval. She smiles and holds out an arm to draw him closer.

'Still a few hours,' says Isla. 'Try to sleep.'

She sits with Beth on her lap and Marcus pressed against her, leaning her forehead on the glass of the window. Her head hurts. She raises her hand to the contused skin around her eye.

'Mum?' Marcus is still awake, watching her.

'I'm OK.' She has been trying to make light of the pain for his sake. 'Please, pumpkin. Go to sleep.'

He closes his eyes obediently. A soft sigh escapes his lips a few minutes later as his small blond head flops sideways onto his sister's shoulder. A lump rises to Isla's throat. Outside, bare brown mountains melt into the rapidly advancing dusk but she does not see this. A different landscape unfurls before her mind's eye as the bus advances into the Andalusian interior, soft and green, an English idyll dotted with landmarks as familiar to her as the lithe hard bodies of her sleeping children. The encroaching shadows smooth away her bruises, the cut on her temple. Isla looks out at the darkening landscape and through the dusty glass of the bus windows a house appears. It stands above a garden flanked by rolling hills, redolent of summer roses and the sharp cries of soaring swifts. This is Marshwood. Marshwood, where it all began.

PART I

SPRING – SUMMER

England, March 1995

Marshwood. Isla's childhood home, a heavy L-shaped house built of honey-coloured stone in the middle of the nineteenth century. Six bedrooms, a large drawing-room, a breakfast room, a dining-room, two larders, three pantries, a cloakroom, a scullery and a complicated warren of semi-habitable attics and outbuildings. Two and a half acres of land clinging to a windy hillside in western Dorset beneath an ancient Roman fort, an orchard, a paddock, and kitchen and flower gardens. A place of infinite possibilities and asymmetrical rooms, sweeping views and curtained window-seats. A fine house, thought a little gloomy by some and romantic by others, perched on Pater Noster Hill a mile out of the historic village of Chapel St Mary and four miles from the nearest market town of Bambridge. Large, isolated, draughty and damp, it had an air of faded grandeur perfectly in keeping with its sole inhabitant, Isla's eighty-year-old grandmother Bella. It had also become, in the early spring of 1995 and for the first time in living memory, the object of a bungled burglary, which 200 miles away in leafy west London had led to yet another argument between Isla and her husband Richard.

Richard had come home late, his briefcase bulging with papers to read for the following morning, his body stiff from a day of unrelenting meetings. Even the sight of his massive west London Edwardian villa, entirely mortgage free since his last bonus, did little to soothe his temper. As he let himself into the hall, all he could think was that it had been a bitch of a day, that his clients were bastards, and that he wished he had never decided to become a lawyer. What he needed was a drink, a hot meal and mindless television, preferably though not necessarily delivered without question by his wife. Instead of which he had found the house in darkness and Isla huddled in bed on the telephone to her grandmother.

'I'll be down tomorrow,' she was saying. 'I'll come with the children straight from school. Will you be all right till then?'

Richard threw himself into an armchair and assumed an air of long-suffering patience. The soft murmur of Beth talking in her sleep floated towards them from across the landing. Isla, still talking, raised an eyebrow towards the door. Richard got up to close it, then resumed his post in the armchair, sighing loudly as he loosened his tie.

The argument began as soon as Isla hung up, although thinking about it later she realized that in fact it had started long before, and that what appeared to be an isolated dispute was just one more link in the chain of a single ongoing quarrel, a quarrel which had become her marriage, or which her marriage had become, she wasn't quite sure which.

'Granna's been burgled,' said Isla.

'Is that what it is.'

'You might at least try to look concerned.'

'I'm not in the mood, to be honest.'

Of the many faces of Richard and Isla's continuing disaccord, Marshwood's was the most familiar. She loved it. He did not. She went often. He did not.

'I'm going down tomorrow.'

'So I gathered.'

They sat facing each other, Isla and Richard, he crushing the fragile period armchair with his massive frame, she in her dressing-gown looking not much bigger than a child, sitting cross-legged in the middle of their king-size leather bed. They sat facing each other knowing that this was not how things should be nor even how they wanted them to be, that there were other gestures, other words which should be coming to them naturally at this moment, anodyne solicitous enquiries about his day at the office and the children's day at school. At this moment he should be dropping a kiss on his wife's forehead or temple or lips, they should be going hand in hand together to the kitchen where his supper, set aside from earlier, sat waiting to be reheated, she should be pouring him a glass of wine and then he should be asking about the burglary at Marshwood, what was taken, what the police had said, how Bella was coping.

'I can't believe you're going down again,' said Richard.

'Richard, she's been *burgled*!'

'Well has she called the police?'

'Obviously.'

'And what do they say?'

'As it happens, they've caught him. The burglar.'

'Well then.' He closed his eyes. She knew it was to avoid looking at her. 'No harm done.'

'She's *upset*. And scared.'

'And what do the insurance company say?'

'They're coming tomorrow. Something about the windows, the burglar broke some windows, the leaded ones in the living-room. Apparently they were the original panes.'

'Oh great,' said Richard.

'What?'

'More expense.'

'Rich, it's not *about* the money!'

'No,' he sighed. 'No, it never is, to you.' He heaved himself to his feet and began to unbutton his shirt. 'I'm tired,' he said. 'I'm going to eat. And then I'm going to bed.'

They lay side by side in the dark that night, unable to sleep and unwilling to talk. It was Richard who eventually broke the silence.

'You didn't even ask if I minded your going away this weekend.'

Isla felt a twinge of guilt. 'You could always come with us, you know. It's been ages since you did.'

'Would you stay if I asked you to?'

'Richard, what is this?'

'If I asked you to choose?'

'It's not about choosing. It's about doing what's right. Come with us, Rich. You might enjoy yourself.'

'I have to work on Saturday.'

'Well then . . .'

'What?'

'What difference does it make if we're here or not?'

'It just does. And I've got the golf tournament, remember? You were all meant to come and watch.'

Isla had not remembered. She withdrew the hand she had stretched out towards him. The covers rose and fell as Richard turned away, a cold draught wrapping itself around her shoulders.

He was still bad-tempered the following morning at breakfast.

'Please don't sulk.' Isla waited for the children to go upstairs to brush their teeth before confronting him. 'I promise this'll be the last visit for a while. You must see why I have to go down.'

'I'm not sulking. I've been thinking. This can't go on. Marshwood. The problems, the endless expense. The bills, the things going wrong, the burglaries . . .'

'Only *one* burglary.'

'It can't go on, Isla. You're going to have to talk to Bella. Tell her I can't keep footing her bills.'

'I mean it,' he told her later on the phone just before she set off. 'Talk to her. I'm not working myself to the bone for a pile of bricks that's not even mine. I'd rather have my own place. My own house in the country, with my own non-leaking roof and my own fully functioning burglar alarm. Don't think I'm not serious about this. I am. I bloody mean it.'

Marshwood was jointly owned by Bella, Isla and Isla's mother Callie, but its upkeep was unfeasible without his substantial lawyer's income. She knew he was serious. He was always serious. Isla, crawling through Friday afternoon traffic towards the M3 with her children spreading crisps and orange juice over the back seat of the family Volvo, tried to remember the last time Richard had *not* been serious. Once, she was sure of it, he used to tell jokes. Jokes which actually made her laugh. Now . . . well.

They arrived in the early evening as the spring dusk

lingered, reluctant to take its leave of the lengthening day. The children shot out of the car and disappeared into the garden, heedless of their mother's cries to follow her into the house. She found her grandmother in the drawing-room, surrounded by the friends her grandfather Clement used to call her Coven: tall, formidable Esther, who had come to Bambridge as a nurse during the war and never left; shy Kitty, forever distracted mother of seven and grandmother of fifteen, always trailing baskets of knitting or needlework; flirtatious, fun-loving Nancy, whose tongue could be as sharp as her heart was kind.

'The children have gone feral already, I'm afraid.' Isla kissed her grandmother's papery smooth cheek before turning to the others. Her heart sank a little. The old ladies had a look about them she knew well. They were in the middle of an argument, and she had interrupted them.

'I hope you'll make her see the light,' grunted Esther.

'You have no heart,' snapped Nancy.

'Well, you have no sense,' retorted Esther. 'I don't hold that against you.'

'Please stop quarrelling,' begged Kitty. 'It doesn't help.'

Bella gave a forlorn sigh, and they all turned towards her. She sat at the centre of her little group, presiding over a drinks tray, elegant and somehow other-worldly in a patterned Indian shawl and her regulation dark red Chanel lipstick. 'We were talking,' she said mournfully, 'about the man from the insurance company.'

Isla suppressed a sigh of her own. The man from the insurance company was the bête noire of Marshwood, almost its resident ghost. Out of the corner of her eye, she glimpsed Beth and Marcus tearing through the garden towards the old fig tree in the middle of the lawn. She had driven down with them straight from school. After three hours in the car, they were beyond hunger, and wild. She felt a stab of envy for their freedom.

'Tell me what he said this time.' She laid a gentle hand over her grandmother's.

Kitty looked up from her knitting and shook her head. 'He was most unsympathetic.'

'Positively brutal,' cried Nancy. 'Although,' she added thoughtfully, 'rather good-looking. In a very *middle-class* sort of way.'

'He was utterly unrealistic,' sniffed Bella.

'He won't recognize the claim,' explained Esther. 'And he's putting the premiums up again.'

'That's rather a problem,' said Isla.

'Well yes, dear,' agreed Esther. 'It is.'

'He was cross because we didn't do what he asked after the last time, and change all the downstairs windows.'

'Well how could you, darling?' protested Nancy. 'When it is so expensive.'

'It does seem so unfair, when you think of the premiums.' Bella pouted, querulous. '*And* what I had to pay for the roof last winter.'

'And there was that little fire too, when you left the gas on.' Kitty, squinting down at her matinée jacket, jumped as Nancy poked her sharply in the ribs.

'Must you bring that up now?' hissed Nancy.

'The whole thing's a bloody disaster,' said Esther. 'You're going to have to move. It's not *safe* here. Today a two-bit burglar, tomorrow an axe-murderer. Mark my words, Belle, it's a slippery slope.'

Later, once the protesting children had been put to bed and the Coven had left, Nancy and Esther still arguing, Isla sat at the foot of Bella's bed and took up Esther's point.

'You *are* going to have to think about it, you know,' she said.

'He hardly took a thing,' grumbled Bella. 'Honestly. All this fuss about a bit of Edwardian silver. He didn't even take the television.'

'No.' It was a matter of personal pride to Bella that she had not bought a new television set since watching Neil Armstrong land on the moon. 'Well, he wouldn't, would he? Realistically.'

Bella looked mutinous. 'It wasn't *me* who called the insurance company, it was Esther. *I* was all for letting it go. She's sorry now, of course. What with the premiums going up again.'

'Which brings us back to my point,' said Isla. She tried not to look at Bella as she launched into her little speech. *It's time to have a serious discussion about this, the burglary's just the tip of the iceberg, maintenance costs to think of and now the insurance going up too, what will happen when you can no longer drive, you can't stay up here on your own, not pleasant but we have to be sensible, we want what's best for you but if things go on as they are soon the property will be worthless* – the phrases drummed into her head by Richard rolled out, miserable, each one feeling like a betrayal, and she tried not to look at her grandmother, whose initial expression of incredulity had given way to one of injured pride.

'Basically, I don't think Richard's prepared to pay up much longer,' blurted Isla as she finished. 'And I don't think I can change his mind. Granna?' she asked, as Bella remained resolutely silent. 'I can sort of see his point,' she offered. 'We all love Marshwood, but . . .'

'Richard does not love Marshwood,' said Bella.

'Well, no,' conceded Isla. 'But he's very fond . . .'

'He has never understood what Marshwood means to me. To us. He has no imagination.'

'I'm not sure that's *entirely* fair . . .' Isla trailed off again, forced by her fundamental honesty to recognize that imagination was indeed not Richard's strongest point. An uncomfortable silence descended on them again. Bella glared out of the window. Isla looked around the room. Her gaze stopped on the far corner where the wallpaper, giving up a decade's battle against encroaching rot, had emphatically parted company with the wall. 'What happened there?' she asked

'Damp. It's all this rain. It'll dry.'

'Oh Granna . . .' She looked beseechingly at Bella, quelling her architect's instincts to examine the damage more closely. 'I don't know what to do. I love Marshwood as much as you do, but please say you'll at least think about what I've said?'

She paused, apprehensive. The mutinous glint in Bella's eye was a sure sign of a firebolt about to be delivered. Past experience had taught her that these could come from nowhere and bear little or no relevance to the subject at hand, but they usually hit home.

'You can remind your husband,' announced Bella, 'that under the terms of your grandfather's will, nobody can throw me out of this house for as long as I wish to live in it.'

'Granna, nobody wants to . . .'

'And you can tell him that he needn't worry about me being so isolated any more. I didn't want to tell you over the phone. Jack's back. He came to tea yesterday, and he wants to see you.'

Bella had wanted to trip her up, of course, to pay her back for her perceived betrayal, but Isla had been pleased with her response. It never ceased to surprise her how, after so many years, just the mention of Jack's name could cause her heart to skip but she had learned to conceal it well. A measured pause, a dignified acknowledgement – *really? I wonder what he's doing here* – and she had moved on, claiming fatigue. Alone in her room though, she pulled a blanket off the bed and climbed with it onto the cushioned windowsill from which she could look out over the moonlit garden to Jack's house beyond.

In Isla's mind, her childhood was divided into two clear parts. Before she was five, in London. Afterwards, at Marshwood. Before was a small flat in a red-brick building with a white porch and cracked marble steps, walks in frosty parks and rides on steamed-up buses, and afternoon naps – she remembered these clearly – when her mother painted and which smelt of turpentine. She remembered also – though she was never sure whether this was just one isolated memory, or many instances of the same thing happening all rolled together by the passing years – Callie tearing round to tidy the flat at the end of the day, a spray of perfume, a dab of lipstick, the stolid daytime nursery atmosphere of their home transformed into something different, something electric and vibrant which included her at its centre, something exciting and full of laughter which meant that Isla's father was coming home. Memories of her father were vague, prompting her to wonder whether those she had of Callie did not in fact date from a later era. Laughter, loud and sudden and clear. A smell of cigarettes and, curiously, eucalyptus. A pleasing sense of warmth and security, that everything was as it should be – though she wondered whether this too might not be a retrospective attribute.

That had been 'before'. Five unremarkable, happy years, unruffled in Isla's memory by the gradual dimming of her father's light. *Before* Daniel died, a period eventually followed by *after* the move to Marshwood, the two separated by a vague period of *in-between* which carried a sour hospital smell and the sound of muffled crying. And then her father and the flat were gone and Callie and Isla were at Marshwood along with most of their belongings – though not their furniture – and Callie was either locked in her room or stalking over hills on her own, and her eyes were always red.

'Your mother is Grieving,' explained Bella when after a fortnight of this Isla enquired timidly when she was to go home. 'Do you know what that means?'

Isla shook her head. Bella often used words she didn't understand. It was one of the things that made her so frightening and so exciting all at once.

'It means,' sighed Bella, 'that she is Depressed. We hoped it would not come to this, but we think that she should Let the Flat.'

'Let the flat what?' asked a baffled Isla.

'Come over here, Isla.' Clement's voice was quiet and kind. Isla went to him willingly. Her grandfather was a different proposition altogether from Bella, gentle and somehow always more accessible. He patted his knee and she nestled into him, inhaling his smell of pipe smoke and sawn wood. 'What Granna is trying to say is, how would you like to come and live with us?'

Jack Kavanagh's parents had bought Marshwood's old coach house from her cash-strapped grandfather in the early sixties and converted it into a handsome four-bedroom home. She had known him all her life, but she dated the beginning of their friendship to then, to the beginning of 'after'. He was brought over for tea soon after Callie and Isla's arrival, and after ten minutes of wriggling at the table asked if she would like to see his den.

He had built it deep in the heart of the laurel hedge which separated Marshwood from his parents' property. The hedge appeared impenetrable from the outside but Jack dropped to the ground and crawled beneath it, followed by a silent Isla, to emerge in a small clearing concealed from prying eyes by a thick canopy of leaves overhead and latticed branches on either side. There were two grubby cushions on the ground as well as a metal box which when opened revealed a torch, a mangled packet of Toffoes and half a bottle of orange Fanta.

'My mum was really cross about the cushions,' said Jack, offering her a sweet. 'She says they're ruined for ever and she doesn't want them back. Is your dad dead then?'

Isla pondered this. *Dead* was not a word she had heard much in connection with her father. *Gone. Departed. Passed over. Deceased.* And yet she knew that he *was* dead, as dead as Clement's old bull terrier who had joined all the other dogs in Marshwood's extensive pet cemetery the previous Easter. The thought of the pet cemetery cheered her up. It hadn't occurred to her until this moment that her father might have company on the other side.

'Yes,' she said. 'He is.'

Jack took another Toffo and they chewed together for a while in meditative silence. He was a robust little boy with permanently grazed knees and dancing black eyes, always tumbling into trouble and charming his way back out of it. He was not used to this sort of situation, and recognized its call for careful words. 'Do you mind?' he asked at last.

'Yes,' she said. 'A lot,' she added.

Another long silence, during which Isla thought quite hard about trying not to cry, and Jack scratched around the den looking for something to do. He turned towards her when inspiration struck, brandishing a small, very grubby penknife.

'We should be blood brothers,' he said. 'Since you'll be living next door.'

When Isla started at the local school in Bambridge at the beginning of the next school year, it was with Jack at her side. When Jack's friends teased him for being friends with a girl, he fought them. When the girls asked Isla why she was such friends with a boy, she showed them the scar on her right hand where Jack had cut her – an ugly scar, the knife having been both very dirty and much sharper than expected. The inhabitants of Chapel St Mary soon grew so used to seeing the two children together that if ever one were to appear alone, they were invariably asked where the other was. They were known locally as the Troublesome Twosome. Most people viewed them with affection. Others – those whose orchards Jack and Isla raided for fruit, or whose flowers they picked for a dare, or who discovered that they had been assigned the roles of witch or child snatcher in the twosome's complex fantasies – muttered that they were wild and uncontrollable.

Jack never replaced her father, of course, but he did make *after* a lot easier to bear. He had a nose for trouble. Bella grumbled that he dragged Isla into it after him, but in truth she was more often a willing accomplice. Once, when they were seven, he dared her to climb the highest tree in the grounds of Marshwood, and the fire brigade had to be called out to get her down. On another occasion, they convinced a gang of Jack's visiting cousins to play pirates.

'We will be the pirates and you will be the merchant seamen,' ordered Jack.

'You can't just have two pirates and five seamen,' complained the oldest child.

'Yes we can,' glowered Isla. Jack, fearing repercussions from his father, had been uncertain about her plan to make his cousins walk the plank, but she had goaded him into helping her and two of the visiting boys had received a thorough dunking before their cries alerted any grown-ups to their plight. Jack's father had whipped him for that. Isla, as usual, had gone unpunished.

Callie, having neither Jack nor a child's stoic adaptability, fared worse than her daughter. Isla cheerfully entered the world of Marshwood, a world of dogs and her own diminutive pony, where her grandfather let her play with his wood-turning tools and gave her a plot of garden of her very own, and her grandmother laid down arbitrary rules which were never enforced. Whereas sometimes it seemed that Callie would never recover. Her period of weeping and solitary walks soon gave way to years of restlessness. India, Thailand, Nepal, Tibet. Greenham Common, Vietnam peace marches. The only times Isla's solid little world was rocked, when the fading memories of her father flickered painfully to life, were when her mother left and when she returned. Departures were always tearful and full of self-justifying explanations Isla did not understand. Homecomings were ecstatic but, once the presents had been given and the stories told, fast followed by a return to brooding anger.

When Isla was nine years old, Callie went to Andalusia on a painter's retreat. She came home fizzing with enthusiasm to announce that she was leaving England for good in order to settle in a small village in the Alpujarras.

'Leaving England?' Bella looked baffled. She had been washing one of the dogs when Callie, with characteristically catastrophic timing, made her announcement. She froze, one soapy hand clasped around a brush, the other restraining a sodden flat-coated retriever bitch. Isla, whose job it was to speak soothingly to the dogs during their monthly baths, looked up curiously. 'But why?'

The retriever broke loose. Isla was sent to catch her and tore down the flagstone passage after a trail of damp footprints, pondering the implications of Callie's announcement. It was the end of June, nearing the end of term. Days were long and adults indulgent. Jack and Isla, playing in Marshwood's garden long after their allotted bedtime, hid in the bushes surrounding the terrace and tried to eavesdrop on Callie, Bella and Clement. *I need to get away . . . can't forget him . . . can't move on . . .* This was Callie. *But are you sure this is what will make you happy?* Clement. *And what about the child?* Bella.

Callie, it appeared, could not cope with the child, and asked that she remain at Marshwood for a time. She would come back for her when she felt stronger. For now, she argued, it was better for everybody for them to remain apart.

As Bella expressed disapproval and Clement gently questioned Callie's judgement, Isla reached out for Jack's hand. He held it firmly. She crept closer and did not let go. Callie never did come back for her.

Their world changed when they turned eleven and were sent to separate boarding-schools but even then distance did not get in the way of their friendship. At thirteen, he convinced her to drink a bottle of Martini stolen from his parents' drinks cabinet, then held her hair out of her face as she threw it back up. She returned the favour during the following holiday, when he tried to smoke one of Clement's cigars. And at fifteen, when Clement suffered a devastating heart attack and Marshwood was plunged into mourning, Jack broke out of school and hitch-hiked home to comfort Isla, bringing her a box of toffees stolen from his dorm mate and marching her out of the house to the top of Pater Noster where he sat beside her and listened as she howled.

'Everybody leaves,' wept Isla. 'Daddy, Mum, Grandpapa. Everybody.'

'I'm here,' he said. And then, because it seemed the right thing to do, he took her in his arms. She rested her head on his shoulder and somehow, from deep within, began to smile.

Deep down, she had always known they were meant to be together. Two more years passed, two years in which they both came home less often, two years marked by exams and holidays divided between Marshwood and the occasional visit to Callie in Spain, two years during which Isla passed O levels with flying colours before setting her cap at a Cambridge scholarship, while Jack ignored his schoolwork and began to experiment with drugs. Two years in which the feeling born on the hill that day blossomed into something else, something she kept secret and hidden and did not acknowledge even to herself until that final summer. Her love for him had exploded rapturously on the last day of the holidays, when she followed Jack through Marshwood's grounds down to the woods below, along the stream and around the bottom of Pater Noster along an alley of beeches to the small private lake which lay beyond, where they stripped down to their swimming-costumes in accordance with the challenge laid down the previous evening.

She hesitated on the edge of the lake, her toes curling with revulsion as her feet sank into soft, fine mud. They had never done this before. She toyed with the idea of calling the whole thing off, but the thought of losing face was worse than that of the water.

'Ready?' She nodded. *As I'll ever be.* He gave the signal and she hurled herself in.

Blinding water. Choking, a mistimed breath. Lungs burning, body sweating despite the cold. The strong, earthy smell of the lake. The conviction that she must win. He was faster but lost speed on the turn when he reached the other side, and she gained on him on the return straight. She threw herself onto the shore seconds before him and lay on the dry hard ground gasping for breath. When she opened her eyes he was lying on his back next to her, laughing.

'I won!' she beamed.

He turned to look at her and smiled.

'You won.'

A dog barked in the distance, but his eyes never left her face.

The dog barked again and the owner of the lake arrived, yelling at them, *can't you read* and *this is private*, and they had gathered their clothes, shaking with helpless laughter as they tried to run and pull on shoes at the same time. Isla's hand was in Jack's as they ran through the sweet coconut smell of the gorse in bloom, brushing aside the tall ferns under which they had hidden as children to emerge on top of the hill, still in their swimwear, where they collapsed against the familiar grassed-over remains of the Roman hill-fort. And then that gesture. Jack's hand cupping her face, his thumb brushing her mouth. His voice, hoarse and full of wonder, saying her name. Her own hand coming up to meet his. Leaning in towards him, the wind caressing her bare limbs, feeling that at any moment it might pick her up and she could fly with it over the hills she knew and loved so well.

She had kissed other boys before, more out of curiosity than anything else, but this was different. His mouth on hers was soft, almost hesitant. A caress, more than a kiss. He moved away from her and she wound her hands around his neck to keep him close. 'Isla,' he repeated, and then his mouth was searching for hers again, and her hands were buried in his thick dark hair, and his were on her back, pressing her against him. She fell back against the soft springy grass. He rolled on top of her and groaned as she moved her hips instinctively under his. She gasped as his hand closed over her breast.

'Should I stop?'

She shook her head. He brought his mouth down to her breast and she thought she might faint. His hand crept lower down, pushing aside the fabric of her swim-suit. It occurred to her that perhaps she *ought* to stop him. Then, as his fingers got to work, she gave up any effort at resistance.

It never crossed her mind that he might not feel the same way as she did. Isla floated off the hill and back to Marshwood in a daze. Back at school, she wrote him long letters describing her feelings for him. The moment when she knew she loved him, the reasons she loved him, the way he laughed, the way he cried, the way he walked, the way he was always there for her, the feel of his mouth on hers, of his hands caressing her body, how she couldn't wait for half-term, how she wished they were at the same school. Even his replies – less frequent, more guarded – didn't ring any alarm bells. Despite her general ignorance about boys, she knew enough not to expect the same level of emotional articulacy from them as she was capable of. The fact that this was Jack, who had never hidden an emotion from her in his life, she refused to see.

They both went home for half-term at the tail end of October, Isla arriving a day before Jack. She could not be still on the morning he was due back and Bella sent her out for a walk. It was a rainy, blustery day. Isla, who always lost her own jackets, donned an old Barbour of Clement's, called the dogs – Bella still kept two in those days, a setter and a Border terrier – and set off for Pater Noster. She walked slowly at first, not wanting the pounding of blood in her ears or her ragged breath as she climbed to interfere with the sound of a car in the lane below. But the dogs were young and energetic. The terrier, Petra, was little more than a puppy. Isla threw sticks for her most of the way up the hill. At the top, tiring of the game, she ran with her up and down the tussocks made in the hill by the old fort. The setter, who was known as the Duchess, emerged from a hedgerow bearing half a fallen tree, making Isla laugh out loud. A soft, steady rain was falling, and her jacket did not have a hood. She raked her fingers through her hair, sweeping it back so that it lay plastered against her skull. Rain trickled down her face, and when she looked at her hands after wiping it off she saw that they were streaked with the bright blue mascara she had applied that morning. She stood still for a moment, her face turned upwards towards the sky, loving the feel of the rain and the sweet smell of the wet grass. Then she shivered as the water began to seep into her collar, whistled to the dogs and began her descent back towards Marshwood. The incline was steep, the ground wet, the going slow. She slipped as she neared the end of the path. Petra, thinking she was still playing, leaped on her, leaving muddy paw prints on her jacket. Isla laughed. And then she heard the car.

It was him, she knew it was him. Pushing the dog aside, giving no thought to her appearance, she ran the remaining distance down to Marshwood. Over the years, she and Jack had expanded their old den to create a narrow passageway between the two properties. Isla flew across the lawn towards it, the dogs racing ahead of her, the Duchess' ears streaming in the wind. She heard their joyous barking and the cries which greeted them a good half-minute before she emerged from the hedge herself, panting but radiant – and froze.

An unfamiliar Morris Minor had just pulled up to the front door. Isla hung back, uncertain. She had expected him to return alone with his parents, but Clive and Tanya Kavanagh were standing in the porch, simultaneously waving to the passengers of the Morris Minor and shooing away the over-enthusiastic dogs now bouncing around them, shaking water out of their sopping fur. Perhaps this was not Jack come home after all, but a random visitor. The door to the passenger seat opened.

Two feet swung out, followed by legs of unfeasible length, a torso in a lumberjack's coat, a shaggy crop of dark hair. It *was* Jack. But now out of the driver's side a girl was emerging, a girl with a mane of ash blond hair swinging down her back, a girl in a tailored leather jacket and impeccable jeans, who walked around the car with perfect composure and slipped her hand into Jack's before taking the few steps which separated them from the house.

Isla gasped and tried to creep away. Not so the Duchess, who adored Jack. Breaking away from his parents, she bounded over to him and leaped straight at his chest to lick his face. The girl screamed. The Duchess licked her too. Jack's father roared and turned towards the hedge.

'Isla! Get these monsters off my property! I swear to God, one day I'm going to shoot them.'

'They're only saying hello.' Isla slunk out of the shadow of the hedge, refusing to meet anybody's eyes.

And then Clive had vanished inside the house, and Tanya had followed him with an apologetic smile, and it was just the three of them. Isla standing in the rain with two dogs panting at the end of their leads, the blonde leaning against the porch appraising her, and Jack hovering uncomfortably in between.

'Who's your friend, Jack?' asked the blonde.

'Amanda, this is Isla,' he mumbled. 'Isla, this is Amanda.'

'Oh,' said Amanda. Cool eyes flicked over Isla. 'I've heard a lot about you.'

Jack flushed and looked away. Isla drew herself up and forced her own face into a sneer.

'Funny,' she said in a voice of ice. 'But I've never heard you mentioned at all.'

She turned on her heel and left them. She would have liked to use their old short cut again but she thought it would look undignified, and so she walked back down the drive with her head held high, conscious of their eyes on her back and grateful that they could not see the hot tears of humiliation which mingled as they fell with the fat raindrops coursing down her cheeks.

Amanda had not stayed long. Jack had come round later, barging past a furious Bella to confront her.

'It's not what you think.'

'You don't know what I think.'

'It just . . . happened.'

'You should have told me.'

'I was going to. I've been meaning to for ages. I . . . I didn't know how.'

She was the older sister of a school-friend, whose attentions had dazzled him. He hadn't known how to refuse. He hadn't meant to hurt anybody.

'You could have told her about me.'

'I did!'

'Of course you did.'

'Isla, we can still be friends, right?'

He had looked so woebegone, so pathetic. For a moment, friendship – second best, but better than nothing – had seemed a tempting option. Then she hardened. Friendship be damned. She wanted to hurt him as much as he had hurt her.

'You're a bastard, Jack Kavanagh, and I hate you.'

The Coven all came to see her that week, Nancy, Esther and Kitty, each bearing her advice like a gift.

'Fight the bitch,' cried Nancy, blowing perfect smoke rings from a cigarette stolen from Isla's secret stash. 'Don't let her get away with it!'

'You don't need men,' said Esther sternly, depositing works by Germaine Greer and Simone de Beauvoir on Isla's bedside table. 'Men are a distraction. You don't know how lucky you are to be growing up now rather than forty years ago.'

'Forgive him,' pleaded Kitty. 'You love each other so much. Forgive him, Isla dear.'

Bella, though less voluble than the others, had agreed with Kitty. When Isla, heart-broken, sobbed that her life was over because she had always imagined she and Jack would be together and now they couldn't be, not after this, she had gently tried to defuse the situation. Words such as *be careful*, *you'll regret it* and *over-reaction* had been spoken, to catastrophic effect. Isla had only wept harder, and that had been that.

Isla refused to see him again that holiday. Back at school, she scraped through her Cambridge entrance, then set to preparing her A levels. She missed him but would not tell him so, and after a few tentative letters to which she did not reply he gave up trying. Isla spent holidays revising and came home little. By the time exams were over and she relented, his parents had fulfilled a long-held dream of moving to Canada, tenants had moved into the coach house, and the Troublesome Twosome were a thing of the past.

Fifteen years later, Isla sat on her window-seat, wrapped in blankets and lost in thought, looking out across the garden towards Jack's house. A light was on upstairs in his old bedroom. He had not been back to Chapel St Mary once in all that time. With his parents in Canada, the house had been let, but it had been standing empty now for almost two years. She wondered what had brought him back. Wondered also at the effect of the news of his presence on her, the stirring of old emotions; excitement and yearning as well as the anger she had thought long buried.

The night outside was inky black, smoothing away masonry cracks and fallen plaster, flaking paint and rotting timber. At night, it was still possible to forget the sorry state of the house and remember only the glory of its position, nestling among the rounded silhouette of the encircling hills. Isla leaned forward to open her window, tilting her head to listen to the murmur of the trees planted by her grandfather sixty years before, soothed by the rustle of wind in their leaves. Damn Richard, for his refusal to understand what the house meant to her. And damn Jack, for coming back now, bringing memories she had no desire to revisit. Isla sighed, and stared out at the night sky, willing away the darkness.

Later, he would tell her that three hundred yards away, in the childhood home to which he had not returned for fifteen years, Jack also sat alone, remembering. What had he been thinking, coming back here? He had thought that now, after the hellish months in Bosnia, a return to his roots might be just what he needed, but the truth was that the house appalled him. Even after the cleaner had been and the dust sheets had all been removed, its emptiness was inescapable. In his memory, he had pictured it fondly as all pristine respectability, wall-to-wall blue carpets, chintz curtains and displays of china. Now he noticed things by their absence: the smells wafting from the kitchen, the logs piled high in the basket by the fireplace, the tap-tap of the dog's claws on the flagstones in the hall. He was in the kitchen now, a quiet symphony of co-ordinated beige units. He filled the kettle to boil water for tea. His mother had been so proud of her new kitchen, installed just a couple of years before the move to Vancouver. 'So modern,' she had crooned, her usual self-effacing demureness forgotten in the face of integrated units and synthetic worktops. 'So clean.' A spark of mischief. 'Not like next door.'

Next door. Even twenty years ago, Bella's kitchen had been an anachronism, battered stainless steel units and a free-standing gas oven, most of the splendid saucepans inherited from Clement's great-aunt gathering cobwebs on the wall, a testimony to Bella's dislike of cooking. 'And the floor!' Jack's mother had sighed, gazing at her spotless new linoleum. 'I'm sure most of the tiles at Marshwood are broken.' Jack could have told her they weren't. Over the years, he and Isla had spent enough time playing under the ancient table to gather a close knowledge of the kitchen floor. The tiles were not broken. A bit cracked, uneven, but not broken. Rather like Bella herself.

Back in his bedroom, he stood in the dark by the window, hands around his steaming mug. The lights were on in Isla's room. He wondered if she knew he was back. He had caught sight of her that evening in the garden, unchanged from a distance, small and slim in jeans and trainers, short auburn curls blowing around her head. Her two children had been with her, the boy tall and fair and serious looking, the little girl resplendent in a bright dress and purple boots. At one point the girl had stopped walking and bellowed *it's not fair* across the lawn. Jack, watching from his upstairs window, had actually laughed out loud because she was so like Isla. And then it had hit him. That the reason he had come back, after everything that had happened, had nothing to do with the place, but everything to do with her.

A movement caught his eye. A figure had appeared, pushing open her window. It was her. He caught his breath. She was leaning out, her head resting against the stone framework. On a whim, he walked back to the door of his room and flicked the lights on and off several times, as he had so often done to signal to her when they were children.

But when he looked back again towards Marshwood, she was gone.

Isla woke late. Beth had joined her at one point in the night, complaining that everybody was sleeping and that she was bored.

'It *is* three o'clock in the morning.' Isla, who was used to her daughter's night-time visitations, still felt obliged to point this out. Beth was asleep now, her face cherubic in slumber, long curls splayed out on the pillow, a piratical one-eyed bear tucked beneath her arm. Isla yawned, stretched as far as she dared, and decided to go for a run.

She had brought trainers but no running clothes. A quiet rummage in the chest of drawers yielded leggings, an old lacrosse skirt and an oversized sweatshirt, all relics of her schooldays. She only noticed half-way down the stairs that the leggings were loudly striped in red and black and wondered, delight briefly lifting her out of sleepy torpor, when she might have bought them. Avoiding the lane which would have taken her out past Jack's house, she jogged down over the lawn velvety with moss, past the disused greenhouses, through a rotting gate and out into the paddock beyond. She never ran in London and only really found her stride when she picked up the footpath in the woods beneath the house. The morning was clear and soft, the ground pearly with dew, the woods budding into spring. She ran at a steady pace, concentrating on her breathing. Her speed picked up as the initial burning in her lungs faded, and at first she was able to focus only on this, the joy of running through the damp sweet-smelling country, with cuckoos and pigeons and blackbirds calling and the occasional dog loping alongside her until it was called away. This was what she craved more and more, this feeling of detachment from her everyday life, the secure, peaceful everyday life she had worked so hard to build and yet which lately she so often sought to escape. She stumbled, lost her stride, stopped for a moment to catch her breath. She ran faster when she started again, but now the spell was broken. Now thoughts were streaming through her previously clear mind, thoughts of Marshwood and its precarious future, of Richard's stubborn refusal to listen, of Jack's light flashing unanswered in the darkness. She stopped when she reached the stile at the end of the alley of beeches and leaned against the gate to catch her breath. From here, through the trees still bare of leaves, she could see the lake shrouded in lingering scraps of mist. She turned to go, and burst into tears.

It was something new for Isla, this tendency to sudden crying. She hated it, the weakness and neediness it implied. People cried when something was wrong or they were unhappy. Whereas her life was perfect, and she *would* not be unhappy. She choked on her tears and stifled her racking sobs, forced her shaky breath to become even again as she resumed her run, marking a slower pace back up the hill. The last stretch took her around the side of Pater Noster to the gate leading back down to Marshwood, and as she ran memories of Jack broke free from their anchor in the deeper recesses of her mind, reminding her that this was the same gate through which they had first escaped alone onto the hill, to gorge on stolen Easter eggs. And that this was the gate through which they had secretly ridden the neighbouring farmer's ponies, to be discovered because Jack fell off during their final gallop and broke his wrist. That this was the gate . . . *oh, bloody hell.* Isla pulled up short and almost fell over.

That this was the gate against which he now leaned with his back to her, in the company of her six-year-old daughter.

His ghost had returned to haunt her often in the

years following their quarrel, on landmark dates such as her wedding and the days the children were born but at random other times as well, brought to mind by nothings, the crispness of an autumnal twilight, a mud-splashed boot kicked into a dark corner of the cloakroom. Its visits had grown scarcer over the years, but their meetings in her mind had still followed a vague but particular pattern in which she combined all the desirable qualities of mid-thirties womanhood – a muted glamour enhanced by the salving experiences of motherhood and marriage, the radiation of self-sufficiency and contentment. And now here she stood dressed in schoolgirl cast-offs, with sweat-damp hair and tear-streaked cheeks, flushed and panting from her run. The sensible option, she decided, good sense slicing through the fluttering of her panicked mind, would be to run away. She turned to go. A twig snapped beneath her foot. Jack and Beth looked up.

Isla squared her shoulders, affixed a smile and walked the remaining yards towards them with hopeful non-chalance.

'I see you've met my little girl.'

She almost laughed out loud at the sight of Beth. Always an eccentric dresser, she had excelled herself today, accessorizing her brother's old Batman pyjamas and her own purple rubber boots with a fuchsia pink shawl of her mother's, worn around her body like a sling and in which nestled a very small, very sleepy silver tabby kitten, the smallest of a litter born recently in Bella's barn. Perhaps, thought Isla, still aspiring to an air of serene superiority, all was not lost. Perhaps there was something rather charming about a family of boho eccentrics. She held out her arms and Beth ran to her, raising her face to her mother's grateful kiss.

'I was hiding,' announced Beth.

'You weren't doing a very good job of it,' replied Isla. 'Since we can all see you.'

'This is Jack.'

'I know.' She looked directly at him for the first time, flashing what she hoped was a radiant smile. He grinned back. She blushed. 'It's a bit cold to be out here in pyjamas, Bettyboo.'

'He thought I was you.'

'Did he?'

Beth considered this. 'Just for a minute,' she conceded.

'I said, I thought she was you for a minute because you are so alike.'

His voice. Was it deeper than when they parted? She tried to remember, hearing snatches in her mind, shouted commands, shrieks of delight, teasing whispers, tearful apologies . . .

'It's still quite cold,' she said to Beth. 'You should go in. I'll follow you.'

Beth left, dragging her feet. She raised her hand in a small defiant salute to Jack before leaving and he responded in kind. The implicit complicity of the gesture annoyed Isla. She raised her chin a small but important fraction and turned towards him.

'I know I look ridiculous.'

He had not moved throughout her exchange with Beth but remained leaning with his back against the gate, one foot hooked behind him on the bottom rung, watching her. *Brilliant*, thought Isla. *After fifteen years, the best I can come up with. I know I look ridiculous.*

Jack's mouth twitched.

'*Distinctive*, I would say.'

And now another memory, two children running naked and caked in mud through the grounds of Marshwood in mid-December. *Why can't you behave like normal children?* an incredulous Bella had scolded. *Because we're not normal, Granna*, seven-year-old Isla had chanted back. *We're distinctive.* She had learned the word from her grandfather, teaching her about the grains of different woods. *Am I distinctive?* she had asked. *Why yes*, Clement had replied with great seriousness. *Most definitely.* She and Jack had appropriated it for a time, enjoying its sound, the sharp explosion of consonants and musicality of its central vowel. She grinned despite herself at the recollection. They had been wild as children. *Uncontrollable*, Bella used to say – another good word, though they had found it harder to pronounce.

'That's better.' Jack's voice brought her back to reality.

'What?'

'You're smiling.'

'I was smiling before.'

'A different smile.'

'Yes,' she acknowledged, because however annoying it was, he was right and her previous smile *had* been different. She tried to study him surreptitiously in the silence that followed, a silence which was neither heavy nor uncomfortable but more a mutual recognition of the fact that this reunion which had taken fifteen years to come about should not now be rushed. He leaned against the gate, his head angled away from her to watch the small retreating figure of Beth. She noted long legs encased in rumpled jeans, strong forearms where the sleeves of his dark red cotton shirt were pushed back, a heavy watch on a leather strap. *No ring.* As a teenager, he had favoured hunched, laconic stances but now he carried his height and stature with ease, an attractive nonchalance. Her eyes flicked upwards, noticing cheekbones sharper than she remembered, a face more lined, more closed too. She thought he looked weary. *Older.*

Beth had reached the front door. Jack turned to look at her. Isla blushed.

'I know what you've been up to,' she blurted. 'Granna kept a scrapbook.'

'A scrapbook?'

'Yes.' *Oh God, she'd done it again! Why was she even talking about this?* Over the years, Bella had taken an enthusiastic interest in Jack's career as a photographic reporter, cheerfully ignoring Isla's stony silence on the subject. *The boy just can't keep still,* she would say whenever his name came up in one of the Sunday colour supplements. Ethiopian famines, Russian environmental disasters, the fall of the Berlin Wall, race riots in Los Angeles . . . It seemed Jack had been present at all the major events of the last decade. The Coven had all felt somehow personally responsible for his meteoric career, a career which had simply made Isla feel inadequate.

Jack gave a little bow. 'A scrapbook! I'm honoured.' His mouth twisted into a quick smile, before he pursed his lips in a very Bella-like expression. 'I'm glad to see the boy's doing *something* with his life,' he drawled in passable imitation. He cocked an eyebrow at Isla, gauging her reaction.

Isla laughed. 'Not bad, but actually we were all very impressed. Even me.'

'Well,' said Jack softly. 'That's the main thing.'

His eyes held hers for a few brief seconds, the coal black eyes she remembered of old, which were not dancing now but burned with a new intensity, as though seeking to convey a message she was not equipped to understand. *I want to, though,* she surprised herself thinking.

'You're shivering.' He pushed himself away from the gate and put a hand on her shoulder, touching her for the first time as he pushed her gently towards the path. 'Time to go in.'

'Will I see you again?'

The smile was still amused, but the eyes now were blazing. 'Of course,' he replied. 'That's why I came back.'

Inside the house, Bella was in a fine mood.

'I've been speaking to the Coven,' she announced. 'And they all agree, even Esther.'

'All agree about what?' asked Isla absently. Her mind was still on Jack and their oddly unsatisfactory meeting. He had changed. Had she? As much as him? Could she ask him? She wasn't sure she wanted to know.

'With what I've decided. I am going . . .' Bella paused for effect '. . . to write my memoirs.'

'Good!' It occurred to Isla that she had been adopting this tone of voice more and more with Bella recently, the sort of indulgent, encouraging lilt she usually reserved for the children.

'I want you to help me.' Perhaps it was because Bella, in her single-mindedness, could be just as tyrannical as Beth. 'I do think you might. I was so upset, you know, with what you said about moving.'

'Granna . . .'

'I want you to understand just what it is you are asking me to do,' said Bella firmly. 'Say you'll do it.'

'I'm not asking you to *do* anything. Just to think about things. And of course I'll help you, if that's what you want. But can I get changed first, and see to the children?'

Bella peered at her. 'You look peaky. Where have you been?'

'For a run.'

Bella shuddered.

'And I saw Jack.'

'No! Dressed like that?'

'Yes, Granna,' said Isla. 'Dressed like this.'

They started that evening after dinner, sitting in Bella's favourite alcove by the French windows, with the view over the terrace and the lawn beyond. Isla, wearing tortoiseshell glasses and wielding a fountain pen, waited for Bella to begin.

'What was the name of that woman who told stories?' asked Bella.

'Beatrix Potter,' said Isla.

'The other one.'

'Enid Blyton?'

'Scheherazade. I feel like Scheherazade, delaying her stay of execution.'

'Don't you think you're being a *little* over-dramatic?'

'It's what it feels like to me.'

'You'd better concentrate,' said Isla, 'or we'll never get started.'

'I don't know where to begin.'

'Start with when you first came to the house.'

Bella nodded. She settled back into her armchair, took a dainty sip of rosehip tea and touched her fingertips together.

'In 1936,' she intoned, 'I was an old maid.'

Isla did a quick mental calculation. 'In 1936,' she said, 'you were twenty-one years old.'

Bella frowned. 'This isn't going to work if you keep on interrupting.'

First memories. 1918, almost four years old. Her older brothers, Harry, Digby and Rupert all sick with the flu, her father's Somerset vicarage a blur of trunks and packing cases and valises as the family prepared its exodus for Switzerland. At some point, somebody must have explained that she was not going. Somebody may have petted her, her mother may have cried, but she did not recall this. She remembered only that her brothers were sick and thus were to go, whereas she was healthy, and must stay. Ever since, she had viewed her robust good health as a source of vexation, especially now that her friends were so obsessed with pills or, in the case of Esther, with serial hip replacement operations. She remembered a large cold house in a place she learned was called Surrey, and a tall cold woman she was to call Aunt, and she found out later that she lived there for over a year before the family returned – healthy, clannish and exclusive.

One by one her brothers left home for boarding-school, and she remembered the tantrum she threw when she was told that she was not to follow them, a fit of such titanic proportions that it penetrated the sanctified hallows of her father's study at the opposite end of the vicarage from the nursery. The unfairness of her subsequent whipping felt like nothing compared to the curt explanation she received for the decision not to send her to school because it was too expensive and *things were different for girls*. She remembered how empty the house was without the boys, but also – a more sophisticated memory this – wondering how it was that she felt even more lonely when they came home than when they were away. And she remembered the joy of a new family moving to their village, with a daughter her own age called Nancy who had a governess with whom she was to share lessons.

'Nancy,' said Bella, 'has *always* been a lifeline.'

Nancy, who was not so much mischievous as downright naughty, who organized midnight raids on her parents' kitchen and put frogs in the beds of visiting guests, who begged that Bella sleep over during the week until she virtually became a weekly boarder at her house, who bullied her indulgent father into buying another pony for Bella to ride. It was at Nancy's house that Bella discovered her lifelong passion for reading. There had been two sorts of books in her own home: the austere theological tracts ordered by her father from specialist bookshops, and the syrupy romantic novels which her mother borrowed from the library and kept hidden in her knitting basket. Whereas Nancy's parents read *everything*. Old classics and modern bestsellers, fact and fiction, romance and crime, philosophy and poetry – books of all kinds jostled for space on the shelves and tables of their bright, comfortable library. At home, to be caught with a book in her hand had been tantamount to being discovered idling. At Nancy's house, Bella had once been let off lessons for an entire morning in order to finish *Great Expectations*.

'What can I say?' sighed Bella, draining her teacup. 'It was paradise. Really. Even after we no longer had a governess, I still spent so much time there. It was a *happy* place. Nancy didn't get the point of all that reading, of course. She always used to cry, *you and your damn books!* She was very outdoorsy, whereas I was more of a mouse . . . Anyway, then she eloped, and it all ended. Right in the middle of *War and Peace*, though her father was a darling and let me take it home.'

Nancy who had taken to wearing too much lipstick, who rode too fast and danced too easily, who kissed every single one of Bella's brothers, came to live in Chapel St Mary when she was just eighteen after eloping with a dull but smitten Dorset landowner, abandoning her best friend to an existence caring for parents who, after years of showing no interest in her at all, were all at once showing far too much. Her father, who was coming up to retirement, was increasingly irascible. Her mother spent her days drifting between her garden, which she tended with assiduous care, and her bed where she sighed over her library books. With the boys grown up, both her parents seemed to view her as the only project they had left.

'They wouldn't let me visit her for a whole year,' said Bella. 'Even married, she was considered loose.'

Isla snorted. 'Shall I write that down?'

'I think so,' said Bella. 'I think she'd rather like it.'

A look passed between them, a slightly wicked understanding.

'I was so bored,' continued Bella. 'My governess had wanted me to apply for university, but my parents wouldn't hear of it – money was still quite tight, and of course the *boys* all had to be provided for. My father found me a dismal little job working for the rural dean, but mainly they wanted to marry me off. A good match. That was why they didn't want me associating with Nancy – the elopement had been quite a scandal. But I had a bit of money of my own, thanks to the job. So I stood up to them.'

'And that's when you first came to Marshwood.'

'And that's when I first came to Marshwood.'

'So now we can begin.'

Clement Langton bought Marshwood in the autumn of 1928, just two months short of the tenth anniversary of the Armistice. Along with the house, he almost immediately acquired the reputation of an eccentric, a recluse with no interest in country affairs and a range of alarming hobbies. Rumour had it – and rumour was correct – that he had joined up on the day he finished school in the summer of 1915, and that he had been demobilized just before the end of the war with a nasty leg wound, the source of his noticeable limp. That he had bought the house on coming into a substantial legacy from his recently deceased Great-Aunt Mathilda, a spinster who had raised him alone in her large house in Hampstead, though he himself had spent little time there, having been sent to prep school at the age of seven and then on to Rugby. That in the years between the end of the war and the demise of his great-aunt he had taken up a place at Oxford, trained as a lawyer and practised in London, but that he had little liking for his profession. That he had not intended to settle in Dorset but had bought the house because he liked the view, that he meant to let the estate's farm and cottage and that he spent his days painting, reading, playing the piano or locked in the barn he referred to with great satisfaction as his workshop. His local friends included a much-shunned homosexual solicitor, a usually inebriated Irish poet and a couple from London who had moved to the country under the mistaken apprehension that they could make a living by raising alpaca goats. His more discerning neighbours noted that although he was not hospitable he was always courteous, and that his excessive absent-mindedness masked a not inconsiderable intelligence.

Gossip – in the form of Josie Bates, Clement's elderly housekeeper – did *not* relate the circumstances leading to his acquisition of Marshwood. In Clement's mind, it was clear that he would never have bought Marshwood, or even sought it out, if it had not been for the Frenchman Antoine Duchesne, but until he met Bella he kept this fact very much to himself.

He had met Duchesne in the spring of 1918 after a joint Franco-British offensive just north of the Vesle, between Reims and Soissons. Clement had taken a shot in the leg and fallen into a shell hole, passing out from the pain. He came round to the sound of a voice calling to him in French and in the flickering light of the fading guns he saw that the other man was trapped from the waist down in a pool of mud.

He did not think that he might actually be able to rescue the Frenchman, only that he did not want to die alone. And so he dragged himself forward and held out his arms, and the two men lay in this strange embrace until the rescue party discovered them at dawn. By this time Antoine had sunk further into the mud. Clement, guessing that they would try to shoot him, had wrapped himself around the Frenchman's body, leaving their rescuers no choice but to haul him out and take him to the clearing station along with Clement.

No, Josie Bates, happily recounting all she knew about her employer to village gossips, knew nothing of the stink of shit and vomit putrid against the sharp smell of gunpowder, the horror of the dark, life-sucking mud, the unbearable beauty of dawn. He did not tell her about the clearing station, the agony of his splintered leg, the ambulance awash with blood, Antoine's silent tears. The Frenchman spent a whole day with Clement before being moved on and in that time, while Clement smoked and tried to concentrate with his schoolboy French, he talked incessantly. He talked about the war, the previous night, his fear, his gratitude, about the parents he had feared he would never see again and the girl he wanted to marry. Most of all he talked about the home he longed for with every inch of his being.

'*C'est plus facile de ne pas y penser, hein, au quotidien. Mais maintenant . . .*' It was easier not to think about it on a daily basis, but now, in the relative safety of the field hospital . . . The Frenchman described woods and lawns, stables and kennels, airy bedrooms and wood-panelled staircases, the smell of woodsmoke and plum tarts . . . It was this talk of home which fired Clement's imagination. Listening to Antoine, he was transported to another world far from the horror of the trenches and the cold memory of his Great-Aunt Mathilda's Hampstead villa. At seventeen, when he had joined up, war had seemed to him a whole future in itself and he had had no thought for what might lie beyond it. Now, in a clearing station behind the front line, he began to envisage what it could mean to think of a place as home.

'Tell me more,' he ordered when Antoine fell quiet.

A dreamy look came over Antoine as he lit another cigarette. 'There is a duck who lives on our bit of river,' he said, 'who likes to lay her eggs on top of the porch. This has always been the case, I am told, even when my father was a boy. Of course, it was not always the same duck . . . In the summer, we take a boat out on the river, but it leaks. No-one has ever repaired it. The leaking is part of the fun. In winter, the staircase creaks so that when you are lying in bed you can imagine you are on a boat with wooden masts. It is a terrible house in a way. Never any peace. But it is home.'

Home. Like a promise, the idea clung to Clement for a few days, until real life took over and shook it from his mind. Clement came out of the war haunted by a shadowy company of mutilated ghosts, who dogged his footsteps by day and filled his distorted nights with horror. They stalked him through his years at university and during his articles, they watched over his shoulder when he started his first job, they filled the public benches whenever he appeared in court and crowded the sofa of his small Battersea flat. He forgot about Antoine and the house which resembled a sailing boat. He forgot, in truth, everything good that had ever happened to him, floating through the strange limbo years between

64

demobilization and the acquisition of Marshwood with attendant ghosts his only company. Even when he came into his inheritance and the question came up of where he wanted to live, the idea of looking for a new house would probably never have occurred to him if he had not stumbled on the photograph from Antoine.

Clement had scribbled down his great-aunt's address on the back of a cigarette packet before leaving the clearing-station, and the Frenchman had sent him the picture at Christmastime in 1919. In it Antoine stood poised and a little stiff, almost unrecognizable in his civilian clothes, one hand resting in inevitable custom on the shoulder of his wife who, equally well scripted, sat before him with a baby on her lap. All wore their finest clothes, the child the most splendid of all in yards of frothy lace. They posed on the porch of a grand-looking house, and for all the rehearsed stiffness of his pose Antoine's look of triumph was unmistakable. The happy domestic scene it depicted was as alien to the anticlimax of Clement's post-war existence as it had been to his life in the trenches and yet he detected, amongst his spectral coterie, a tremor of excitement as if his ghosts sought to remind him of something once glimpsed and long forgotten.

He had no idea what sort of house he wanted to live in, or indeed where he wanted it to be. He came to Marshwood quite by chance after months of frustrated dealings with estate agents infuriated by his vague assurance that he would know what he was looking for when he found it, led there by an acquaintance from his Oxford days, an amateur archaeologist who for some unexplained reason had decided to take Clement under his wing. They spent the afternoon exploring the remains of the old Roman fort on Pater Noster. Wandering off on his own, Clement walked over the brow of the hill and there was the house nestling in its lee, its honey-coloured stone aglow in the afternoon sun, dark windows closely hugging the steep slope at the back but its south-facing façade turned towards the valley. A local agent informed him that the house had been virtually unlived in since the war. Its owners, tracked down to Scotland, had not previously considered selling but were persuaded easily enough by the amount of ready cash – much more than the market price – that Clement was able to offer them. He gave not a moment's thought to the house's isolation or general air of neglect, to the smell of damp in the closed rooms or the steep slope of the garden. Here was a place which had remained unchanged for generations, built on the Englishman's love of the land, at one with its surroundings. Clement immediately recognized Marshwood for what it was. He had come home.

He took possession of the house in early summer. He owned no furniture of his own, and had sold most of his great-aunt's, keeping only what he liked, an eclectic collection which included her baby grand piano, two walnut bookcases and a collection of fine copper pans. These, along with a few crates and cases containing his own belongings, sat expectantly in the middle of the vast empty drawing-room waiting for their assigned place while Clement, with little thought for unpacking, took a celebratory brandy and soda out onto his new terrace. As he admired the view which swept down the valley towards the hazy blue of the sea beyond, peace settled on him at last, softly, like a fine dusting of powdery snow that drew a veil over his ghosts and blew away the lingering nightmares of the past.

By the age of twenty, Bella had all the outward trappings of a country parson's daughter. In nearby Brighton, haircuts and hemlines grew shorter by the day, but in her father's country vicarage Bella had grown from adolescent mouse into a grave young woman of apparent docility, her legs decently covered, liquid brown eyes free of kohl liner, her heavy locks of curling hair imprisoned by an armoury of pins. Despite this, she was something of a hit with the local village boys, a fact which amused her chiefly because it baffled her father. She could have told him, had he bothered to ask, that he had nothing to fear from them. Behind her serious façade, Bella dreamed of falling in love as much as any girl. But somehow in her fantasies love and marriage were never an end in themselves but a gateway to independence, which the boys who filled the pews of her father's church could not hope to offer. Unlike Nancy, Bella did not rebel. She did everything her parents asked of her until her twentieth year with barely a demurral, but she never lost the sense that somehow she was just biding her time. There was a world beyond the village and the vicarage, a future which did not involve endless meetings of the Women's Institute and the Mothers' Union or the typing up of her father's dreary sermons. Her mind wandered as she listened to those same sermons on Sunday mornings, carried sometimes by the words of the gospel, sometimes by the song of birds outside. Surely Jesus wanted something *more* than this? A life of subversive teaching, of courage and defiance, a death of such cruelty, a sacrifice of such magnitude – surely He would have wanted her to embrace life, to savour and cherish it? And yet here she was, slowly suffocating with no idea of how, precisely, she was to do this. It was all wrong. Something must be done. But what?

Biding her time, Bella endured. She endured her mother's adulation of her brothers when they came home and her father's obvious pride in them, realizing that for as long as she lived at home her place must always be in their shadow. She endured the boys' noisy, well-meaning superiority towards her, her father's cold lack of interest and her mother's timid affection. She endured the terminally dull job they found her when in an uncharacteristic burst of temper she declared that she must find work or die of inaction. But the day the rural dean put his hand on her thigh and suggested she stay on a little later was the day Bella finally had enough. She told her startled boss what he could do with his job, ignored her father's anger and her mother's tears, packed her bags and announced that she was leaving to stay with Nancy in Dorset, after which she intended to go and stay with her oldest brother in London, who could do that for her if nothing else, and get herself a 'real job'. The day after her arrival in Chapel St Mary, she attended the village fête, where Clement quite literally ran into her.

She was to find out later that Clement liked the village fête immensely. There was an easy camaraderie here and a festive spirit which only just prevailed over the fierce underlying competition between exhibitors. Just before Bella burst into his life, he stood in the produce tent admiring the extravagant display of oversized vegetables, finding the spectacle at once touching and reassuring, a simple manifestation of man's faith in the renewal of perishable matter. He would try it himself, he vowed. He had been as lax in the cultivation of his land as in the furnishing of his house, keeping both in their virgin state and allowing the one to grow wild while the other remained marvellously uncluttered. *I must put it all to good use*, he told himself as he did every year at this same event. He would have the grounds landscaped, take on a gardener, let the fields to a farmer. Lost in these delicious thoughts, he decided to go in search of tea, cake, and some kind soul to advise him. He marched out of the produce tent and straight into Bella, who had just spent a delightful half-hour browsing at the second-hand book table and now stood in the middle of the crowded aisle, an inconvenient obstacle lost in the opening pages of *Crime and Punishment.*

Her sensible handbag and her parcel of books went flying. She cried out, clutching at Clement. He staggered and trod, twice, on her foot, causing her to stumble and upset a small stand displaying knitted children's toys. Somehow, in the confusion that followed – Clement on his hands and knees gathering woollen animals, Bella retrieving books and straightening her dress – he contrived, through a stream of apologies, to offer her a cup of tea.

'I am an idiot,' he sighed again and again as they repaired to a table in the corner of the tea tent. 'I could never forgive myself if I had hurt you.'

He was rather sweet, thought Bella, this awkward bachelor in his mid-thirties fussing over her with tea and a plate of cakes. As a rule she was irritated by the tongue-tied stammerings of admiring young men, but in Clement she found it rather touching.

'It was my fault entirely,' she told him. 'Of all the places to choose to read! But sometimes you can't help yourself, can you? You read a sentence and you are transported.'

'Yes!'

Bella laughed, startled by the effect of Clement's sudden beam on his very ordinary features. He leaned forward, frowning now. 'I remember once, many years ago, just after the war . . . I was on a train, and I began to read *The Count of Monte Cristo*. A fellow officer had given it to me, and I didn't get round to it until I'd been back in England for a few months – couldn't bring myself to, somehow, it reminded me of too much, the actual physical book, because he'd had it in the trenches you see, and it wasn't what you might call pristine. But that all fell away with the opening paragraph – the little boy sighting the *Pharaon*, the dock at Marseilles . . . I missed my stop. In fact I missed several stops. I was going from London to Oxford, and I ended up in Birmingham . . .' Bella laughed again. He blushed, obviously pleased. 'What were you reading when I bumped into you?'

'*Crime and Punishment*.'

'That seems curiously appropriate,' he chuckled, and she thought it was a nice sound, well modulated, neither too loud nor too quiet but just right.

Dressed in white, with her mass of gently waving brown hair released from its pins and tied loosely in the nape of her neck, she looked, he told her later, like one of the Pre-Raphaelite Madonnas he had seen in the art books he had begun to order to bridge the gaps in his education. They talked for a long time about books

71

they had read, not noticing the surreptitious glances they attracted, the arched eyebrows and knowing smiles which heralded a promising booty of local gossip. They were still pleasantly ensconced almost an hour later, reciting opening paragraphs to each other from memory with a fresh teapot between them and the remains of what had been a hearty cream tea, when Nancy finally tracked Bella down and chivvied her away.

Nancy had put together a punishing schedule for her friend of lunches, teas, dinners, and assorted activities in between. Clement was never a part of these. The lunches were exclusively female affairs, the tea parties predominantly so. The dinners included friends of Nancy's husband Peter, younger men who spoke of shooting and hunting and the money markets and interested Bella not in the slightest. She suspected they did not interest Nancy either, seeing how her friend's eyes drifted and conversation lagged. Clement took to calling in the afternoons, in the lull which followed tea. An awkward moment, frowned Nancy, because it was too early for drinks and what on earth was one to serve him?

The first time, he brought a book. 'The *Wessex Poems*,' he said, almost apologizing. 'I thought, since you are in Dorset, Thomas Hardy . . . Perhaps you know them. It's . . .' – he looked suddenly shy – 'it's a first edition.'

The second time, he brought news of an exhibition in Dorchester which he thought might interest them. And the third time, he brought an invitation to Marshwood.

'He *is* a bit strange,' said Nancy as they bowled up the lane in her little red sports car. 'So reclusive. No-one's ever been to his house, that I know of anyway. I rather think he's stalking you.'

'I like him,' said Bella. 'He's different.'

'Hmm,' said Nancy. 'Well, don't like him too much, or you'll encourage him. I do hope Peter joins us soon.'

In time, Marshwood would echo with voices calling out to each other down its corridors, feet would thunder up and down its stairs and the chaos of shared existence would spread into every nook and cranny. Hundreds of people would come here, would become, however infinitesimally, a part of the house's living fabric. But Marshwood was still in its infancy at the time of Bella's first visit, a haven but not yet a home, a perfect antidote to the crowded miseries of Clement's war, marking a pause before the onset of a future when it would cease to be entirely his. He had looked after the house since moving in, of course, put in a new roof, run damp courses, redone exterior pointing and repainted interior walls. But beyond the work necessary to assure the solidity, the *permanence* of his home, he had done nothing.

The walls of the drawing-room were bare, its wooden floors unadorned, its windows uncurtained. They sat on straight-backed chairs around a plain low table, and

Bella found herself more saddened than surprised by the austerity in which her jolly tea companion chose to live. He was nervous. The housekeeper had laid out drinks in the drawing-room by the French windows and he served them himself, fussing over ice and lemon, and how much gin, and would they like vermouth or bitters or just plain tonic water? Conversation was stilted until Peter arrived. Tall and lanky, with the insouciant arrogance of those born to money, Nancy's husband loped into the room and was immediately set upon by his wife.

'Where have you *been*?' she hissed. 'We got here *hours* ago.'

Bella caught Clement's eye and gave an apologetic half-smile. He asked shyly if she would like to look around the grounds.

He led her to the edge of the terrace and she stood without knowing it in the very spot which Clement had occupied on the day he moved in, drinking in the same soaring view. Thoughts of a new life seeking work in London, which had so occupied her when she left home, were quite gone now. Standing here she fantasized about a different future, tied to this house. She saw windows thrown open to the sweet Dorset air, carpets and cushions and paintings and clutter. She saw her children, two boys and two girls whom she would love equally. They would go to local schools for as long as possible, and when the time came for them to be sent away she would write every week, and visit, and always be there for them, and always be close.

'May I show you something else?' Clement's shy question cut into her reverie. He stood a little distance from her on the edge of the terrace, one shoulder turned away, as though inviting her to follow. 'It won't take long but it's . . . well, it's what I'm most proud of, really.'

He led her towards the low outbuildings grouped further down the hill between the garden and the paddock.

'This is the garage . . . my housekeeper's little cottage . . . this one is for the gardener, such as he is, I must do something about that, landscaping and so on . . . Here.'

She followed him into the low barn and blinked, waiting for her eyes to grow accustomed to the watery light which filtered in through a bank of small, rather dusty windows.

A solid workbench, some twelve feet long, ran along the wall of the barn. Bella spotted what she thought was a lathe, and a selection of wood-turning tools. The hard-packed earth floor beneath the bench was strewn with curly wood shavings, and the air was redolent with the sharp sweet smells of sawdust, spirits and linseed oil. Cloths, tins and bottles jostled for space on shelves cut into the wall, but it was the table in the centre of the room that caught Bella's attention, an ordinary round oak table on which rested a whole menagerie of carved animals. Horses, dogs, cats, mice . . . she stepped closer. The carvings, rich and glossy, had a rounded naïvety which breathed life into them more surely than a more precise rendering of detail might have done, each little statue seeming to carry within it the essence of the creature it represented. Bella stretched out a hand, her fingers itching to touch them. She glanced up at Clement, who stood against his workbench, fiddling with a piece of wood which looked as if it might one day become a badger.

'You made all these?'

'I . . . well, yes.'

'Do you . . . do you sell them?' It seemed a poor question compared to those she would have liked to ask.

'No, I . . . well, I'm still learning. I take classes. I want to learn to make furniture as well. I'm . . . you see, I'm a solicitor actually, or rather I was . . . No heart for it, really. Whereas this . . . well, there's plenty of money, and I do love . . . *enjoy* it.' He stopped, hot with embarrassment.

'Well, I think they're beautiful,' declared Bella.

'Take one.' He left the security of his bench and advanced towards her, hands extended out to the table. 'Please.'

'I wouldn't know which to choose.'

'Here.' His tone was suddenly decisive. He plucked a small bird from the table. 'This one's yours.'

'How do you know?'

'It just is.'

The bird was sleek and round-breasted. It seemed to gaze back at her, the expression in its glossy wooden eye at once mischievous and solemn.

'I love it,' said Bella.

He blushed. 'I know the house doesn't look like much. I don't care so much for interiors. I spend most of my time here. The library is comfortable and the piano is tuned, and beyond that . . .'

'I think the house is lovely,' said Bella, and it was true, because in her mind it had already become something other than what it actually was.

'It was a strange conception – the house and me. A curious path which led me here . . .'

Inside, in the inhospitable drawing-room, Peter droned tonelessly on about his day's meetings while Nancy drained her second gin and tonic. Outside, Clement walked Bella slowly around his estate, pointing out a fine rose, a promising fruit tree, a family of rabbits on the edge of the woods, all the while telling her about the Vesle, Antoine and the photograph that had led him here.

'I've never spoken about this to anyone before,' he told her. 'It's not something I have ever wanted to talk about.'

'Why did you now?'

'Because somehow I find that I can.'

And so it began.

Nancy did her best to talk her out of it. 'I suppose you

think you're Charlotte Brontë,' she said gloomily. 'But honestly darling, he's hardly Heathcliff material. And think how messily that all ended.'

'I like him,' repeated Bella. 'And Heathcliff was Emily Brontë, by the way. Not Charlotte. Charlotte wrote *Jane Eyre*. Which,' she mused, 'somehow feels more appropriate.'

'*I* think he's perfectly sweet.' Kitty had recently moved to the area after her marriage to a young Bambridge doctor, and she had become friends with Nancy and Bella. 'I like him too.'

'Oh God!' cried Nancy. 'Don't encourage her!'

Clement was seventeen years older than Bella. He did not cut a remotely romantic figure, being on the small side of average in height, with sandy hair, muddy eyes and a slight limp, his legacy from the war. But his whole face lit up when he smiled, and he adored her. He fell in love with her gladly, absolutely, believing her to be the final step towards his salvation. She had never dreamed of a husband such as he, but she would never admit that she married him for any material reason. She liked and respected him, enjoyed his conversation and his peaceful outlook on life. She convinced herself that her fondness was in fact love, and although she had a secret liking for the sunset endings of her mother's clandestine novels, even at her young age she had the good sense to realize that these were quite irrelevant to the business of getting on with life.

*   *   *

The sky was heavy and overcast on Sunday morning, spitting occasional rain from sullen clouds. Bella, wrapped in shawls, settled on the sofa with the sports pages of the weekend paper. An inveterate gambler, studying the racing selection was one of her favourite activities. Marcus knelt at a low table, pinning dead insects to sheets of coloured paper. Beth lay on the floor, twitching pieces of string in an attempt to coax her kitten out from beneath an armchair.

Isla fidgeted, unable to keep still.

'Doesn't anybody want to go out?'

'Darling, look at the weather.'

'Children?'

'Did you know,' frowned Marcus, 'that woodlice are crustaceans?'

Bella gave a shout of laughter. 'You go,' she said. 'I'll look after the children.'

'I don't want to go on my own.'

'You always used to.'

And then the doorbell rang and it was Jack, asking if they would like to go out for a walk.

Will I see you again?

That's why I came back.

In the twenty-four hours since their meeting at the gate to Pater Noster the uneasy excitement provoked by their closing exchange had given way to anger, anger which swelled now into self-righteous rage at his apparent assumption that nothing between them had changed.

'No,' said Isla. 'We wouldn't.'

'Who is it?' called Bella from her sofa.

'It's Jack,' spat Isla.

'I was just wondering,' said Jack amiably, side-stepping Isla to wander into the drawing-room, 'if anyone wanted to come for a walk.'

'Jack!' cried Bella. 'Isla was just saying how much she wanted to go out. Take her away and let us be lazy in peace.'

'I'm not lazy,' remarked Beth. 'I'm very, very busy.'

'Busy being lazy,' snorted Marcus.

'I'll get my boots then,' said Isla through gritted teeth.

'I'll wait outside,' said Jack.

Bella peeled herself off the sofa to see them off.

'Why did you *do* that?' asked Isla in a furious whisper as she tied her bootlaces. 'Supposing I didn't want to go?'

'But you did want to go,' said Bella comfortably. 'I must say I think he's grown rather dashing. I shall enjoy having him as my neighbour again. And *Nancy* will be beside herself with excitement.'

'Well *you* go for a walk with him. The pair of you.'

'Tut tut. Have fun!'

Bella closed the door. Jack ambled over. 'Ready?'

'Sure.'

'I thought maybe we could do the St Ann's walk,' he said. 'Then back over the top of Pater Noster. If that's all right with you?'

'Fine.'

The steep primrose-clad banks which bordered the road down to Chapel St Mary gave way as they entered the village to stone walls enclosing cottage gardens cheered by daffodils, bergenia and fritillaria. Tight buds on the apple tree at the entrance to the churchyard hinted further at the promise of spring. Jack walked easily beside Isla, slowing his long easy strides to her pace. They did not talk and the silence between them grew thicker until she thought that it must be almost visible, like the drops of moisture which shimmered in the damp morning air. She racked her brain for words to break the tension. None were forthcoming.

They turned into the footpath bordering the churchyard, where the dripping branches of the uncut hedgerow brushed their sleeves and shoulders.

'Lucky we're wearing waterproofs,' said Isla.

'You're angry with me.'

She understood from the calm simplicity of his statement that denial would be pointless.

'Yes,' she admitted.

'For coming back?'

'Partly.'

'For staying away?'

'That too.'

'I'm sorry.'

And now the anger was like a darkness welling up from deep within, blinding her with more unwanted tears. They had arrived at the stile into the field which led to the foot of St Ann's. Isla grasped the wooden fence and swung herself over. A bramble, snaking out of the overgrown hedgerow, snatched at her gloveless hand, drawing blood.

'Show me?'

'I'm fine.' Isla raised her hand to her mouth. Blood, ferrous and salty, coated her tongue.

'I've got a handkerchief . . .'

'I *said* I'm fine!'

'Isla . . .'

She was crying openly now, words spilling out without control. 'I *trusted* you. And I *missed* you. And you just . . . you just *waltz* back, like none of it mattered, like we're best mates or something . . .'

She stopped, drew a breath, sniffed loudly. Jack took her arm and led her away from the hedge, to the middle of the field and the shelter of a large oak tree.

'Here, sit down, catch your breath.'

The ground beneath the oak was dry. They sat with their backs against its trunk, a careful distance from each other, not touching. They had been climbing slowly since joining the footpath, and from their vantage point beneath the tree they looked down on the village dominated by the square tower of the church.

Behind them, only half a mile away, was St Ann's Hill. Two horses stood nose to tail in a corner of the field, ignoring them.

'Now,' said Jack.

'I'm sorry,' mumbled Isla. 'I'm being absurd.'

'I don't think so.'

'It's not like I've spent the last fifteen years . . . I mean, I'm *happy*, you know? Married, with lovely children . . . It's just, seeing you, it brings things back.'

'I missed you. That's why I came back. I wanted to see you. I *needed* to see you.'

His comment struck her as dangerously emotional. She followed his gaze down the hill and wished she had not started this.

'It was great though, wasn't it?' said Jack.

'What was great?'

'You and me. Us. Everything how it used to be . . . you know, before. Running wild, king and queen of all we surveyed. Getting into trouble, not caring. I wish we could go back to being children. Before I fucked up.'

'You didn't *really* fuck up.'

'Sweet Isla.' He smiled and reached out a hand to touch hers briefly. 'You're too generous. But we both know I fucked up. And I really am sorry.'

Isla, confused by the touch of his hand, said nothing. 'Isla?'

'It doesn't matter.' She closed her eyes and rested her

head against the trunk of the tree. *No*, she thought. *It doesn't matter. Because that was then, and this is now, and the fact that we are here and able to talk about it somehow cancels out that fifteen-year-old hurt.*

'Granna is dictating her memoirs,' she told him. 'She's convinced that they are all that stand between her and being forcibly ejected from Marshwood.'

She peered round the tree at him. His eyes were closed, but there was a distinct upward curve to his mouth.

'Explain?'

She told him everything: the burglary, the insurance, Richard's decision, Bella's reaction. She began to lose her inhibitions as she talked, embroidering the facts a little, exaggerating just enough to make the story funny, gently poking fun at Bella in the way they always had together. 'I'm not entirely clear how exactly the memoirs will help,' she concluded. 'But they *are* fascinating. I never knew about Grandpapa and the war.'

'Yeah well. Some things people don't talk about. What does he do, your husband?'

'He's a lawyer.'

'So he *has* money.'

'Yes, but not endless supplies.'

'And *you* don't want to sell Marshwood?'

'Of course not! But if we can't afford to keep it . . .'

'Don't you get a say in the funding question?'

'I don't work.'

'But still . . .'

'It changes things.' She followed his gaze down the hill, unwilling to talk about Richard. 'Tell me about your love life.'

'You're changing the subject.'

'Not at all. It's a logical progression from our earlier conversation.'

'There's nothing to say.'

'No woman?'

'There was. It ended.'

A new silence settled between them, heavy with secrets.

'I'm sorry,' said Isla.

'Yeah well.' His voice was rough, but she thought she heard it catch. 'It's been a fuck of a time.'

A pheasant took off nearby in a cackle of beating wings, making them both jump. Isla laughed. Jack jumped to his feet, looking very much his old self as he laid down his challenge.

'A bet!' he announced. 'That I can get to the bottom of St Ann's Hill before you.'

'Hardly a *fair* bet,' countered Isla. 'You're way faster than me.'

'I'll give you a headstart.'

'Two minutes.'

'One.'

'One and a half!'

'Done.'

She grinned. 'What's the forfeit?'

'The forfeit?' His eyes sparkled with a wicked gleam. 'A kiss.'

Isla laughed again. 'No forfeit,' she shouted as she began to run.

She ran as she had not run for years, yelling and screaming, stretching out to grab him when he passed her, scrambling through thickets to find short cuts, bent on victory. She arrived at the foot of St Ann's less than a minute after him and out of old habit collapsed into his arms, gasping with laughter with her hair over her face. They stood in the shadows beneath the hunched mass of the oak-flanked hill, and as she drew in deep breaths she felt that she could taste its smell, so different from Pater Noster's, the dark sweet smell of humus and bluebells. Her body tingled and her eyes shone as he held her by the shoulders, helping her recover her breath after the run. In that moment Isla forgot Richard who had stayed behind in London, the children back at Marshwood, Bella and her memoirs. She forgot the past fifteen years and the way her story with Jack had ended.

'Well, sir,' she smiled, reverting to the language of their childhood challenges. 'Do you claim your forfeit?'

And then a shadow crossed his face which told her that unlike her he had not forgotten, which on the contrary showed that he was far away from here, in a place she did not know, caught in memories which were not of her.

He was so much taller than her. It had never failed to surprise her as a teenager, after so many childhood years of feeling that their bodies were almost inter-changeable. She stood on tiptoe and pulled his face down towards hers.

'There,' she said, trying not to mind that he barely seemed to notice the kiss she planted on his cheek. 'Forfeit paid.'

Isla met Richard at a house party in London two years after she graduated from Cambridge, and she married him eighteen months later after a whirlwind romance. None of Isla's few previous boyfriends had measured up to their secret comparison to Jack, but Richard almost immediately obliterated any of her lingering feelings for him.

He was leaving just as she arrived at the party, and he was very drunk. He took one look at her and refused to let her pass.

'Your eyes,' he informed her, his massive frame blocking the doorway, 'are like the Aegean Sea just after sunset.'

'You mean pink?' she asked.

'Blue,' he slurred. 'Wassyourname?'

Even drunk, he was gorgeous. She told him.

'Isla,' he murmured. His face lit up with triumph. 'Like an island. In the Aegean!'

She laughed outright, then realized that he had passed out, still standing slumped against the wall. He called her the following day, ostensibly to apologize, actually to ask her out. On their first date he took her to a restaurant on the South Bank with breathtaking views of the Thames, then kissed her after dinner pressed up against the railings along the riverside walk. Their second date was at a boutique hotel in Bath where they made love almost continuously for an entire weekend, at the end of which he asked her to marry him. Two weeks later, he flew her to Paris, where they fucked standing up under an evil-smelling bridge and he presented her with a ring. A month after that, when she still hadn't given him an answer, he took her to meet his parents. And in their mock Tudor mansion in a quiet part of the New Forest, Isla fell in love.

His father, Hugh, was a chartered accountant with a gouty leg and a passion for Hemingway. His mother, Elizabeth, served home-made steak and kidney pudding for lunch, followed by a lemon meringue pie she had also made herself.

'I can't believe you actually cooked all this,' sighed Isla happily between helpings.

'It's terrifically easy.'

'*Nobody* in my family cooks. My grandmother thinks the Marks & Spencer ready meal is the pinnacle of

Western civilization. And my mum's idea of a hot meal is a cup of coffee.'

'Isla grew up with her grandmother,' interjected Richard, smiling fondly. 'And her mother lives in Spain.'

She braced herself for the inevitable further questioning, but it never came. 'I can teach you if you like,' smiled Elizabeth. 'When you come again.'

After lunch they took the dogs for a walk, two sprightly golden Labradors who ran tirelessly after the sticks Richard threw for them.

'You're different here,' she told him. 'More gentle. Actually, nicer.'

'Does that mean you *will* marry me?'

'It means I'll think about it.'

She fell in love with Richard because at twenty-five he looked like a Nordic god and she couldn't get enough of him in bed, because he was clever and impetuous, because she adored his family and he was nice to his dogs, and because once, during a night of unusually tender love-making, he whispered to her that their children would be beautiful. And when she did think of Jack on her wedding day, it was only to giggle at the mental picture of him not as a lover but as a little boy again, wide-eyed with delight at the sight of the vintage Rolls hired to carry her to the village church.

'It's not too late to change your mind.' Bella, who had

taken against Richard from the beginning, looked up at her hopefully from inside the car.

'I'm not changing my mind.'

As Isla turned to walk back down the aisle on Richard's arm, she paused to survey the congregation. She saw Bella sitting with the Coven and a weeping Callie, her parents-in-law with Richard's brothers, and a crowd of friends and colleagues. She saw all of this as well as her radiant future, and as she stepped out of the church into the weak spring sunshine, her love for her new husband was overwhelming.

'You haven't forgotten about this evening?'

Twelve years after her perfect wedding day and two weeks after her walk with Jack, Isla stood bleary-eyed in her kitchen on a typical school morning willing herself to rise above the familiar pandemonium of a family weekday breakfast.

'Hello! Earth to Isla?' She started. Richard was looking at her impatiently. 'Reception. Tonight. Waldorf,' he enunciated.

'Of course,' she replied unconvincingly. 'I'm really looking forward to it.'

Marcus marched into the kitchen and thrust a hand at her. The pale yellow mucus which covered it dribbled onto her jumper.

'Leo's been sick. We have to take him to the vet.'

'I have to take *you* to school.'

'If *I* were sick, you'd take me to the doctor.'

'Not unless you had a temperature.'

'I know how to take a cat's temperature. I saw the vet do it. What you do is, you take a thermometer, and you stick it up his—'

'School.' Isla gave her son's nose a playful tweak, aware that she had snapped and that this had been unfair. 'I promise I'll make sure Leo's all right. Where's your sister?'

'She's gone back to bed. Like she does every morning.'

'Oh for Christ's sake,' said Richard. 'Isla, she can't *keep* refusing to go to school. You're going to have to do something about it.'

I can't do this any more, thought Isla. The realization was as sudden as it was absolute. *I actually, physically cannot carry on doing this every single day . . .*

Richard was still talking to her, pulling on his jacket. 'You will wear something appropriate?'

'Excuse me?' Even her own voice sounded distant to her now.

'For the reception?' His eyes flicked over her, taking in the random selection of clothes she had pulled on after sleeping through the morning alarm. It was not fair, she thought in a burst of silent anger, to judge her appearance so early on a school day.

'Right-o,' she said. 'Appropriate. No leather, no whips.'

Richard frowned. *Once upon a time*, she thought, *that would have made him laugh.*

He shrugged. 'Whatever. Just don't be late.'

Isla, a trained architect and the winner of several small professional prizes, gave up the job she loved and at which she excelled when she fell pregnant with Marcus. Looking back on this decision in the years that followed, it struck her that this was the first compromise of their married life which was entirely one-sided, and she wondered if this fact, even more than the amount of time she spent alone, was at the root of her growing loneliness.

'There's no *point* you still working,' Richard had insisted when she protested that surely, like so many women, she could do both. They had researched various forms of childcare and been appalled at the cost. 'It'll eat up all your salary. It doesn't make sense.'

She protested that she loved her job, that she had trained hard for it, that it brought her pleasure. She had ambitions, dreams of award-winning public buildings, of developing a model of social architecture which would revolutionize modern living space, of contributing to journals and debates. He countered with idyllic descriptions of family life, implying that his own upbringing – healthy, conventional, happy – put him in a better position than hers to judge what was right for their children and for them. His mother had never worked. His father had provided for them. Social stereotyping existed for a reason, and that reason was that it was a solid functioning model.

Isla gave in because she wanted to please him and because pregnancy awakened in her resentments and insecurities she had never known existed. Awash with hormones, she wept bitterly for the father she barely remembered and brooded angrily over her mother's desertion. They visited the New Forest often in the months leading to the birth and every home-made scone, every well-cooked meal, every little attention of her mother-in-law's screamed at her that this was what she had missed out on, this cosseting, this security. Later she would feel ashamed of herself for such thoughts, which she would come to see as a betrayal of Marshwood and of her grandparents. At the time, they all conspired to her capitulation.

The first years of parenthood had felt like a partnership, an adventure in which both Isla and Richard pulled equal weight. They had been happy – not just pleased with their lot, contented, peaceful, but genuinely, soul-stirringly, get up singing in the morning happy. Whereas now – when had it taken root, this imbalance between them? When had the politics of money so invaded their relationship that Richard became implicitly acknowledged as the provider, she as the receiver? When had every non-essential expenditure – and God knew they could afford them – begun to be met with raised eyebrows and pursed lips and little throwaway remarks, more often than not in front of other people, spoken with rolled eyes and shrugged shoulders, *women, you know what they're like, what can you do?* Sometimes she thought that their entire relationship revolved around his work: how much he was earning (a lot, though in his view not enough); how long his hours were (he was rarely home before ten o'clock); more lately, who was going to fill the shoes of one of his firm's senior partners after his upcoming retirement (Richard, clearly, was the more deserving, but there were two others in the running). Isla, the children, their life as a family – all felt very secondary compared to the overwhelming energy Richard put into advancing his career.

The trouble is, thought Isla, having extracted Beth from her bed and wiped the cat-sick off her jumper, dropped the children at school and returned via the supermarket, *that there's nothing I really have to do. Every day is like the one before, punctuated by dropping the children off at school and picking them up again. And I'm sure it is good for them to be with me but in the hours when I am alone I could literally be anybody – the cleaner Richard won't let me have, a secretary, an interior designer.* It had been bearable until Beth started school full time, but now her days were so empty she could scream.

Isla put away the shopping and wandered into the study to compose a list, less because she needed it than to give herself a sense of purpose.

Car MOT – book service too

Bake cake for school sale – remember baking powder!!!
No nuts!!!

Check cat is not dying of feline flu. And if he is <u>do not flirt</u>
<u>with the vet as it embarrasses EVERYONE</u>

She smiled glumly as she re-read her list. Isla had not
been prepared, when she agreed to give up work, for
the curious contradiction which was her experience
of motherhood: overwhelming love on the one hand,
on the other blind panic before a life reduced to the
repetition of routine chores, to a largely absent husband,
to the fear of loneliness so constantly haunting that she
thought not in terms of good and bad days but of good
and bad moments forever succeeding each other. She had
her own way of dealing with the dark thoughts which
crowded her mind with increasing frequency, having
discovered within herself an ability to switch off and
enter a state of floating non-emotion in which nothing
could touch her. As long as there were no surprises, no
breaks or upheavals in their day-to-day lives, she could
cope. As long as her children were happy. As long as
the house was well run. As long as Richard did not
complain. As long as all this balance was maintained,
then she could pretend that this detachment was in fact
a form of serenity, and ignore her occasional random
tears. And yet now . . .

Isla, lost in a reverie all her own, smiled as her pen

flew across her list of chores. A messy shock of hair, high cheekbones, the hollow curve of a once round face, a mouth both sensuous and melancholy, black ink eyes which stared intensely out at her. Unbidden, Jack's face appeared from the tip of her pen. She blew on it gently to dry the ink then, still smiling, drew a cloud of love hearts around it. The phone rang, making her jump.

'About tonight,' said Richard.

'Tonight?'

'You'd forgotten!'

Their breakfast conversation came back to her as a hazy memory. 'Waldorf reception. Seven. Nice dress. Of course I hadn't forgotten.' She glanced guiltily down at her to-do list, scratched out her sketch of Jack and wrote *book babysitter* beneath it in big letters.

'Something's come up. I have to work instead.'

She drew a line through *book babysitter* and drew a smiley face.

'You'll have to cancel the babysitter.'

'Not a problem,' said Isla.

'You sound cheerful,' said Richard suspiciously. 'Are you OK?'

'God I'm not *that* grumpy, am I?'

'I thought you might be looking forward to it.'

Isla, who hated Richard's work functions, resisted the temptation to snort.

'Anyway, whatever. I'll be late. Don't wait up.'

She ran into a friend at the school gate that afternoon and accepted her invitation to tea. It was growing dark when she finally came home with the children. Marcus and Beth, wildly excited, ran shouting to evade her half-hearted attempts to wash them. In the end she slid into their bath herself and they tore off their clothes, hurling themselves in after her and flooding the bathroom floor. Later she let them sleep in her bed. She lay between them after reading their story, wide awake in the darkness. A soft silence descended on her bedroom, broken only by the remote hum of west London traffic and the barely perceptible sound of their intermingled breathing. Beth sighed and threw an arm around her mother's neck. Isla inhaled the sweet baby smell which still clung to her daughter, trailing her lips like a lover down the rose-petal softness of her arm, recognizing in this painful, magical moment that glimpse of something greater than herself, when she rode her love for her children like the crest of a wave and the landscape of her existence was flooded with light. The morning's to-do list with its silly portrait of Jack was safely consigned to the shredder. And really nothing could come close to making her feel as she did then, in bed with both her children: this adoration of the flesh, this devotion begotten of sacrifice, this intimacy born of sharing every detail of existence. Even as she was aware, throughout such moments, of their heart-breaking undertow, their fragile transience, she clung to the certainty they offered that she was living her life as she was meant to.

Bella chose the following evening to dictate the next chapter of her memoir. She called late, as Isla and Richard were getting ready for bed, and declared that she couldn't sleep.

'Who the fuck is it?' shouted Richard from the bathroom.

'Shh!' hissed Isla. 'It's Granna.'

'Well tell her to call back tomorrow like a normal person.'

'Of course it's not too late!' carolled Isla into the phone. Richard came in and glared at her. 'I'll just take the phone down to the study.' *Sorry*, she mouthed. *It's important.*

Richard's introduction to Bella had been as disastrous as Isla's first meeting with his parents had been positive, and had resulted in mutual and unwavering disapproval.

'Do you enjoy Pepys?' This, after a brief exchange of innocuous pleasantries, had been Bella's opening salvo.

'I beg your pardon?'

'Samuel Pepys. Do you enjoy him? I am re-reading his diaries. I find it fascinating how much of what he writes is still relevant today. Don't you agree?'

'I'm afraid I've never read him.'

'Never read Pepys!' It had taken Bella a while to digest this piece of information. 'Well, what *do* you read?'

'Newspapers, mainly. Sometimes thrillers. I don't really have time for books.'

'No time for books! But what do you *do*?'

'I work.'

'What, all the time?'

Isla had been furious, and Bella had defended herself with vigour as soon as Richard left the room. 'Darling, he can't be right for you. He hasn't read Pepys!'

'I hate to break this to you Granna but *most* people haven't read Pepys.'

'*You* have!'

'Only because you made me!'

'What would your grandfather have made of it, you being with a man who didn't read?'

'Well, probably, if he saw that I loved him, he would have been happy.'

'What did your grandfather actually do?' asked Richard later. They lay together on her bed, but for the first time she could remember they were both fully clothed, and arguing.

'He inherited a lot of money from his Great-Aunt Mathilda, who raised him after his parents died.'

'That was it?'

'He invested it – rather well, as it happened. And he bought land. And he, er . . .'

'He didn't work?'

'Well, he did, sort of. He was a local magistrate, and he made beautiful furniture, and sometimes ran wood-turning workshops, and he loved gardening, and he . . .'

'Let me guess. He read a lot.'

Even then, before Isla had asked him for a penny towards the upkeep of Marshwood, before the stock market crash when there was still sufficient money in Bella's funds to keep the house going in something resembling good repair, he had made it clear what he thought of her living there.

'It's absurd.'

'It's her home!'

'It's a museum.'

'She loves it. *I* love it. I hoped you would too.'

'It gives me the creeps.'

She had silenced him with a kiss and as they finally made love she had put his peevishness down to hurt pride, and told herself that in time he would come round to her way of seeing things.

They had exhausted Isla ever since, these two people who purported to love her more than anyone else, in their attempt to pull her over to their side, away from the other. It was typical of Bella to call at this moment, when she should have known that Isla might be with Richard.

'I wouldn't want to interrupt anything,' said Bella.

'You're not,' said Isla. Richard had had a quiet, almost

resigned look of expectancy about him, the look which she knew preceded sexual overture and consequently either dissimulation on her part or disappointment on his. *With any luck*, she thought, *he will be asleep by the time I go back upstairs.*

'Only I couldn't sleep.'

'It *is* only half-past ten.'

'I know I wouldn't be able to,' said Bella in a small voice.

'It really doesn't matter,' Isla assured her. 'I love hearing about all this.'

She curled up at one end of the study sofa, wrapped in a blanket. 'I'm going to put you on loudspeaker. Then I can take notes.'

There was married life before the war, and married life once the war started, and there was life before Louis, and there was life after Louis. There were gentle satisfactions and petty frustrations, innocent pleasures and guilty secrets, and then there were emotions which crushed and overwhelmed, emotions which spoke of a life far beyond Chapel St Mary and Bambridge, a life which belonged to no place but was an ache of longing and desire and pain and joy which lasted a few brief weeks and which marked her for ever.

'I suppose it's only to be expected,' Clement's old housekeeper had said mournfully to all and sundry when he announced his wedding. 'There are going to be changes up at the old house.' And changes there were. Clement had given Bella free rein to renovate Marshwood and she threw herself into the project with gusto while he looked on, besotted and not a little bemused. Miss Bates, as lavish with her tongue as Bella was with her spending, informed all who cared to listen (and they were many) of every new development. 'Suede cushions,' she told her friends over tea and buns. 'Pink. Brown leather sofas, *and* she's got rid of the settee.'

'It's a pity you're not opening a hotel,' drawled Nancy on one of her frequent visits. 'That woman is giving you no end of free publicity, the whole of Bambridge is agog and longing for an invitation. There are the most amazing rumours going round. Ghastly Mrs Pinkerton asked me this morning if it was true you had two stuffed peacocks mounted above the drawing-room mantelpiece. *Alas no*, I told her. *Only the one, but it's ever so big.'*

Builders, plasterers, carpenters, painters. Upholsterers, decorators, stylists. Clement joked that more people came to Marshwood in the first six months of their marriage than in the ten years he had lived there alone. Deliveries streamed in, of carpets and lamps, furniture and paintings. Bella knocked down the wall between the drawing-room and the old parlour, repainted bedrooms in soft pretty colours and covered beds with quilted counterpanes. She curtained windows and hung pictures, threw rose-patterned rugs over the bare oak floors, opened up fireplaces and modernized the kitchen. She hired a housemaid to help Miss Bates and gave precise instructions of what they were to do. Under her orders the house gleamed, glass sparkled, wood shone, the darkest corners were energetically dusted. The rooms smelt of beeswax and fresh flowers, the bathrooms of Jif and Yardley's Lily of the Valley, the wardrobes of starched linen and lavender. Outside she oversaw the overhaul of the orchard and the planting of a herb garden, the sowing of new flowerbeds and the pruning back of the many creepers – honeysuckle, clematis and wisteria – which had grown rampant under Clement's neglect. The garden at Marshwood never did quite shake off its air of semi-wildness, but under the watchful eyes of Bella and her newly appointed head gardener it acquired the look of a more kempt wilderness.

They had both come to marriage with certain expectations, and were pleased to find that these were met. Clement had Bella. Bella had her autonomy. They both had Marshwood. Once the frenzy of renovation had abated, life settled into a pleasant routine. Mornings, on the whole, were spent at home. After breakfast – which they always ate together, with Bella reading aloud from the newspaper – Clement went to his study to talk to his stockbroker while Bella had her daily consultation with Miss Bates and the new cook. After this she telephoned orders to the shops in Bambridge, dealt with the post, wrote letters and read as much as she could. In the afternoons she changed her clothes and either went visiting or received visitors while Clement tended to his own affairs. In the evenings, they entertained or went out. *Life*, she wrote in one of her weekly letters home, *is a never-ending round of coffee mornings and afternoon teas, tennis and bridge parties, parish meetings and lectures, visits, dinners and receptions. You must come and stay again soon*, she added, not without an element of satisfaction because although she knew it was childish, she loved to show off her new circumstances to her family.

Bed, an inevitable part of what Nancy referred to as her *wifely duties*, was punctual and courteous, involving much asking for permission and profusion of thanks, generally performed in their nightclothes with the lights out. It was a far cry from the passionate embraces described in her mother's library books, and she could not help wondering what all the fuss was about. She longed for children but it took nearly three years for Bella to fall pregnant, three years during which she grew secretly obsessed with the thought that she might not be able to conceive at all. On the day she finally found out she was expecting, in the early summer of 1939, she went into Clement's study to tell him and wept. Then, seeing his look of alarm, she laughed. Then cried again. Then laughed, and carried on laughing for days.

Although she couldn't be sure, she liked to think that it had happened in Rome, in a hotel overlooking the Spanish Steps during their annual holiday abroad. Bella loved these trips, which to her mind summed up just how far she had come from her father's sombre vicarage: she loved the cadences of different languages, the unexpected smells, the taste of new food. The art, the landscapes, the people . . . It seemed entirely fitting to her that her first pregnancy should come to symbolize her own twin passions for travel and for home. When the time came, she decided, she would order the baby's layette from Italy. In the meantime, she bought new gramophone records of Italian opera.

'He can't hear you,' said Clement tenderly.

'Kitty says she can.' It was a little joke between them, one of the many that had sprung up since the pregnancy, this alternation of 'he' and 'she' when talking about the baby. 'Kitty sang to both her babies in the womb, and she says they're extremely musical.'

Marshwood, the garden, the pretty bedrooms and the new kitchen, it had all been done for *them*, the four children she had imagined on the terrace on that first visit. *All anyone can talk about is the coming war*, she noted in her diary in the closing days of August. *And all I can think about is this baby. I have never been so happy. Ever, ever, ever.*

She miscarried a week later.

Everything changed with the war, but Bella barely noticed this in the early months. She had lost a lot of blood with her miscarriage, and a secondary infection dragged on into the autumn, leaving her weak and depressed. She kept to her bedroom all through the bitter winter, re-reading old favourites and warmed by hot-water bottles. The cook left to join the Women's Land Army and the housemaid, giddy with young love, got married and resigned to follow her new Navy husband to Dartmouth. Josie Bates announced that she too would leave as soon as Bella was better, to do her patriotic duty keeping house for a colonel billeted in Bambridge. In the meantime she struggled to keep the house going alone and cooked starchy meals which Clement and Bella ate off trays, sometimes together, more often not. He had moved out of their bedroom and slept on the sofa in his study, an arrangement Bella was too tired to question. By the time she came downstairs again, Marshwood felt like a very different house.

'I had to close off most of the bedrooms,' said the old housekeeper mournfully. 'Couldn't keep them going on my own. And Mr Langton, he don't use the dining-room no more, nor the drawing-room, so they've been shut up too. I go in once a week to do the dusting.'

'It's so cold.'

'Well, what with fuel rationing, and the house being hardly used . . .'

'But where is Mr Langton?'

'In his study most of the time, else in that workshop of his. I don't see him except for when I bring him his meals. I've been that worried about him, all alone in there, but of course I didn't want to say anything until you were better.'

'Of course,' said Bella. 'Well, that's very kind of you.'

She was aware that at this moment she was being judged, though she did not understand what for. 'I think I'll go down to the workshop now,' she said with a touch of hauteur. 'We'll eat in the dining-room at lunchtime. Nothing complicated; whatever you had planned. And we shall need a couple of fires, don't you think? To cheer us all up.'

She had seen little of Clement during her convalescence. At the time, this had not troubled her. She had cried bitter tears on many of Kitty's visits, and surprised herself by laughing during some of Nancy's but she felt only lassitude and a kind of discouragement whenever Clement entered the room. He never stayed for long and when he spoke it was never about their lost baby but always about the war. This had irritated her. On one occasion, she had snapped at him that she couldn't care less about the stupid war, and to stop coming to see her if that was all he could talk about. She had felt only relief when he left.

Now that she was better, she felt ashamed of her behaviour and determined to make it up to him. His study was empty. She pulled on a warm coat and for the first time in three months stepped out of the house.

The air was cold and damp, the sky dull, the

countryside devoid of colour, but the mere fact of being outside brought a rush of unexpected sensations. Fresh air in her lungs and on her face, the sound of birdsong, the smell of woodsmoke and the rustle of the wind . . . She was alive. Battered and sadder than before, but alive, and ready to face the future. She would go and find Clement in his workshop and tell him this. They could try for another baby. They could open up the house again. Maybe, she thought vaguely, they could take in some evacuees, do their bit for the war effort.

'Guess who?' she called out. She felt almost elated as she stepped into Clement's workshop. 'I'm up at last!'

The workshop was empty. Bella stood in the middle of the dark room, feeling foolish, then wandered over to Clement's worktable.

Soldiers. Dozens of them, carved in wood, placed on a bed of damp earth. Soldiers with one leg, with no arms, with their heads blown off. One with his hands in the air in surrender or despair, another lying face down, a third kneeling in prayer. This one in particular moved her. She stretched out her hand to pick it up.

'What are you doing here?'

Bella gave a guilty start and dropped the wooden figure. Clement stood in the doorway, glaring at her.

'I came to tell you I was up,' she said.

'You shouldn't be here.' He entered the workshop and came to stand between Bella and the worktable, blocking his model battleground from view.

'I thought you'd be pleased to see me.'

'You shouldn't be here,' he repeated. He ran his hands through his thinning hair. 'You have to go.'

'Clement, those carvings—'

'Get out! Get out! Get out!'

'I don't understand.' Kitty, when Bella relayed this scene, was upset. 'It's so unlike Clement. Did he apologize?'

'In a way,' said Bella. 'I think. He said he was getting attacks of what he calls *moodiness* and I should ignore them.'

'Sounds like more than moodiness to me,' said Nancy darkly. 'I did try and warn you he was odd. I mean, terribly nice, and he's grown on me ever such a lot. But still, odd. What d'you suppose is wrong? Is it the baby?'

'I don't know. He says that all he wants is to be left alone. I found out that all the time I was in bed he didn't speak to his stockbroker once, and he's talking about giving up being a JP. Oh and his call-up papers for the OC arrived yesterday, and he says he won't go.'

'Can he do that without being court-martialled?'

'*I* don't know! He says it's a pointless waste of time and if the Germans are going to bomb us they're not going to be stopped by a few geriatric cripples.'

'Gosh!' said Nancy. 'Strong words from our Clem.'

Kitty looked distressed. 'Belle, you have to make him do it. Imagine if he went to jail! And even if he doesn't, he has to do *something*. It's not good to be idle, especially not these days, when everyone's so busy.'

And so this became their new life, Clement and Bella's. After much nagging, he stayed on as a local magistrate, joined the Observer Corps and resumed contact with his stockbroker while she got on with running Marshwood. She would have liked to find a job in town, something involving other people which would have taken her away from the oppressive atmosphere of home, but there was nobody left to care for the place. She turned Marshwood into her war work instead, expanding the kitchen garden beyond the herbs and summer fruits they had previously grown for enjoyment into a veritable business concern. Their head gardener had left with the other servants, but Josie Bates' elderly father lived in the village and had tended a vegetable plot all his life. With his help Bella dug rows of potatoes, turnips and swedes, cabbages and sprouts, cauliflowers and carrots. In the summer months she grew tomatoes and beans, lettuces and radishes. She planted gooseberries and currants, she learned to prune fruit trees and to bed strawberries, to make jam and to bottle vegetables. She sold as much as she could at local markets, and distributed any surplus she and Clement did not need for themselves in Chapel St Mary.

When she wasn't working outside, she taught herself to cook and to do housework, to wield saws, axes, hammers and brushes. She and Clement had as little to do with each other as was possible for two people living under the same roof. He did not return to their bedroom once she was better, and she began to understand that he had never left it with her comfort in mind but for himself, because he could not bear to be touched. Dark rings circled his eyes and his skin was grey from exhaustion. She knew that he was not sleeping, but he snapped at her again when she asked him why not. She guessed that he was afraid. They all were – of air strikes, of invasion, of the bell on the bicycle of the telegraph boy. But Clement's fear was somehow more animal. On one occasion, when a low-flying plane had passed directly overhead, he had actually been sick. On another, the sound of an air-raid siren had reduced him to tears. Each time, when she tried to comfort him, he pushed her away.

The war followed its course, tightening its stranglehold upon the world, from the verdant pastures of occupied France to the searing deserts of Africa and the azure of the Mediterranean. Towns were destroyed, the skies were filled with burning metal, the seas with the cold bloated bodies of the drowned. This war – the one Bella thought of as the *real war*, which took place far from her little world and in which people fought and died – the real war, then, seemed very unreal to her, something implausible that happened to other people but not to her. She did not mind her daily rounds of chores. On the contrary, she clung to them. She felt that in working as she did for Marshwood she was somehow validating her existence, not just now but before the war, when she had thought herself so successful and *important*. But she could not help wishing for something more, some greater sacrifice to bring legitimacy to her solitary life.

Later she told herself that she had known she would love him from the moment she saw him. Louis appeared out of the fog on a January morning in 1942, when all sense of relative perspective was lost in the thick white mist which had risen from the valley. She saw him as she swung herself over the gate from the paddock coming back from her morning walk with the dogs. He stood uncertainly before Marshwood's massive front door, and there was something exquisitely vulnerable about his posture. He did not hear her approach. She noted long legs and a slim build, a finely shaped head beneath closely cropped dark hair, a navy blue uniform over a thick wool sweater.

'Can I help you?'

He started and turned to face her. 'I hope so,' he said and his smile, too big for his face, gave him the appearance of a child. He spoke English with a strong French accent. 'My name is Louis Duchesne. I am looking for Clement Langton. He once knew my father.'

She had never known a man who could talk so much. His story had seemed completely implausible to Bella, living out the war in the dull safety of Chapel St Mary. They sat waiting for Clement at the small round table by the doors to the terrace, their minutely rationed tea laid out before them in Worcester china and silver pots, and he told her how he came to be here. It had never occurred to Bella that Clement might be a legend in Antoine Duchesne's household. Louis told her that he had always known the name of this village, had had it pointed out to him on a map as a boy as the place where his father's rescuer now lived. He himself had trained as a fighter pilot in France, but was now retraining to fly British planes. He had been passing through Bambridge with friends and, recognizing the name, had decided to stop.

'I should perhaps have called before coming,' he apologized. 'I did not realize we would be so close.'

'Not at all,' said Bella. 'A surprise like this is just what we need.'

He told her how he had escaped from France via North Africa with a band of airmen determined to carry on fighting when defeat seemed inevitable, about the vast columns of refugees fleeing their homes in northern France before the invading army, and about the plane he had stolen to fly from Algiers to Gibraltar. *Zero visibility . . . sabotage . . . altitude 800 metres . . . anti-aircraft fire . . . crash landing . . . British convoy . . . U-boats* . . . On and on he talked, eyes shining, punctuating his words with extravagant movements of his hands. Bella thought he looked like an exotic child, and poured him another cup of tea.

'Do you miss home?' It was all she could think of to ask. He had stopped talking to drink his tea, and she found that she wanted to hear his voice again.

'Of course.' He looked dejected now and she was surprised by a strong desire to hug him. 'But if I go back, I'll be shot.' He shrugged, a supremely Gallic gesture. 'Not a fate I relish.'

'Shot by the Germans,' she said, and immediately felt stupid.

'I'm just as worried about my own countrymen, to be honest.'

His face had darkened, and his voice had taken on a new wry quality which did not suit him.

'I don't understand,' Bella ventured. 'Why would your countrymen want to shoot you?'

'Because I'm a traitor.'

'But you're fighting with us!'

'I fight with the Free French. As far as the current French government is concerned, we are outlaws.' He frowned. 'It's curious how few people really understand the concept of collaboration.'

'I'm sorry,' she said humbly. 'I do read the papers. It's just . . .'

'No,' he said quickly. '*I'm* sorry. My comment was not meant in any way to make offence.'

She smiled, a little embarrassed. 'There's no need to

114

apologize. And it's *give* offence, by the way. Your English is excellent, but we say *give* offence. You give it, I take it. Except I haven't. Taken it, I mean. Offence, that is. I was going to say, it's just difficult, isn't it? Do go on with your story.' She was not used to being so flustered and found it hard to concentrate on what he said next.

He was haunted by the thought of his parents, with whom he had had no contact since leaving France.

'I would like to write, but it is dangerous.'

'Dangerous?'

'They hate us. If they can use our families to get to us, they will. It's not unheard of, you know, for the families of traitors like me to be executed as an example to others.' He sighed then smiled apologetically, as if reproaching himself for being too serious. 'Do you know,' he continued, 'I have been at war for over three years and I have not fired a single shot! And now I have to retrain, and still can't fight. When I feel I would like to cross the Channel and beat them away with my bare fists!'

He was beautiful, she thought, with his hazel eyes and olive skin and heart-breaking childlike optimism. He talked of honour and vindication, patriotism and comradeship, and she thought, *he is something of a miracle, this child whose life was made possible by that chance near-death encounter between his father and my husband, risen from the mud and suffering of that battlefield.* As she listened to him, this war which until now had felt so

115

parochial to Bella took on a different hue. Places she had loved on her holidays abroad, churches and village squares, sleepy towns and bustling galleries all robbed of their identity, turned by war and occupation into something *other*, no longer parts of a landscape taken for granted but something worth dying for. Her head swam with the vision he gave her of a raging, disinherited continent, and still Louis talked on.

'You look just like your father.' Clement's quiet voice from the entrance to the drawing-room startled them. Louis jumped to his feet and started towards Clement, hand held out.

'It is such an honour to meet you, sir. I am—'

'I know who you are.' The two men stood facing each other, Clement silent, Louis disconcerted.

'Darling, how long have you been standing there?' Bella slipped her arm through her husband's. 'Come and sit down. I'll make some more tea.'

But she knew that Clement would not join them. His body remained stiff against hers. He did not respond to the pressure of her hand on his arm and she dropped it, feeling foolish, as he continued to stare.

'Clement . . .' She was using, she thought, her married woman voice, able to load a single word with supplication, threat, concern and disapproval all at once. He took the Frenchman's hand but still said nothing, staring at him instead with a hostile expression until Louis, embarrassed, looked away.

'I should go,' he said.

'No, please, stay.' She managed to smile at Louis and glare at Clement at the same time.

'Really – my friends. I'm meeting them soon. They are taking me back.'

She saw him to the door. 'I'm sorry about Clement,' she said. 'He's not always like this. At least, he is, but he didn't use to be. Please come and see us again. I'm sure he'd be very pleased to see you.' He smiled faintly and Bella, poised, cool Bella, felt shy.

'We would *both* be very pleased to see you. And if you have time, if you need to get away for a few days . . . well, please use this house as your own.'

'Thank you.' He left then, walked off down the long drive in his navy blue jacket and cap without looking back, which was just as well, she chided herself later, because she had stood and gazed at his retreating back until he was swallowed up again by the fog.

That night she shouted at Clement for the first time in their married life.

'How *could* you be so rude!' she stormed. 'The poor boy, after everything he's been through. Everything *you* went through, with his father. I've never – I really don't think I have ever been so embarrassed in my whole life.'

Clement did not shout back but sat slumped in the chair Louis had occupied, gazing out beyond the terrace at the night sky, where heavy clouds advanced inexorably towards a plump and shining moon. This had been the war's gift to Clement, this apathy. She had not expected an answer, and was distressed by the weariness in his voice when he did finally speak.

'The boy,' said Clement, 'doesn't know the first fucking meaning of war. War's mud, and lice, and damp, and the smell of piss and shit. It's screaming shells and being bombarded twenty-four sodding hours a day. This isn't war. These *fighter pilots*. It's easy for them, isn't it? They just point, and shoot. And if they come back, they're heroes. And if they don't – pff!' He flicked his right index finger against his thumb. 'They just fucking disappear.'

'Clement . . .' He had closed his eyes and did not reopen them. She stood helpless before him.

'Don't swear,' she finished lamely. She got up, intending to go to him, but then realized that he had not listened, had probably not even heard, as he repeated softly, over and over until she left the room, unable to listen any longer, *they just fucking disappear . . .*

Louis sent a brief thank-you note after his visit. She did not expect to hear from him again but he wrote in March, a jubilant letter explaining that he had managed to smuggle a letter to his parents and had had a reply. His father sent his regards and was delighted that they had met. Might he take her up on her offer and come and stay? He had twenty-four hours' leave the following week, if it was not too soon . . .

Bella telegraphed at once to tell him he should come, then flew into a panic. Nobody had stayed at Marshwood since the beginning of the war. There was the house to clean from top to bottom, there were spare bedrooms to be aired, a bed to be made, flowers to be cut . . . She had to choose wine from the dwindling stock in the cellar, and what – oh, what was she to cook? It was a lean time of year in the garden, and she was not clever enough in the kitchen to do anything appetizing with their limited rations, especially for a Frenchman. A Frenchman! She remembered with agony the food she had eaten with Clement in restaurants in France.

'That's what comes of asking people to stay,' grumbled Clement as he watched her leaf through hefty cookery books borrowed from Kitty. He had not taken kindly to the news of Louis' visit. 'I don't know what possessed you to say he could come.'

'I told you, I felt sorry for him.' Bella stared in despair at a photographed pavlova. I wish it was summer!'

'You might have asked me before saying yes.'

She closed the book with a loud snap. 'I might have,' she sighed. 'But you would have said no.'

In the end, she decided to sacrifice one of the hens they kept for eggs, stalking it herself around the coop for some time before finally pouncing on it to break its neck, to her own, and its, astonishment. Once killed, the creature had to be plucked, and its giblets removed, feats which she performed more or less adequately by concentrating hard on the plight of the boy who made this all worth while. When the time came, she roasted the hen with sprigs of rosemary from the kitchen garden, and served it with potatoes mashed with swedes. She had never cooked a roast before, and was rather disheartened to note how much it reduced in the cooking, but the truth was that even the most accomplished feast could not have made a success of that first dinner with Louis.

He arrived in the early evening. Bella had changed out of her gardening clothes and pinned her hair up in his honour, but Clement made his feelings about the visit clear from the outset.

'Thank you for inviting me at such short notice.' Louis, who had travelled on a borrowed motorbike, overflowed with exhilaration as he stepped into Marshwood's entrance hall. 'I can't tell you what it means to me to be with you here, in a real home.'

He looked endearing and very young, with his goggles pushed up into his hair and his cheeks flushed pink from the ride. Bella smiled. Clement surveyed the motorcycle with distaste. 'Kill yourself with one of those,' he glowered. 'And I didn't invite you.' The formal atmosphere of the dining-room did little to lift their spirits. Bella had hoped that Clement would prove more sociable than on Louis' previous visit, but he responded to all attempts at conversation with monosyllables. Bella – hoping to God she did not look as flustered as she felt – chatted. Her smiling exterior gave nothing away of her seething rage towards her husband, or of the general turmoil of excitement and apprehension she felt towards Louis, but her best friends would have recognized the signs: Bella was anxious, and was behaving accordingly. She chatted about the articles she had read about De Gaulle in the papers, she exclaimed prettily when Louis said that he had met him, she giggled at his impersonation of the great man. And when that topic ran out, she fell back on village gossip.

'And so the new teacher has been called up and I've no idea where they'll find another one, have you, darling?' she asked desperately, after Clement had failed to speak for a full ten minutes.

He did not answer, did not even look at her. Bella caught Louis' eye and knew that Clement's snub had not gone unnoticed. What must he think of them? Sitting in their handsome dining-room, eating badly cooked food off her finest china, the pretty young chatterbox and her sullen older husband. What did he eat, normally? And with whom? Did he stick with fellow pilots, or were there girls, pretty WAAFs (they were *all* pretty, something to do with the confidence of wearing those uniforms) who joined them at table? She had no idea, none at all, but she couldn't help thinking it must be jollier than this. Was he wondering how this strange situation had come about? Did he pity her? Did he wish he hadn't come?

'This wine is excellent,' said Louis, and she almost let herself believe that he had not noticed a thing after all. 'You must have bought it before the war? It's been a long time since I tasted anything so good. It reminds me of home.'

'Yes,' she said gratefully. 'Before the war. Clement imported it straight from Bordeaux.'

'What it is, a Château-Lafite?'

'Actually, it's from a small vineyard owned by an old university colleague of Clement's. He used to send us a couple of cases every year.'

'Really? A friend of mine . . .' He was off, telling a long, not very funny, nor very interesting but excessively normal story about late summers helping with the *vendanges*. She could have hugged him for his tact.

Clement had left them after supper. It was cold in the house. Bella, feeling extravagant, lit a fire in the drawing-room. She sat primly at her worktable, studiously mending an old dress while Louis reclined in one of the leather sofas by the fireplace, his long legs crossed at the ankles, reading. She racked her brain for an appropriate topic of conversation. She could think of nothing and began to worry that he must think her both dim-witted and rude. He yawned, and she thought, *what can I possibly say that will not sound ridiculous and that will not be disloyal to Clement?*

'I'm sorry about supper,' she said finally.

He had the grace to look taken aback. 'Sorry? Why? It was splendid. A treat.'

'You're very kind, but it was dreadful. I know I can't cook. I mean I'm learning, but there's no-one to teach me. The food in France is so wonderful, and I dare say all French women cook beautifully, but I am quite, quite useless, or at the very best I am a complete beginner.'

'No, no, it was splendid. Really. A feast. The chicken was . . . the chicken was . . .' He tailed off, his finger and thumb rounded to emphasize the exquisite, clearly lost for words.

'The chicken was tough, rubbery and about half its original size. Which was pretty diminutive in the first place. All the bigger ones got away.'

He looked at her solemnly. 'You did not let me finish my sentence. What I was going to say was, the chicken was worthy of the greatest Paris chefs . . . never have I tasted such a chicken . . .' There was such a wicked gleam of enjoyment in his eyes as he looked at her that she forgot to feel sorry for herself and joined in his game.

'After the war, I shall write a cookery book, a compilation of my best chicken recipes . . .'

'After the war, you shall open a restaurant . . .'

'A hotel . . .'

'People will queue for days for the pleasure of eating chicken at your table . . .'

'Now you're exaggerating.'

His laughter was warm and rich. It came from deep within him until his whole being seemed to smile, lighting up the space around him, the whole room, engulfing her. He leaned forward in his chair, elbows on his knees, and now her heart seemed to have stopped beating altogether.

'Bella,' he asked. 'Do you play cards?'

She was surprised again. 'I . . . well, I play whist. Not particularly well, but anyway, we need more players. I don't really know any games for two people. We could play snap.' She blushed. 'But that's not what you meant. It's a child's game.'

He grinned. 'Come.'

She could not believe that to be with him could be so simple. He produced a pack of cards and they began to play, with hilarious rivalry. She made tea, and they drank it with dry Marie biscuits which he devoured as they played. He cheated quite openly, a fact which he denied vigorously, and she laughed and thought *I don't think I have ever felt so happy in my entire life. Not even when I was pregnant. No, I have never been so happy.*

Richard's light was still on when Isla crept back into their bedroom. She tiptoed to her side of the bed. He stirred. Her heart sank.

'What did she want?'

She climbed into bed, still wrapped in a blanket.

'I told you. She's dictating her memoirs.'

'Yes, but why *now*? And what the fuck does she think she's achieving with these memoirs anyway? It's not as if anyone's going to buy them. Does she think she's going to get them published?'

'I doubt it. I think she just wants people to listen. To understand her, I suppose. It makes her happy. She's upset because she thinks she may have to sell the house.'

'Not that again.' Richard threw an arm behind his head and glanced at his alarm clock. 'Bloody hell, Isla, it's nearly midnight. You've been on the phone for bloody hours.'

'Granna said she couldn't sleep.' Isla stiffened as he rolled over to put his hand on her stomach. 'Richard . . .'

'What?'

'I'm tired.'

'You're always tired.'

Isla had grown to love the darkness. At night, with the house quiet and Richard asleep, she could let herself think about Jack. She closed her eyes and saw him looking at her, the gleam in his eyes as he threw out his challenge. Felt his arms around her as she fell into them. She had tried to find the right word to describe her reaction to his touch. Excited, elated, light-headed – all were right, and yet none were enough. She banished these thoughts during the day but at night, for the few minutes before she fell asleep, they crept up on her and she let them come . . .

'We *never* have sex any more.' Richard's voice cut accusingly through Isla's daydream. 'Isla? I know you're awake.'

'I told you. I'm tired.'

And then, because she felt guilty, she turned to him. She turned to him, and she did everything she should. She climbed on top of him, she moaned as she rode him, she gasped when he thrust harder, she cried out at his climax. But afterwards, when she could tell by his breathing that he was asleep, she cried silently into her pillow, thinking not of Jack now but of Richard, and what they once had together but had somehow lost. And then it came to her, the word she had been searching for to describe her feeling at Jack's touch. The missing word was *alive*.

He called the following Saturday as Isla, Richard and the children were preparing to go out.

'Is this a good time?'

Isla was in the study, hunting for a missing boot. Just outside in the hall, a half-dressed Beth was wailing because an ill-sorted wash had turned her favourite violet T-shirt a sludgy green. Directly above, Richard was flooding the shower room as he did every Saturday morning, clouds of steam rolling out onto the landing.

A loud crash from the basement told her that Marcus was back in from the garden and likely to be treading mud all over the new seagrass carpet.

'We're going out to lunch,' she told Jack. 'Our friends live forty-five minutes away, we're expected in half an hour and nobody's ready. Except me, but I've lost a boot.'

'I can call back.'

'No, no!' She dropped down onto the study's sofa, jumped back up again as something hard dug into her back, beamed when she realized that it was her errant boot and sat back down again to pull it on. 'I found it,' she told him. 'Is everything OK?'

She closed her eyes to savour the sound of his voice, cool and caressing with a husky catch to it she did not remember from before. Opened them again, smiling, staring without seeing it at the bright butterfly print wallpaper she had put up against Richard's will but which the children adored.

'What do you think?'

'About what?'

'Isla, have you been listening?'

'I got distracted,' she admitted. 'Tell me again.'

'Promise you'll pay attention.'

'I promise.'

'I ran into Esther in Bambridge. She said one of the houses on that estate she lives on is up for sale.'

Esther lived in one of six cottages on a converted farm

on the edge of town. The old farm buildings nestled around a landscaped courtyard, and a huge granary barn had been converted into flats, one of which housed the caretaker whose duties included keeping a watchful eye on the elderly inhabitants. Bella, she knew, despised the arrangement.

'One of the cottages is up for sale. I thought, in the light of what you were telling me last time you were down, you might be interested in looking at it.'

'For Granna, you mean?'

'No, for you. Obviously, for Bella! I just thought, if the worst came to the worst. You know, if you had to sell . . .'

'She hates those cottages.'

'Ah, come on, Isla!' She smiled again at the sound of his laughter. 'Come and have a look at it. You never know, it might be perfect.'

'Richard'll hate it if I go down to Marshwood again so soon.'

'It's what he wants though, isn't it? For her to move?'

'I suppose so, but . . .'

But we both know that's not why I would come down. But I can't use this as an excuse to see you. But you really shouldn't be quoting what Richard wants at me . . . Another crash from downstairs, followed by a high-pitched screaming and the thunder of footsteps down to the basement.

'Next weekend? The agent doesn't think it's urgent.'

'Isla!' Richard's voice roared up from the kitchen. 'For Christ's sake, I could hear the kids from upstairs! They were trying to kill each other down here!'

'That's not fair!' Beth's voice, loud with indignation, bellowed over her father's. 'I'm not trying to kill *anybody*! *Marcus* is trying to kill *me*!'

'I have to go,' said Isla.

'But you'll come?'

'I'll come. But just for heaven's sake don't tell Granna about the cottage.'

'But we're supposed to be in the New Forest that weekend!' As predicted, Richard had not taken kindly to the news of another trip to Marshwood.

'We can all go together as planned on Friday night, then I'll just go on to Marshwood for the day on Saturday.'

'But we're meant to be spending the weekend with my parents. They'll be disappointed.'

'I'll be back by teatime.'

'I don't understand why it can't wait.'

'I thought this was what you wanted.'

'What? How?'

'If Bella likes the cottage, perhaps we can sell Marshwood.'

'She'll *never* move into a cottage.'

'She might.'

'She won't. You're deluded even to think so. And who is this Jack bloke anyway?'

'I told you. We grew up together.'

'The one you shagged who buggered off?'

'I did not *shag* him. We kissed once, a very long time ago. Sort of . . . experimentally.'

'I thought you hated him!'

'That's not really the point.'

Really, she had lied to everybody. To Bella, telling her she was coming to hear more about her memoirs; to Richard and his parents about her motivation for going; to the children, who had wanted to accompany her. Beth and Marcus waved her off, gathered around Elizabeth by the gateway to the drive. A little to one side, Hugh was engaged in a detailed conversation with Richard, who nodded as he listened, scratching the head of one of the ancient, drooling Labradors. *This* was her world, she told herself. Pleasant homes and round-limbed children, every day the same, calm and happy. She toyed with the idea of turning back, but how would that have looked? No, she would go, but she would stay for as short a time as possible. She would look at the cottage, make a thorough inspection, pretend that she didn't know what she was really doing there, and then she would make her excuses and leave. And anyway, she thought, suddenly beset with doubt, what was to say Jack actually wanted her? Whatever *that* meant. There had been that moment when she thought he would kiss her, and then that shadow across his face, that closing off. If he *had* wanted her, he would have taken advantage of that moment, wouldn't he? By the time Isla pulled into Bambridge, she was thoroughly confused but almost certain she was lying to herself as well.

He was waiting for her by the entrance to the cottages. The breeze coming off the hills blew the hair back off his face revealing, beneath the marks of time, the clear stamp of his boyhood features. He had also driven and was wearing glasses, which had the unsettling effect of making him look both younger and older than his thirty-four years. There was something touching, intimate even, about those glasses. *Stop it*, she told herself. She deliberately slowed to a sedate, almost regal pace until she stood before him. They brushed cheeks. She tucked her hair behind her ears, rearranged her jacket and twiddled with the straps of her bag. Then, praying that he could not see the shaking of her hands, she followed him towards the inner courtyard where the estate agent was waiting.

The cottage stood a little apart from the others, a pleasant three-bedroom house with a thatched roof, a large living room and a small kitchen. It was brighter than its exterior suggested, with big casement windows giving onto a walled garden where fat pink peonies were in full luxuriant bloom. The views beyond were of playing fields and a huddle of rooftops clustered around the church spire. It was a far cry from the decaying splendour of Marshwood but Isla dutifully went through the motions. She enquired about buildings insurance, council tax and yearly service charges, inspected non-slip tiles in the bathroom, the brand new kitchen, the alcove in the sitting room wide enough to hold a bed. Jack did not walk around the cottage with her but made a desultory inspection of his own. She found it almost impossible to concentrate on the estate agent's chatter, her mind occupied with him and with the ever more pressing question, *what the hell am I doing here?*

'Drink?' asked Jack when the visit was over.

'I have to go. I'm having lunch with Granna.'

'For old times' sake.'

'I really shouldn't. Thank you for organizing that. It was very interesting.'

Before she knew it, he had ushered her into the bar of the George Hotel and was ordering drinks at the bar.

'I did say no . . .' she protested.

'But you didn't mean it.'

She asked for a lime and soda. He ordered whisky, which he drank neat.

'It's not even midday,' said Isla reprovingly.

'Then I've made an early start.' He took another sip and grinned at her. 'Alone at last.'

'Tell me about your job.'

'You're trying to change the subject again.'

'What do you mean, again?'

'You're always doing it. As soon as you think the conversation is at all dangerous.'

'I hardly think *alone at last* is *dangerous*. Just . . . stupid.'

His grin grew wider. 'Darling Isla. Always so direct.'

'Jack, don't insult me by trying to flirt with me.'

'Is that what you think I'm doing?'

'Yes. No.' She gripped her drink, suddenly unsure. 'I don't know.'

'Isla.' He raised his hand and brushed away the strand of hair that had fallen over her face. She flinched. He moved away.

'All right then, what do you want to know?'

'About what?'

'About my job. That *is* what you asked.'

'Where were you last? Before you came here?'

'Bosnia.'

'Bosnia?'

'You sound surprised.'

'That's not the answer I was expecting. I didn't know you did wars.'

'I didn't.'

'Was it tough?'

'Let's just say that like your grandad there are some things I don't talk about.'

She looked up at him, her expression serious. He sighed.

'Don't do that.'

'Do what?'

'This is the bit when you say, *you can talk to me, Jack.*'

'That isn't . . . you don't know that.'

'Say it isn't true.'

She was silent. He drained his glass, then signalled to the barmaid for another.

'It's where I met her.'

'Who?'

'The woman. The woman you were asking about. The woman I was with, before.'

'Do you want to talk about it?'

He glanced up at her. She bit her lip. 'Sorry. That wasn't meant to be funny.'

Black and white. That was how he had wanted to shoot her. He had been in Sarajevo for less than a week, had met her for the first time just after being shot at by a sniper, and all he could think of, when he saw her, was that to shoot her in colour would be a crime.

'Go back a step,' interrupted Isla. 'You were shot at by a sniper? How did that happen?'

Jack shrugged. 'Stupid. I was with some Canadian journos, they had this ridiculous open Jeep, we stopped to ask for directions, *bang.*'

'But was anybody killed?'

'Nah. I think he was just trying to frighten us. Did a good job. Anti-sniper unit arrived on the scene about ten minutes later – we were still cowering under the car – but he'd long gone. This'll make you laugh: the anti-sniper bloke, a Dane, he goes up to these Bosnians sitting playing cards outside a café and he asks, *where'd the fire come from?* And the Bosnians don't even look up, they just keep on playing until one of them asks *what fire?* They hadn't even bloody noticed!'

'I'm not laughing,' said Isla.

Jack shrugged. 'It seemed funny at the time.'

In fact he was still shaking by the time he arrived at the Holiday Inn. The basement bar was dimly lit, the fog of cigarette smoke obscuring it still further.

'What do you want?' One of the Canadian journalists, Jeff, was offering to fight his way to the bar for drinks.

'What is there?'

'Whatever you want.' Jeff grinned. 'As long as you can pay for it.'

'What's cheapest?'

'Vodka.'

'Vodka it is, then.'

She was sitting at a table in one of the furthest corners of the room, surrounded – as always, he would learn this – by men. Her hair, loosely tied back, was coming undone and a dark coil wound around her neck, mirroring the white smoke of her cigarette which spiralled upwards. Jack stared, entranced.

'That way danger lies, my friend.' Jeff was back with a tray of vodka shots. 'Many have strayed up that path, believe me. Few have come back alive.'

'I was just thinking I wanted to shoot her.' The

Canadian raised an eyebrow. 'You know what I mean. Black and white. Colour would kill it.'

'Yeah.' Jeff nodded. 'I know. Come on.' He gripped Jack by the elbow and propelled him across the room. 'Hey, Elena!'

She looked up. Her eyes, he noticed, were huge, almond-shaped, fringed with long dark lashes which swept her high cheekbones when she blinked. They had reached her table. She did not stand up.

'My friend here is a bit soft in the head.' Jeff was laughing. Jack realized that somehow he was already drunk. 'He just missed getting shot by a fucking sniper, and now he wants to photograph you.'

Elena stubbed out her cigarette and smiled. 'Journalists are crazy,' she said. 'But photographers are worse.' She raised her arms in a lazy gesture to tie back her falling hair. 'So,' she said, striking a pose. 'Is this better?'

There was something about her, something honest and frank which cut through the heavy eye make-up and the admiring male retinue and which made him tell her that no, this was not better.

'It was the smoke,' he told her. 'And your hair. They mirrored each other, the one curling upwards, the other down. For a moment, it was perfect. The composition was perfect.'

'Ah well.' She sighed and lit another cigarette. 'Momentary perfection. Who can aspire to more?'

One of her friends produced a pack of cards and

shuffled it impatiently. 'They want me to play,' Elena informed Jack. She smiled, a funny impish grin which caught him off guard and made him smile back. 'Perhaps I'll see you around.'

'And then?' Jack had fallen silent. Isla waited for a moment, then nudged him gently. 'What happened then?'

'I'm sorry?'

'Elena. What happened next?'

'Oh!' He picked up his glass, made to drink, put it back down before it touched his lips. 'We got together, but then it ended. It ended, and I came home for you.'

Isla was still shaking by the time she let herself into Marshwood. She found her grandmother sitting by the door to the terrace, absorbed in reading the letters which covered the little round table before her.

'They sent mine back,' said Bella in lieu of greeting. 'After Louis disappeared. Of course his are a lot more interesting.'

'He disappeared?' Isla shrugged off her jacket and threw herself into a chair.

'Well what did you expect?'

'That's so sad.'

Bella harrumphed. 'I've been going through them all again. I thought they might interest you. We can look at them after lunch.'

'Lovely. Granna, I'm not sure I can do this today.'

'They're really very fascinating. Descriptions of flying, fighting and suchlike.'

'I'm sure they are. Only the thing is, I promised Richard . . .'

'Did you have a good journey? I was expecting you earlier, I must say. It's such a shame you can't stay the night. We'll have lunch now, shall we? Bring your notebook I think, darling. I'll fill you in on the next bit and then we'll come back for the letters.'

He is just a child, she told herself firmly after Louis' second visit, ignoring the fact that he was only a few years younger than herself. *He is so far from home. This fondness I have for him is the affection of a parent for his child. Protective.*

And yet that night the screaming. The terrible shriek which tore her from sleep (and, dare she admit, from dreams of him), echoing round the house so that in her confusion she could not identify its source. The sobbing which followed and the low, ghastly moaning. The murmur of voices tracked, once her mind cleared, to Clement's study. Louis on the bed with his arms around her husband, stroking his head as if *he* were the child, Clement clinging to him while the tears of twenty-five years poured down his cheeks in torrents of grief, soaking his striped flannel pyjamas, and all the time Clement repeating, sounding lost and pathetic, *I'm sorry, I'm sorry, I'm sorry.* They did not notice her standing petrified in the doorway. After a while, Clement's tears subsided and he leaned back into his pillow. Louis sat on the end of the narrow bed, elbows on knees in the position she would forever associate with him.

'Do you want to tell me about it?' he asked quietly.

She stayed in the shadows as Clement began to speak.

'It's a new dream,' he said. 'The funny thing is, I had this feeling they were going to change when you showed up. They were always the same before. Bombardments. Trenches. Blood and gore, memories, really. The fucking cheek of the sun rising in the morning. The rain. All real.' Clement's voice grew stronger. 'And then after you came, it's been the same, every night, well, most nights, anyway. Empty trench. Silence. No mud, but would you believe it the rugs from the drawing-room. And at first – every night – I'm relieved, because it's so quiet, and it's all over. And then I'm terrified, because I think that I'm the only one left. And I start to run, like a duck, you know, in dreams? And I'm trying to find the end of the trench, and it keeps curving away from me. And just when I think I can't go on any more, I turn the corner, and then I stop. And it's completely different from my other dreams. It's lush green countryside, nothing to do with the landscapes of the usual dreams. There's a young man sitting on the floor with his back to me, and he's perfectly still. He's looking at the view. I shout at

139

him to turn round, but he never does. I don't know who he is, and yet I know I've failed him.'

He closed his eyes. She took a step towards him. Clement did not hear, but Louis looked up. He shook his head, an almost imperceptible gesture of such authority that she turned and left, ashamed of herself because she felt embarrassed for Clement, angry with him too, for unburdening himself not to her but to this boy who had come to them for relief from the traumas of his own war. Louis had left his cigarettes on the landing table. She took one now in a small act of defiance and returned to her room to smoke it. She left the light off so that she could pull back the blackout curtain, and she sat curled on her window-seat glaring moodily out at the night sky. She was jealous, she realized. Jealous of the bond she had just witnessed between the two men, of her husband's open heart before this stranger, of the boy's compassion and understanding, jealous of all brothers in arms and their wealth of shared experience.

She sat for a long time before he came to her door and knocked softly before half entering the room.

'May I?'

She waved him in. There was only just enough light from the moon for him to see her indicate the armchair by the window. *How should I feel about this?* she wondered, and then was furious with herself for blushing as she wrapped her shawl more tightly around her shoulders.

140

'What was all that about?' she asked.

'Clement had a nightmare. He shouted, I heard him. I am a light sleeper. It's not the first time I hear a man crying in the night.'

'And do you always go to them?'

'Most do not want to be comforted.'

'I've never seen Clement like that. I didn't even realize he was capable of such emotion.'

'Sometimes these things are best expressed between men.'

'Of course.'

He looked at her, his expression quizzical.

'I think perhaps he feels that it is easier to talk to me. For one thing I am a stranger, and for another . . . well, I have seen nothing, nothing compared to him, but still . . .'

'More than me,' she snapped. 'I know.'

'Please don't be angry.'

'I'm not really.'

They smoked together in silence.

'It wasn't always like this, you know,' she said at last. She waved her hand vaguely to indicate the room. 'This was *our* room once. We were happy.'

Were we? She remembered the feeling of the night before, playing cards with Louis. Light-headed, alive, electric. Unlike anything she had ever felt with Clement.

'But you have no children.'

Even without seeing her reaction, he must have realized how that sounded. She could almost feel him blush.

'I was pregnant,' she said, 'but I lost it just before the war. I thought that was the trouble with Clement.'

'Perhaps it is, partly.'

Bella lit another cigarette and they smoked for a while in silence. 'Isn't it curious,' she said at last, 'how grief can divide people? Even when they most need each other.'

'I have noticed this too,' agreed Louis. 'The instinct is to shut everything out. Whereas perhaps, if one shared . . . Bella, there will be other babies.'

'Do you think so?'

'I am sure of it.'

Her eyes pricked with tears. 'Look,' she said. 'You could always see other lights before, in the village and in Bambridge. But now there are just the stars.'

He looked, his forehead pressed against the window pane, and he smiled his glorious too-big smile.

'So the war has given us something after all,' he said softly, and looking at him she was consumed by the innocence of a gaze which spoke only of pure delight and quite belied the heavy experiences of his exile.

'Yes,' she answered, and found herself smiling back.

'It's been years since I read these,' said Bella. 'But I've kept them all.' Lunch over, they had returned to the alcove by the terrace. Isla carried the coffee tray. Bella bore a large box of soft-centred chocolates. She perched on her favourite chair, unwrapped a chocolate and gave it an absent-minded nibble. 'Here we are. This was his first letter after the visit I just told you about.'

The envelopes had the silky fragility of dried petals but Louis' fine spidery writing, though faded, was still legible. The letter in question was formal, a little thank-you note disappointing in its blandness, except that in it he asked if he might visit again, a request which even all these years later Bella remembered sent her pulse racing. She smiled as she read her reply before handing it to Isla. 'So proper,' she said. 'So friendly. When my heart beat twice as fast just writing to him.' *Of course you may write to us, whenever you like. I feel that we are, in a certain way, responsible for you while you are in our country. We are, I suppose, the closest you have to family, and so as with family, you must never feel that you are imposing, and write and visit as often as you like.*

'Your grandfather was quite transformed by that visit,' said Bella. 'They went out walking for hours the following morning. He showed him the garden, the flowers, the kitchen garden, and then he marched him off to look at the orchard and the paddock and the fields which had all been let to the farm next door. You know, we had to. To grow crops for the war. They spent the rest of the afternoon in the workshop.'

'Were you still jealous?' hazarded Isla. It seemed a very daring question to ask of Bella, except that this was not Bella as she had always known her, strong and slightly daunting, but a new Bella, vulnerable and rather disconcertingly open.

'I would have been, except that the change in Clement was so extraordinary. Do you know what he said? When we sat down to dinner after Louis had left, he said *there is something of an angel about that boy*. And of course I agreed, though I had different reasons for thinking it. I was worried that once he left your grandfather's mood would change again, but it didn't. He wasn't quite back to his old self, and he still slept in the study, but he did start to take an interest in things again.'

Louis had asked for news to distract him. *Clement is astonished because the honeysuckle is flowering already*, Bella had written.

He is also worried, because it seems to be mildewed, a condition very common to honeysuckle, apparently. He has half a mind to pull it out, except that I know he can't bear to. Mildew or no mildew, it smells divine, and I have forbidden all interference until the flowering stops. The bluebells are out in the woods, and you must come back soon to see this sight, it is glorious, and I am not sure if you have bluebells in France? We have adopted a cat, or rather she has adopted us. She is huge, very heavily pregnant, and she has made her home in the garage. So soon we shall have kittens, I fear, and knowing Clement, we shall have to keep them . . .

Had Bella really written this? In the middle of a war, to a man who was not her husband and whom she was beginning to love: written of mildew and bluebells and cats? The letter went on to village gossip. Kitty's husband had been home on a short leave a few months earlier, and she was expecting again. Nancy was planning a dance, was excited at the prospect of a glamorous Free French fighter pilot, longed for him to come. Had he thought Bella silly, in all her frivolous detail? When he asked for distraction, had he expected something else? Or had he read between the lines of her letter? He had answered in much the same vein, with a slight relaxation of tone from his previous letter. To Isla, his reply seemed much more characteristic of the man Bella had described to her, quick and happy, bubbling with life.

'You're still *Mrs Langton* though,' said Isla. 'I mean, he still calls you that.'

'Of course,' said Bella primly. 'But I made him drop it on his next visit.'

Isla could almost see him as she read, imagine the pen flying over the page.

I write quickly, as these clear days are perfect for flying and we are in the air more often than not. We are being trained – at last! – on our new Spitfire. Our poor old Hurricanes seem very sluggish in comparison. I am finally beginning to glimpse a time when I may be allowed to see some real action, and I cannot wait. I am so desperate to get on and do the job I came here to do!

He read her letter with relish, he told her. When he had finished reading, he closed his eyes, and smelt the honeysuckle, and saw Clement standing beside it in his delightful gardening hat (for *delightful*, read *awful*, chuckled Isla, who remembered her grandfather's hats well). He was excited about the kittens, asked her if she wouldn't keep one for him because he loved cats, wondered about his own Minette, the she-cat which had been his from childhood, left behind in France.

I have some leave at the end of June. May I come and visit you again? Perhaps, to please your friend, to coincide with her dance?

Yes, do come, we'd love to have you. She could only imagine the suppressed excitement that went into Bella's friendly, formal little reply. And when Bella began to describe the visit, Isla forgot about the time and about Richard. She even forgot about Jack and the way he set her own pulse racing as Louis had once set Bella's. She forgot everything, and she listened.

He came for a whole week, a week which marked a pause between training and war-making, a turning-point when despite all circumstances he was still a boy who believed in his future, and the summer holidays were still a sacrosanct part of the yearly calendar. A week which sped by, and which she always thought of as one of the happiest and most intense of her life.

The prospect of his visit threw her once again into panic. How could she make it a success? She could not reasonably sacrifice more hens. Clement had still not completely forgiven her for the last one, and anyhow they were good layers. Cooking apart, how were she and Clement, in all their splendid isolation, to provide sufficient entertainment for a young man not yet twenty-three, bursting with life and the promise of a whole week's leave?

In the end, of course, she enlisted help from Nancy, who devised an entire social programme for Louis' stay. If he liked cards, there must be a bridge party. At least one, possibly more. And there must be tennis; she – Nancy – just needed to get someone to cut the lawn. And croquet, so English, he would love it, they could play at Kitty's, Marshwood with its sloping lawns was hopeless for anything like that. There must be tea parties, since he enjoyed tea. The eggs from Marshwood's hens would come in very handy for cake, and she was fairly sure she could get hold of some extra butter. There were records she could bring, it would be good for there to be some modern music in the house. And would an evening of charades be too hopelessly old-fashioned, or rather jolly? What did Bella think? She, Nancy, thought that played in the right spirit they could be quite a lark. And if with all this the Frenchman had any spare time left, he could always help with the dance, which was to be the crowning event of the week's festivities.

Nancy's enthusiasm began to irritate Bella within hours of Louis' arrival. She turned up unannounced shortly after lunch, jaunty despite her faded cotton dress, her pretty blond curls blowing around her head, and suggested they all walk down to the woods.

'We've got a whole programme of events set up for you,' she confided merrily as they set off. 'Didn't Bella tell you? Devised mainly by *moi*. I hope you're ready for a good time. By the end of the week you'll want to go back to your base for a bit of peace and quiet!' Louis looked back to the house as she linked her arm through his, and shrugged helplessly at Clement waving them off from the front step. A look of knowing understanding passed between the two men. Bella caught it and cringed.

The woods lay tucked in the valley beneath Marshwood. Their access was not as picturesque as it had been before the war, and to reach them they had to walk through planted fields which had previously been used as pasture. But soon the fields gave way to a water meadow too marshy for cultivation, a soft, quiet place with tiny white flowers decking emerald grass, and tall reeds where the stream, liberated from its banks, spilt and gurgled its way through the pasture. They walked

148

to the end of the meadow and all the time Nancy chattered and laughed and pointed, while Bella walked a little behind, assuming an air of intense enjoyment of her surroundings and hoping that her irritation did not show.

'Look!' Louis stopped abruptly. The two young women looked.

'What?' asked Nancy.

'An orchid! Would you believe it? A minuscule, wild orchid!'

'Gosh, Louis, you scared me for moment! Don't do that again . . .'

'Bella?'

She crouched beside him to inspect the flower. It was tiny, its delicate pink petals virtually hidden in the grass.

'Are you sure it's an orchid?' she asked. 'I can't believe you spotted it.'

'Certain.' He grinned at her happily. 'My mother would be proud of me. Years of patient lecturing in the garden. Or not so patient, actually . . .'

'You like gardening?'

'Does that surprise you?' He was looking straight at her and she felt herself begin to blush.

'A bit,' she admitted. 'It's not a pastime one associates with most young men.'

'Ah well,' he laughed. 'I am not most young men. Here.'

'No, don't!' she cried, but he had already picked the tiny orchid and was handing it to her. She raised it to her face. Its scent was delicious, faint but sweet. She closed her eyes to inhale it better.

'Take it home and dry it. As a keepsake. A reminder of me, when I am gone.'

'Don't talk like that!'

He looked puzzled, then laughed as understanding dawned. 'When I am gone from *here*,' he corrected.

'Come on, slowcoaches!' Nancy had wandered on to the end of the field. 'Hurry up!'

'Take the orchid.' His big smile lit up his face and everything around him. 'Now that I have picked it, you have to.'

Bella threaded the flower through her buttonhole. 'There. Is that all right?'

'Perfect.' The eyes which held hers for a few brief seconds were serious. 'Now I am happy.'

'For heaven's sake!' screeched Nancy. 'Are you coming or not?'

For the rest of the walk, Bella and Nancy behaved almost as caricatures of themselves, the one's imperturbable serenity contrasting to the point of comedy with the other's bubbling exuberance. But all through that first afternoon, Bella hugged the knowledge to herself that he had not looked at Nancy as he had looked at her, and that he had given *her* the flower.

They did everything Nancy had suggested during

Louis' holiday, and much more besides. For they could not have planned the delicious hours spent in his company working side by side in the garden, or the country walks early in the morning before the rest of the world was up to admire flowering hedgerows, the lazy games of snap on the terrace when the sun made an appearance, the joy of evenings free of charades or dinners, reading quietly while Louis lay on the sofa listening not to Peter's jazz collection but to Haydn's choral music, saying, *do you know, I had never realized before how absolutely perfect music can be.* Clement adored him. Every evening, when they were alone, the two men lingered together over a bottle of port opened especially in his honour at the beginning of his stay. Bella heard them from the kitchen as she cleared away the dishes. Clement questioned Louis tirelessly. What did he think of the Malta campaign? Of developments in Russia, at Sebastopol? Had he heard these reports that now French Jews were being made to wear the Star of David? She lingered over her chores despite wanting to return to Louis. She never thought too much of the significance of what they were discussing. It mattered only that he was there. It was not unusual for their talking to tip into argument, but Clement sounded more animated than she had heard him in years. She joined them when she could no longer bear to keep away, and the conversation turned then from war and battles to books and plans for the following day.

Her own feelings were in turmoil. She wanted to be with him all the time, had to force herself not to follow him out of rooms, not to gaze at him continuously. She felt breathlessly aware of herself when she was near him, entirely conscious of her physical being and the space it occupied in relation to his. Everything she did became tinged with meaning, whether it was preparing a meal that he would eat, or laying a table that he would sit at, or cutting flowers that he would admire. When they were with others she longed to have him to herself, yet the moments alone with him sped by before she could truly appreciate them.

During that week time stood still, and yet it passed in the blinking of an eye. Bella prepared for Nancy's dance with a heavy heart. How much better, how infinitely better it would have been to spend this last evening alone listening to Haydn, playing cards while Clement read the paper and puffed on his cigar and said *well, there's a thing* and Louis and Bella rolled their eyes affectionately, because how many times in this brief, endless week under the same roof had they heard him say that? But instead, she thought as she stared at the reflection of her pre-war evening dress in the looking-glass, tonight she was to share him with the whole of Bambridge and its surrounding villages. Tonight he would wear his uniform, and tomorrow he would leave, and he would once again be sucked into this war she was coming to view as exciting and hateful in equal measure, for having brought her Louis and for taking him away. It was all too confusing. This gratitude she felt to him for saving Clement (she did not think the word too strong), this instinct to protect him, this awakening of her emotions, her mind, her very being to the possibilities of existence. No, she did not want to share him. She did not want him to leave. And yet she had a feeling that his continued presence, cherished as it was, might wreak havoc in their lives.

They watched her walk slowly down the stairs, in her old wine-coloured velvet with the plunging neckline and wide satin shoulder straps, and for a moment she saw them, the three of them, in all their permutations, as if somehow she had nothing to do with them and was looking at a photograph of strangers, trying to guess the connections between them. She saw two men formed by war, and a young woman trying to understand them; she saw a husband and wife and their love for a beautiful boy; she saw the terrible illusion of security and confidence, and she understood that this moment held everything that was dear to her, longed to hold it, perfectly still, and never to move on, but already it was slipping away from her, and Clement was saying how beautiful she looked, a car was hooting impatiently outside and Louis was stepping forward to take her arm, asking Clement *if we really can't persuade you to come too* and promising to *take very good care of her.*

On a pleasant evening in late June in the middle of the war, Bella stepped out of her house to go to a dance, and everything changed again.

Yes, everything changed on the night of the dance. Louis felt it too. His next letter was guarded, a sensible precautionary measure which left her feeling frustrated at the time, though later she let herself read between the lines.

How can I thank you enough for your hospitality? The country walks, the games of cards, the croquet, the tennis . . . so English and yet somehow so reminiscent of home. It is the innocence, of course. At home we play boules and we sail, I play chess with my father and draughts with my sisters, but the spirit is the same. And that is your gift to me, this spirit. There is a common bond which unites humanity, do you not think? Which can be summed up by early morning walks, and late night musings, and preparations for a dance. Ah, the dance! I shall not forget in a hurry the night of the dance.

They had all flocked to him that night, the local women and the land girls and the Wrens stationed nearby, in party dresses and uniforms, and he had danced with them all, attentive and good-natured. This promiscuity had upset her but had not prevented her from taking up his suggestion, at the end of the evening, that they walk home rather than take up the lift arranged by Nancy.

'Except of course your shoes.' He looked worried as he glanced down at her satin pumps.

'Nancy can lend me some boots. She always keeps some in the car.'

'Keeps what in the car?' Nancy glided towards them, flushed and radiant, a besotted officer in tow.

'Gumboots. And possibly, if you have one, a jacket. I'm cold.'

She walked home beside him, the velvet dress hitched to her knees, one hand holding onto her dance shoes and the other to his arm, a battered Barbour around her shoulders. 'I fear I'm somewhat less elegant at the finish than I was at the start,' she laughed.

'But isn't that always the sign of a good party?' She sensed him smile in the darkness.

'I'm glad you had a good time.'

'Did you?'

'I'm sad that you're leaving tomorrow.'

And then, almost nothing. The velvet night, a soft drizzle, the fading sounds of the last revellers. A crescent moon dipping in and out of clouds. His arm beneath her hand, their breath coming faster as they climbed the hill towards Marshwood. Slowing down as they entered the drive. Stopping before the front door. The quick brushing of lips. No more than that, but it was enough.

'I suppose I was pleased with my answer at the time,' sighed Bella.

Isla stretched out a hand to take the letter Bella held out to her.

It was delightful to have you here, she read.

And since we are in the business of throwing protocol to the winds, I must tell you how much your friendship means to us. Clement frets for you constantly, and gathers what news he can of your activities from the papers. I think he sees you in some ways as his own son, and he alternates consequently between anxiety and pride, behaving, in short, like a dear old mother hen. And I do not exaggerate when I say that only through you have I truly understood what it is we are fighting for, what freedom and the lack of it can mean. You are right not to stand on ceremony with us. I will do the same in return, and say dear Louis, never hesitate to come and visit us. You know that our door is always open to you.

'We never talked about it,' frowned Bella. 'Not properly. I sometimes think if we had everything would have turned out differently. Up and down the country people were throwing away the rule books and rewriting them to suit their own ends. But not us. No, we were sensible right to the end. Old-fashioned, that is what we were.'

'He came back, then?'

'Oh yes,' said Bella sadly. 'He came back.'

*　　*　　*

Isla left late, of course, and she drove slowly, her mind preoccupied. Jack, Elena, the anguished intensity of his gaze. Bella, Louis, her grandfather . . . By the time she arrived the children were already in bed. Richard and his parents were in the drawing-room with pre-dinner drinks.

'I'm sorry,' she said. 'I couldn't get away, and the traffic . . .'

'Run upstairs to see them,' said Elizabeth. 'Hugh will get you a drink.'

In the children's room, Beth was working her way through a pile of picture books while Marcus read one of his father's old *Beano*s.

'I don't see why we have to go to bed so early,' he complained.

'Daddy's cross,' said Beth. 'Not with us,' she explained, looking up at Isla. 'With you.'

'I still don't see why that means we have to go to bed so early,' grumbled her brother.

'I expect Daddy's just tired,' smiled Isla. She sat on the end of his bed and hugged him. 'My darling boy,' she said. She went over to Beth's bed and kissed her. 'My princess.'

Beth flung her arms around her mother's neck.

'I don't want to be a princess any more, I want to be a villain.'

Isla laughed out loud, holding her daughter close,

flushed with relief that the afternoon had passed and that nothing after all had changed.

'My villain, then,' she said. 'Good-night, villain.'

"Night, Mummy.'

Richard was alone in the drawing-room when she came back downstairs. 'Mum's in the kitchen,' he said. 'Dad went to make a phone call.'

'I'll go and see if Elizabeth needs any help.'

'She doesn't,' he snapped. 'She said she knew you'd ask, but to sit down and make yourself comfortable, that you should rest after your drive. And Dad made you a gin and tonic. *Lots of lemon. Just how she likes it.*'

Isla's heart sank as she sensed danger. 'That's nice,' she said cautiously.

'Jesus!' he exploded. 'Is that all you can say? You swan down here, hours after you said you would, and all you have to say for yourself is *that's nice?*'

'I hardly *swanned*,' protested Isla. '*And* I apologized!'

'Oh, big deal! I just wish, sometimes, you could see things from *their* point of view.'

'Excuse me?'

'Isla, it's been over two months since you came down for a weekend! They know you're forever squirrelled away at Marshwood. They know how often you go there. And the one weekend we come down here, as a family, the one weekend that's for them, you bugger off for the day!'

'I explained!' Isla, in her indignation, forgot about

Jack and her true motive for the day's visit to Marshwood. She felt only the immediate urgency to defend herself from Richard's sanctimonious anger, matching it with a self-righteousness of her own. 'I went to visit a cottage! Because of the burglary.'

'There's always a reason, isn't there?'

'She needs me!'

'The mercy dashes. The hours on the telephone.'

'Richard, I'm all she has.'

'No you're not. She has friends. She has your mother. She's manipulating you.'

'*She's* manipulating me!'

'What's that supposed to mean?'

'My whole life . . .' Isla paused mid-sentence. *My whole life is manipulated by you*, she had wanted to say, but honesty compelled her to recognize that this did not have to be true. She had left Jack almost immediately following his extraordinary statement that he had returned to Chapel St Mary for her, refusing to rise to it, practically fleeing in her desperation to get as far from him as possible. It had been a panicked, undignified retreat, but now she saw that behind it had lain a real choice, for *her* life, her real life, the one she shared with her husband and family. The realization elated her because if she was able, at a subconscious level, to make such an emphatic choice, then surely it was within her power to make others, equally positive, which would ensure their common happiness?

'Your *whole life* what?' prompted Richard.

'I think I need to go back to work,' said Isla.

'Excuse me?'

'I said, I think I need—'

'What does that have to do with anything?'

'Everything! I've been so unhappy, Rich. Unhappy and lonely. You must know that. But working would help. It's so obvious. I've been fighting against the idea because I thought it was somehow a sort of admission of failure, and I know it isn't what we both wanted, but it's time. I need to do it. I need to feel . . . oh, it sounds stupid . . . *Useful.*'

Richard was frowning. 'I don't see what this has to do with your being late.'

'Richard!' She stared at him incredulously. 'Aren't you listening to me? I've just told you how unhappy I am, and you're still going on about me being a bit late?'

'You're just saying that. Isla, you've got everything you could possibly want. I've *given* you everything you could possibly want. Everything you could possibly need.' He hesitated. 'Maybe we should have another baby.'

'No!' Her own vehemence startled her, and she saw that it had shocked Richard too. 'I don't want another baby,' she continued more softly. 'And since when has not needing anything been the definition of happiness?'

'You know how I feel about working mothers.'

'But if it makes me happier! Surely that would be

160

a good thing for all of us? Now that they're both at school?'

'What about *after* school?'

'We'll get a nanny! Or I could work part time. I haven't thought it through yet.'

'But what's the point? And what about holidays?'

She was going to cry again. *Oh God, please don't let me cry. Not now.*

'Isla.' His voice was gentler now. 'You see? You can barely cope as it is. Let me look after you, eh? We're all right. We're fine just as we are.'

On Sunday morning, despite the unseasonal cold, Richard took the children riding. Hugh went to church. Isla stayed behind to help Elizabeth with lunch.

'Good,' laughed her mother-in-law as Isla expertly rolled out pastry. 'You're better than me now!'

'Do you remember the first time I came down? And you said you'd teach me?'

'Not a lot I can teach you any more. I'm very proud of my student. Isla?'

A large tear splashed from the end of Isla's nose onto the flat disc of pastry before her. 'Bugger,' she swore. 'Now I'll have to do it again.'

'Nonsense,' said Elizabeth briskly. 'It's only a bit of salty water. Have a tissue.'

Isla took the tissue, blew her nose and, like a child, handed it back.

'I'm sorry about yesterday,' she said. 'Being late and everything. I know it was unspeakably rude. Richard was very cross with me.'

'Ah, Richard.' Elizabeth lined a dish with the pastry and poured in a prepared mixture of breadcrumbs and golden syrup. She slipped the tart into the oven and pulled a bottle of tonic water out of the fridge. 'I think we deserve a drink,' she said. 'Let's go next door.'

In the drawing-room, Elizabeth poured large gin and tonics and lit the fire already laid in the grate. 'I know we shouldn't this late in the year, but it's such a miserable day. And you look like you need warming up.'

Isla sniffed. Her tears, now they had started, would not stop. 'It's so stupid,' she said. 'Just he was so cross. And we had an argument. Well, a sort of argument. I told him I wanted to go back to work.'

'And what did he say?'

'That he doesn't want me to. And that I should have another baby. But I don't want another baby. I mean, I would die or kill for my children, but I *don't* want another baby. Another baby would drive me mad.'

She gave a long juddering sigh. 'I know how lucky I am. I do know that, Elizabeth, really. It's just that I feel so useless half the time. Really useless, like I have no purpose. It's been creeping up on me, and now I don't know what to do about it. I haven't even considered going back to work until now because we agreed that this was what we both wanted, but actually now I think, I really think, that it would help. I need to get out and be busy with something that isn't the kids and the house and the school, to see people who aren't other parents, to not be completely dependent. Sometimes I feel – this might sound mad, but sometimes I feel like I'm disappearing. Does that make sense?'

'Darling Isla,' said Elizabeth when Isla finally ran out of steam. 'You are so far from useless or from not having a purpose. You are a marvellous mother and a lovely wife, and Hugh and I love you as if you were our own. But can you not see that marriage is a partnership? You both depend on each other for different things. Earning money is only one of them.'

'But I'm so *bored*!' wailed Isla.

Elizabeth's mouth twitched. 'It *is* awful when your children start growing up, isn't it? When you are no longer needed – what's that terrible expression you all use? Twenty-four seven.'

'Did *you* find it difficult?'

'Of course I did. And just think, when he went to boarding-school . . . I thought my life had ended. I thought I'd never be happy again.'

'What did you do?'

Elizabeth shrugged. 'I just got on with it.'

'Is that what you think I should do?'

Elizabeth gazed at the fire before raising her eyes back to her daughter-in-law. 'Hugh would say that you should make the most of the gifts God has given you.

And with your brains, and your education, and all that training . . . Your marvellous drawings, all those prizes . . . I think you could be anything you wanted. But there *are* two of you. You can't just ride roughshod over Richard, you have to win him over.'

'I *want* to win him over. I want him to understand.'

'Richard,' said Elizabeth gently, 'is chasing a different dream. He'll come round in time. Right now he's completely focused on this promotion. His father was just the same. What you must do, Isla dear, is exercise patience. Wait until he hears about the senior partnership. Would you like me to talk to him then? I'd be happy to.'

'No,' said Isla. She wiped away the last of her tears with her hand and attempted a smile. Elizabeth leaned over to hug her. 'My fight. I'll deal with it. But thank you for listening.'

Richard's promotion was announced a month later. Two parties were held – one at work, which she did not attend. One at home, which she hosted with careful grace. The morning after the latter, he announced that they were all to go shopping.

'You can all have exactly what you want!' he announced grandly over breakfast. 'And then we can go out for lunch.'

'I had plans for lunch,' said Isla.

'Then cancel them, Mrs Hampton! For today we feast on other meats!'

This should be fun, thought Isla later that morning, trying on piles of beautiful clothes in the women's department of a large central London store. *So why isn't it?* She had left Richard with the children in the toy department, being fawned over by two shop assistants to whom Beth had explained in lordly tones that her daddy had promised her *whatever* she wanted. It alarmed Isla to realize how much this had annoyed her. Richard the magnanimous, showering gifts upon his family. She should be grateful. At the very least, she should enjoy the moment. So why was she hating it? Dresses clung in all the wrong places, high-necked sweaters made her breasts look too big, pretty cardigans looked mumsy and unglamorous. She glared at herself in the mirror, knowing that none of the clothes were at fault but that the problem lay with her and her general discontent. In the end, she picked up a huge burnt-orange cashmere shawl shot through with gold silk ribbon. She draped it over her cotton T-shirt. It was big enough to wrap twice around herself, and very expensive. The soft fabric slid over her skin, comforting and elegant at once, the strong colour and gentle sheen bringing a warm glow to her face. *Jack would like this.* She smiled at the thought which stole uninvited into her mind.

'That's pretty.' Isla jumped. Richard was leaning against a wooden pillar, watching her.

'It's the only thing I can find,' she offered. 'I'm sorry, I'm not really in the mood for shopping.'

'Just as well, given the children. Beth's insisting on a giant polar bear. *And* her cub. And Marcus wants Scalextric.'

'You're spoiling them.'

'Yes, well. Doesn't happen very often. Shall we get you that scarf?'

'Richard . . .' She felt a sudden urge, like in a bad Hollywood movie, to take him by the hand and say *honey, we don't need all this. Let's go to the park and play ball. Let's eat pizza. Let's be together as a family.*

'I don't want the scarf. I don't want anything.'

She had spoken sharply, and she didn't know why. A knot was forming inside her – of rage, of frustration, of resentment.

'But *I* want to buy you a present. Come on, Isla. It's a big day. I want to spoil you a bit.'

'Maybe I don't want to be spoiled.'

They stared at each other across the shop's colourful display, Isla and Richard, husband and wife, lost in the subtext of their conversation, aware of a power struggle they did not understand.

'I'm buying it.'

'I won't wear it.'

'I don't care.'

Later that afternoon she broached the subject of going back to work.

'I spoke to Michael last week.'

166

'Michael who?'

'Michael my old boss.'

'Do you think it's too early for a drink?' He was peering into the fridge. 'Only there's a bottle of champagne in here which is just begging to be drunk.'

'He said he thought he might have an opening for me after the summer. Richard, are you listening to me?'

'I am.' He came back to the table where she was sitting, champagne bottle and two glasses in hand. 'I suppose this is what this morning was about.'

'A bit. I think.'

'So what is it, some sort of feminist notion that you won't let me buy you presents because I don't want you to get a job?'

'I'm not sure it's feminist . . .' This was always the problem of arguing with Richard. He was so much better at it than she was, weaving and twisting, attacking in ways she could never dream of. 'But I suppose it does have to do with being independent,' she admitted.

'I thought we'd decided against it.'

'*You* decided against it.' She glared at him defiantly. He stared back, thoughtful.

'OK.'

'OK?'

'Isla, you're a grown woman. I can't stop you doing what you want. Only hear me out.'

There was something mildly threatening about him as he leaned towards her. She had a flash of how he must come across to opposing parties around the negotiating table. A formidable adversary, not to be crossed.

'I know I've always painted a picture of an idyllic childhood, but remember I was sent to boarding-school at the age of ten. It was horrible. I hated it. I was picked on and bullied and miserable. All I remember from prep school was how much I wanted my mother.'

'I'm not suggesting we send the children—'

'And she was always there for me. Always. Every holiday, every visiting day, making me feel that whatever else the world had in store for me, with her I always came first.'

'A part-time job . . .'

'So no. I don't want my children to be cared for by some Kiwi on her gap year or a Polish girl with a dodgy boyfriend while my wife works herself to the bone for a couple of shekels . . .'

'Richard, it's not like that!'

'It *is* like that,' he thundered. Isla jumped.

'You're not *listening* to me!' she yelled.

'Try not to shout, you'll upset the children.'

'*I'm* upset. Doesn't that count? How *I* feel?'

'Tell me something.' Richard uncorked the bottle, poured out two glasses, drained his, refilled it. His movements were slow, deliberate. They told her that he was in no hurry to speak, that he knew he was in control. She watched, fascinated and revolted. He was talking now but it took her a while to focus on what he was saying. Something about going away to Dallas for three weeks in July, and how would she manage things like that if she was working?

'You're never around anyway,' she said, confused. 'So what difference would it make?'

'You've not been listening.' He sighed. 'I said it would be more difficult for you to come with me if you were working.'

'Come with you?'

'That's what I said.'

'But it's the holidays. That's when we normally go to Marshwood.'

'*Must* we talk about Marshwood now?'

'But what would we do all day?'

'Go to the pool. Sightsee. I don't know. Isla, it's the US, for Christ's sake. There'd be loads to do.'

'But you'd be working . . .'

She knew nothing about Dallas, but she had a sudden, clear vision of what those three weeks there would be like. Of days spent alone with the children, of hotel meals and stifling heat, waiting for him to come back from work. Just like home, only hotter and more lonely. And yet he had asked her to go, and that must surely mean something.

'Why do you want us to come?' she asked.

I came back for you. Jack's voice, low and husky. Bella, talking about Louis. Lips brushing in an almost kiss in a moonlit garden. A longing, a need, a yearning for love. *If Richard says he wants me to go because he can't be without us, without me for three weeks, I'll go. If not . . .*

Richard shrugged. 'You're my family,' he said. 'Why wouldn't I want you to come?'

If not, I'll go to Marshwood.

June passed, as it always did, in a flurry of sports days and end-of-year plays. They spent a weekend in the New Forest to celebrate Richard's promotion. Isla spent two days baking for the school fête, where Beth won the fancy-dress line-up and Marcus and his best friend came first in the three-legged race. After a furious row over her decision not to go to the States, the subjects of Marshwood, Dallas and Isla's return to work were studiously avoided. Isla did not let herself think about Jack or the upcoming holiday at Marshwood, and she hardly spoke to Bella.

The children's school broke up in early July. Richard left for Dallas shortly afterwards. Isla piled cases, children and cat basket into the car and drove down to Marshwood full of apprehension.

'You're robbing them of a fantastic opportunity,' Richard had roared when she told him she would not be going with him to the States.

'What opportunity? You'll be working.'

'You can show them round.'

'Well I don't want to.'

It had seemed an important point to score at the

170

time but she could no longer remember exactly why. Something to do with not being dictated to or taken for granted.

'Would you have liked to go to America with Daddy?' she asked now.

'Yeah!' Marcus bounced on the front seat next to her. 'Could we have? Why didn't we? Can we still?'

She reached over and ruffled his hair, pulling it into his eyes. 'Daddy has to work the whole time he's there,' she said.

'Like when he's at home?'

'Just like that.'

'Then that's boring. I don't care. Marshwood's cool. I want to find a stag beetle for my collection. Only it has to be dead. And I can't kill it.'

The thought of seeing Jack again terrified her. *I came home for you* . . . Had she misunderstood him? Would he be disappointed with her for running away from their last meeting? Or take her presence at Marshwood – normal enough during the long summer holidays – as encouragement? Would he want her? Did he not? Did she want him to? She could not resist a glance down his drive as she went past. No car. Curtains drawn. The general air of a closed house. Perhaps he was away. *Good!*

Bella was sitting in the little alcove by the terrace when they arrived, playing cards with Nancy and Kitty with her right foot wrapped in a bandage and resting on a footstool.

171

'I twisted my ankle,' said Bella as Isla kissed her. 'Slipping on the steps on the terrace. Before you ask.'

'Why didn't you tell me?'

Bella assumed her most martyred expression. 'I didn't want to worry you.'

'Excuse me?' Isla raised incredulous eyebrows. 'Since when have you spared me dramas so as *not to worry me*?'

'Probably,' said Bella, already bored with playing the victim and acid dripping from every word, 'since *you* started visiting Bambridge properties without telling me.'

'We should go.' Kitty began to gather her things.

'Nonsense,' said Nancy. 'Things are just getting interesting.'

Isla was blushing. 'How did you find out?'

'Esther told me last week. She ran into the agent in town.' Bella assumed a high falsetto, presumably to represent the estate agent. '*Mrs Langton's granddaughter came to visit Church View the other week. I didn't know Marshwood was up for sale.* Apparently the old fool – the agent – thinks it's a splendid idea. *So much more suitable.* Esther, of course, completely agrees. Which is why Esther is not here today.'

'Actually, I didn't think it *would* suit you, which is why I didn't tell—'

'I knew from the moment she turned up that something was up. She has never, *ever* turned up unexpectedly. Not in fifty years. And then up she popped, asking to borrow a book I know for a fact would never interest her. On Catherine de' Medici.'

'The one I gave you for Christmas?'

'Does it matter? I'll grant her this, she did look excruciatingly uncomfortable. Fidgeting and mumbling and so on.'

'So what happened?' asked Isla resignedly.

'Well she told me about this cottage, of course.' If Isla hadn't known her grandmother, she would not have thought it possible to inject quite so much scorn into two syllables. 'She said *Isla and Jack have been to see it and they think it is perfect.*'

'I never said it was—'

'Perfect!' Bella's voice quivered with indignation. 'Perfect to grow *old* in! Perfect for me to be cut off from everything I love in! Perfect for . . .'

'You don't like it.'

'I hate it! And I'll tell you what I hate even more, is you and Jack sneaking off to look at it behind my back. It's all Richard's fault, of course. Part of his plan to kick me out of Marshwood.'

'Richard had nothing to do with it.'

'Ahem!' Nancy interrupted with a loud cough. A tall, severe-looking woman marched into the room bearing a tray. 'Mrs Langton's dinner,' she announced. 'Do you need to use the toilet?'

Bella grimaced.

'Nancy, we really *must* go,' pleaded Kitty.

'Fair enough. Come on then, KitKat.' Nancy gathered the deck of cards, straightened them and slipped them back into their case. 'Darling, I do think you have to forgive Esther. Three's no good for cards, and I miss bridge. We'll see you tomorrow.'

Isla followed them out of the room. 'Who's that?' she asked when they were out of earshot.

'The nurse,' said Nancy.

'She has a nurse! I can't believe she never told me.'

'She really is very cross,' sighed Kitty. 'I spoke to Esther, and she said they had an awful argument. A quarrel, really. Esther was terribly upset because of course she was only trying to help.'

'Where did the nurse come from?'

'I found her,' said Nancy. 'She managed Esther after her last hip operation. She rather agrees with you and Esther, by the way. Thinks Bella should sell up and find something smaller.'

'I *don't* think that!'

'And between you and me, I'm rather coming round to the same way of thinking myself. I never used to, but Mrs Harbinger – that's the nurse's name – does make sense. Marvellous woman, really. So capable.'

Kitty giggled. Isla and Nancy both turned to stare at her. 'I'm sorry,' she said. 'It's just that Nancy's so in thrall to the woman. I haven't seen her with a crush like this for years.'

'What rubbish,' scoffed Nancy.

'Well she certainly changed your mind,' said Kitty daringly.

'She talks sense.'

'Of course she does. And you've always been such an *admirer* of good sense.'

They always argue, thought Isla. *Ever since I have known them, the four of them have argued like old lovers, and yet they have never quarrelled. Until now, because of me.*

She did not have the chance to speak to Bella alone until much later, when the children were asleep and the formidable Mrs Harbinger had retired. Bella, wearing a frayed silk dressing-gown and her favourite Indian shawl, sat up in bed against a pile of pillows. Isla, feeling nervous, stood against the mantelpiece playing with Bella's collection of carved birds, all presents from her grandfather.

'I know you're cross with me, and I know we were wrong not to speak to you first. We should never have gone behind your back. I'm sorry.'

Bella glared at her. 'Well no, you shouldn't have,' she said. 'You treated me like a fool, and I must say that's unlike you.'

Isla bit her tongue, conscious that Bella was enjoying the spectacle of her repentance a bit too much.

'I didn't *want* to lie to you. It's just that . . . well, Jack suggested it, and I thought why not. I didn't actually *like* the cottage.'

175

'Ah, Jack,' mused Bella. 'Now what on earth does it have to do with him?'

'I suppose he cares about you.'

Bella gave a derisive snort. Isla blushed. 'Well anyway, I'm sorry.'

'That's all right,' said Bella cheerfully. 'No real harm done. I'll forgive Esther too in a day or so. I just wanted to make my point.'

'Which is?'

'I'm not moving.'

'Right.' Isla bit her lip. 'I think we got that message loud and clear.'

'I know what you're thinking. Sitting there, not saying it. What if I had broken my neck?'

'Hadn't crossed my mind,' lied Isla.

'I told Jack too before he left. Didn't mince my words with him, either.'

So she had been right. The house was empty.

'Where did he go?' She tried to keep her voice as casual as possible.

'Who?'

'Jack.'

'Northumberland, I believe. Some friends near the Scottish border lent him a house. He said something about needing time out. About Dorset being too crowded. If you ask me, that boy's not well. He looked dreadful when he left.'

'Right, well. I hope he finds what he's looking for.'

'In Northumberland?' Bella looked at her thoughtfully. Isla blushed. 'It seems unlikely. Darling, do stop fiddling with those birds.'

Isla left the mantelpiece and came to sit on the end of Bella's bed.

'Granna, I've already said I'm sorry. We thought we were doing the right thing. We were concerned, because we care about you. The burglary, the insurance . . . I didn't think it would upset you. I promise never to mention moving house again.'

Was she as transparent as she sounded to herself? She burbled her half-truths, aware that Bella was not really listening. She looked down at her grandmother's hands, which had reached up to take her own. They were gnarled with arthritis and age, the nails yellowing under their thick coat of dark red varnish. Bella followed her gaze.

'He wrote to me once about hands,' she said. 'A whole letter. Quite short, mind. One of the men he flew with, his squadron leader I think, had just had a baby girl, and he went to visit her. He wrote about her hands, how she gripped his finger. He said that he could see her whole life, looking at her hands, imagining all the things they would do. Eating and playing, working, loving. It's a lovely letter. I'll find it for you.'

She gave Isla's hand a hard squeeze before dropping it back into her lap. 'Your mother has artist's hands,' she said. 'I suppose you have inherited them, with your talent for drawing.'

'I suppose so,' smiled Isla. 'I've never really thought about it.'

Bella was sleepy. Isla kissed her gently and sat with her a moment longer, her auburn head resting on her grandmother's frail shoulder.

'I love you,' said Bella unexpectedly.

Isla laughed. 'I thought you were so cross with me.'

'I *am* cross with you. But I love you too.'

Bella dismissed Mrs Harbinger a few days after Isla's arrival.

'Peace at last!' she cried. 'I don't know what Nancy sees in that woman. I only kept her on to help me with the stairs.'

'She wasn't so bad,' said Isla. 'You're not exactly the most conventional of patients.'

'Well I'd much rather have you. Now we can get on with the memoirs. I didn't want to while she was here, in case she eavesdropped.'

'Can I eavesdrop?' asked Beth.

'No you cannot,' retorted Bella.

That evening, when Isla went to her grandmother's room with her pen and notepad in hand, she found her looking disconsolately at her desk, a sheaf of papers spread out before her.

'I'm not sure there's much point doing this after all,' said Bella.

'Then let's stop.'

'No, no . . . I want you to understand . . . Richard to understand . . .' She stopped, confused.

'I don't need to read your memoirs to understand what Marshwood means to you, Granna,' said Isla gently. 'And as for Richard . . .' She shrugged, then grinned. 'He'll do what we say. Come on. Why don't you go to bed?'

'He won't though, will he? You won't be able to make him. And then there'll be no money and I'll be destitute.'

'You're tired.'

'No I'm not,' said Bella with a tinge of asperity. 'Why do people always say that? As if being tired explained anything.' She rummaged on the desk for her reading glasses and pushed them to the end of her nose, looking instantly eccentric. Her mouth settled into what Isla recognized as its most stubborn line. 'Ah, I've found it. His diary. It's the key, really, to understanding him.'

When the bell rang for his first sweep across the Channel Louis was in such a heightened state of readiness that he beat all the other pilots to the planes by several seconds, and was belted up and ready to go before the last stragglers were even sliding into their cockpits. *That keen, eh, Lewis?* John Henry, the squadron leader with the small daughter, was a kindly man and a seasoned fighter. Louis, who liked and respected Henry and so didn't mind his name being massacred by his English pronunciation, gave him the thumbs-up and grinned back. *Good luck!* Henry yelled over the roar of his engine and fluttered his hand in a royal wave before lowering the hatch of his Spitfire.

This is it, then, thought Louis. In nearly three years of this strange war, his first taste of active combat. The early months of waiting, the crushing defeat, the mad flight to North Africa, the anger and humiliation at being ordered to lay down arms, the convoy back from Gibraltar through the mined Atlantic waters, the long frustrating months retraining on English planes, leaving home, meeting Bella, all of the disparate events of the past two years since France had fallen had built up to this heart-stopping exhilaration, taking off in perfect formation in the sweet-smelling English countryside to fight the enemy in his land. Louis had always loved flying but he felt that until this precise moment he had only ever glimpsed a fraction of its glory. The anticipation of danger, the possibility that these could be his last moments on earth all sharpened his senses to the piercing wonder of being here and now, a migratory bird in complete harmony with the rest of his flock and at one with the sky. When they reached the Channel they dropped with a single swoop to a mere few feet above the sea and he noticed, or thought he noticed, every sunbeam refracted on the waves. He felt exultantly alive. He thought that if this moment were to be his last, he would die happy.

They were within a few miles of the French coast

when the radios erupted. He caught his first sight of the enemy, thirty Focke Wulfs, 800 feet above. Higher still, the occasional glint of sunlight on a wing gave away the presence of further planes. *You are outnumbered, come home*, came the call, but already the Focke Wulfs were raining down on them out of the sun.

Louis' first victory was a fluke. Isolated and surrounded, he climbed and spun and manoeuvred his plane as if it were an extension of himself. He did not hear the command to retreat. Over the airwaves, he heard Henry swear. *Bloody left wing . . . See you back home, boys . . .* Out of the corner of his eye, he saw a lone Spitfire falling in crazy circles towards the sea. No time to make sure Henry had jumped. Louis was staring at his own death down the barrels of what seemed like a hundred planes. He was a stag at bay, a fox waiting to be torn apart by the pack. He was every creature who had ever been tracked and hunted, and he believed only in his own survival. German planes tumbled towards him and he spun to meet them, teeth clenched, his whole body tensed.

He did not fight well but fired indiscriminately, without thinking that he might hit friendly aircraft. His victory flew straight at him through the fray, and for some reason at this point Louis remembered his training and stopped firing. Despite the odds, he was the hunter now and he waited, holding his breath. *The white of his eyes*, whispered the voices of countless instructors, rising to meet him from the airfields of England and France. *Attendez de voir le blanc de ses yeux* . . . He wore a red scarf, Louis noted. He must feel the cold, unless it was a mascot, a good luck charm. He was young, he guessed, from what he could see of the face between the scarf and the goggles.

He was young and wore a red scarf and with one perfectly targeted missile Louis reduced him to a spinning ball of fire and red-hot metal. There was no time to savour or ponder his victory. His line of vision was clear. A bad sign. They must be behind him. He pulled back the stick and almost blacked out as his Spitfire surged upwards. It was his one chance, he knew this. He could climb faster than them, and hopefully this, together with the element of surprise, would give him enough of a head start.

It took him a while to notice that they were not following. He looked back and saw to his amazement that the enemy, back in ragged formation, were melting away towards France. Confused, he briefly attributed their withdrawal to his victory, until he grew conscious that his was the only plane in sight, and he remembered the order to retreat.

The radio was silent now. They must have changed the frequency. Louis flew back over the Channel alone through the golden light of evening. It was dark when he arrived home and the airbase was in chaos. He left his plane where he could and walked over to a group of pilots huddling on the edge of the airfield. They greeted him with a few slaps on the back, but overall the mood remained sombre.

See you back home, boys. Henry's body was never found, but his voice haunted Louis all through the long night which followed his first battle. In his mind it merged with the memory of a red scarf beneath the youthful line of a half-covered face, and a twisted ball of burning metal plummeting through the evening sky to the waiting sea. Louis mourned Henry that night, and his German pilot. He mourned his boyish dreams of glory brought to an abrupt end by his first kill three years into the war, and he mourned the country he had come so close to seeing again today. But the following morning, when the bell rang ordering them to scramble halfway through breakfast, he ran to his plane to start it all again.

I will get used to this, he wrote in his diary, over and again, in the weeks following his first battle. They were short of pilots and pressure was high. They were flying more than they should have been, more than was deemed safe, but what did safe mean anyway? Louis preferred it this way.

I have fought many battles since my first victory, coming under merciless fire in skies black with burning smoke, and I have witnessed the many manners of dying which face those who fight in the sky. I have seen pilots jump with their parachutes on fire, and others whose parachutes have not opened at all; I have watched planes slowly spiralling out of the sky, and heard the last cries of men unable to jump. I have seen planes explode mid-flight. I have seen the manner of my own death. I have killed again and derived no satisfaction from my victories. Other pilots return triumphant from their sorties, but I am afraid. Afraid of dying, and of killing. Afraid of forgetting who I am, and of what I am becoming. I am afraid, and I am ashamed of my fear. But I will get used to it.

Four times. It always seemed extraordinary to her, given the impact he had on their lives, but he only came to them four times. There was one more visit after the week-long holiday. He was to be transferred to Anglesey, from where he was to form part of a squadron protecting Atlantic convoys. Two short days' leave, and he was gone.

She went with him down to the lake on his last afternoon. They entered the woods through a wide tunnel of whispering beeches, walking on the faded copper carpet of last year's fallen leaves. Above them, arched branches intertwined like lovers. Two months had passed since his last visit. The season was on the cusp between summer and autumn, and though the trees still retained their leaves, there was a fragile quiver about them as they prepared for the sparseness of the months ahead.

They stopped when they reached the lake and sat side

by side, close but not touching. All she could think at first was how much he had changed. The lightness had gone. He was keeping himself back, where before he had been so generous of himself. Over the past months, he had acquired an air of introspection so that where previously he had delighted her, he now frightened her a little. She had thought before he came that she would be embarrassed to see him, but nothing was said of their last meeting. There was a new harshness to him, a sort of contained urgency, and she was a little ashamed to find how quickly her embarrassment at his presence turned to excitement. They had sat here together before, but never until now had she been so aware of his body close to hers. His high spirits then had been infectious, and with him she had felt a hunger for living which manifested itself in action, in laughter, in their energetic games of tennis and raucous games of snap, in evenings talking under the stars and days working in the garden. He did not move so much now, she realized, and his stillness seemed to absorb his surrounding space, drawing her in. In this moment, profoundly aware of the reality of his situation – that he was leaving, that she might never see him again – she stopped caring about what was right or wrong or inappropriate. She had always loved him, but now she knew that she could not resist him. And anyway, she reasoned, wasn't this partly her due? Had she not nursed Clement like a child, and lived with him like a sister, for years before Louis appeared? Did he not still now, when he was allegedly so much happier, choose to sleep in his study? And was it so wrong to give in to this love, this young, strong, vibrant love? All these thoughts flashed half-formulated through her mind, as her hand moved towards him of its own volition. Fascinated, she watched it settle gently over his, her fingers curling around his knuckles, opening his fist so that his palm lay in hers, facing the sky. He sighed. She quivered as he turned towards her.

It does help, you know, when there's chemistry. That day down by the lake, she understood what Nancy had meant all those years ago. She felt that she must be made up of every element that ever was. She was mercury, all light and movement, and when their fingers intertwined, she was pure phosphorus, about to ignite.

And then he spoke.

'Did I tell you we stole a plane?'

'A plane?'

'In Algeria, when we escaped,' he explained. 'But they sabotaged it.'

'They sabotaged it?' Why was he telling her this now? She tried to remove her hand but he would not let her. She curled her fist into a ball beneath his palm instead as his long tapered fingers closed firmly around hers. 'Who?'

'The air force. Our superiors, I suppose. The fleet had

to be grounded. Part of the deal, the occupation agreement.'

'I . . . Yes, you did tell me, I think. The first time we met. You told me about it.'

'My friend, Xavier, he was brilliant. We trained together, did I tell you? He was piloting. So calm. A hero. We were all heroes then, destined for glory. It was still a game. Sort of. Did I tell you about my friend Xavier?'

He looked distant, almost feverish. Their brief moment had passed, that much was clear. 'You told me about Henry,' murmured Bella.

'Henry . . . Poor Henry. Xavier was killed last week.'

'I'm sorry.'

'So stupid,' said Louis. 'He was on exercise. I saw him crash. So unnecessary. My best friend, really. The only one left of that mad crew who took that crazy flight from Algiers to Gibraltar.'

'Apart from you.'

'Apart from me.' She stole a covert glance at him, and was pleased to see a small ghost of a smile playing around his mouth. 'Do you know, Bella, I have been thinking about what I should do after the war.'

She removed her hand and placed it carefully in her lap. 'Which is?'

'You will laugh.'

'Try me.'

'Excuse me?'

'It's an expression.'

'Oh.' He looked thoughtful, and she knew that he was searching for a French equivalent. She nudged him.

'Well?'

'I would like to become a priest.'

'A priest!'

'I knew you'd laugh!' She was relieved to see his own eyes glint with something of their old merriness. 'But it's true. A country *curé*, with a black cassock and a little felt hat. In a sleepy village with a big square where the acacias bloom in the spring, and the men gather in the afternoons to play *boules*, and I learn all the local gossip at weekly confession.'

'You wouldn't last a minute!' teased Bella.

'I would! Every morning, I would say matins impossibly early. In the summer months this would be wonderful, because I would be up with the sun, and when I came out of church it would be already warm, with birds singing and farm workers going about their business. Of course in winter it would be more difficult, because it would be dark and cold, but afterwards I would go back to my priory to drink hot chocolate from a bowl.'

'Piled high with cream,' mocked Bella. 'A guilty secret which must *never* get out.'

'Of course I should need a housekeeper.'

'Perhaps you could ask Josie Bates.'

'Perhaps,' he said. He leaned forward with his arms resting on his knees. 'Or perhaps I could ask you.'

She caught her breath. He still did not look at her, but she noticed the side of his mouth give a definite twitch. 'You could cook for me,' he said. 'Every Sunday, you could roast a chicken donated by my parishioners.'

'That's not kind!' she laughed.

'What?'

'I've made huge progress in the kitchen . . .'

'Come with me then.'

'Well all right, but I don't know *what* your parishioners would make of it.'

'Come with me now.'

'Oh.'

Later she would tell herself she knew even then that they would never laugh together again. *Come with me.* She closed her eyes and glimpsed possibilities of passion and sweetness and love she had never dreamed of. A world reduced to a room, a bed, two people alone. *Come with me.*

'Where would we go?' This was not her, surely, this little voice, hesitant but so trusting, so full of longing.

'There is a place I know. A hotel.'

'A hotel . . .'

He turned to look straight at her and for the first time she noticed that his hazel eyes were shot with gold. 'Actually, what I want really is to go home.'

The air by the lake was damp and smoky with the

189

smell of early bonfires. Home for Louis was a town by the sea with an ancient port flanked by two towers and a tangled garden full of raspberries, but this was the smell of Marshwood.

'I can't go with you,' faltered Bella. 'It's not that I don't want . . . it doesn't mean . . .'

He looked away, back over the lake dark with shadows in the fading light. 'I know.'

'The dance,' she said. 'Everything . . . I . . . what I felt . . .'

'It was another world, wasn't it?' He turned his gaze to her again. 'Another life, almost.'

'Yes.'

They sat for a long time watching the late summer shadows lengthen over the water. After a while, she moved closer to him and rested her head upon his shoulder. Then, in the gathering twilight, Bella and Louis walked back to Marshwood, silently and without touching. The house was empty when they returned. Louis donned the jacket he had discarded for the walk and picked up his belongings. She followed him out to his waiting motorcycle.

'Must you go so soon? Clement'll be sorry to have missed you.'

'Tell him I'm sorry. It's late, I . . .' He trailed off. His unspoken words hung between them.

'He'll understand. Next time.'

Still he said nothing. .

'How will I know?' she asked, suddenly afraid. 'If anything happens to you, how will I know?'

He raised his hand and rested the back of two fingers on her cheek. 'You'll know.'

'I'll write.' She swallowed the painful lump in her throat and attempted a smile. 'I'll send you news to distract you.'

'Dear Bella. I think perhaps that you should not.' The fingers lingered a moment longer. Then he pressed his lips briefly to her forehead, and was gone.

Silence had fallen around the little table. Bella was the first to break it. 'You look troubled.'

'I was thinking about Grandpapa.'

'Ah,' said Bella.

'I miss him so much,' said Isla. 'And he is so much a part of this house, of Marshwood, of all of us. I always thought you were so happy together.'

'I suppose we were, in our way.'

'But you loved Louis!'

'It would have been very difficult,' said Bella sharply, '*not* to love Louis.'

'So Grandpapa . . .'

'Life is long.'

'But with Louis . . .' It felt very, very important to Isla to know the answer to her next question. 'Did you have . . . do you have any regrets?'

Bella began to gather the papers scattered on

her desk. 'Regrets are the product of an overactive imagination.'

'*Do* you?'

'Really, Isla. It often seems to me that your generation is *obsessed* with the question of happiness. We didn't think like that.'

The spell cast over them by Bella's recollections was gone. Isla offered to help Bella to bed, Bella desisted. They chatted, briefly, of other things and parted for the night on a cheerful note which struck Isla as forced.

She stopped at the door, wanting to apologize but not knowing for what. Bella still sat at her table. She had her back to the door and Isla could not see her face. But the tenderness with which she gathered the papers on her table told its own story.

Marshwood came into its own during the school holidays. Music played through the open windows, children called out to each other, toys littered the lawn. The cloakroom floor was a permanent jumble of discarded trainers and sandals, badminton rackets and footballs, the fridge groaned with food, clothes fluttered on a line in the garden. Plans were made every morning, for picnics and walks and day trips, plans which were discussed animatedly over breakfast but which rarely materialized because, with the garden a riot of flowers and the sorry state of the house hidden beneath a blanket of sunshine, there seemed no need to go anywhere. There was no more talk of selling up or moving to conveniently located cottages. Instead Isla took the house to task, vacuuming dead flies and woodlice, polishing the windows, removing cobwebs. Bella normally survived on a diet of gin, crackers and tinned soup. Under Isla the kitchen, scrubbed and functioning, took its rightful role as hub of the house. Cakes, roasts, picnics, snacks, cold drinks, hot drinks, plasters, Calpol, suncream, raincoats, cat medicine, lost items, found items, gossip, confidences, news and views, all were dispensed and exchanged within its walls. Away from home, in this house which craved the attention she gave it, domesticity ceased to be a burden and became something more, a sacrament. No Richard, no Jack. Just the Coven, reconvened with Esther in their midst, playing cards by the open doors of the terrace; neighbours dropping in to chat; the children running half wild; Bella apparently happy, showing no more desire to delve into the past; and Isla, keeping it all running, bringing the house back to life, feeling useful and at peace, no longer asking questions.

And then, on 16 July, Jack came home.

Up in Northumberland, he had lived with no TV, radio reception or newspapers in a remote cottage by the sea with wild views across to Lindisfarne. He had spent his days in a boat, unsuccessfully fishing, or tramping along beaches with the North Sea wind whistling in his ears. On one occasion, following the enthusiastic example of a hardy family from Newcastle, he had swum. The experience had been brisk but cleansing and he had repeated it several times. As he prepared for the drive back to the south, he told himself that he felt well. Really well, and ready for anything. It had been a mistake to go back to Dorset after Bosnia. It wasn't a return to his roots that he needed, but a new place, light, sea air, big horizons and total solitude. His body still tingled from his final early morning swim – he hadn't washed since the beach, wanting to prolong the sensation of well-being which came of salt-caked skin and wind-whipped limbs. He whistled to himself as he swung the car out of the narrow private lane that led to his friends' cottage, and switched on the car radio just in time for the first item on the news.

Jack came slowly back to his senses to realize that somebody was hooting at him. Where was he? He thought he must have fainted but he was still driving, hunched over the wheel, crawling along a fast A road at twenty miles per hour. He pulled over onto the verge and opened his door to throw up. The car behind shot past with another angry blast of the horn. Jack closed his eyes and listened to the end of the news report. When it was finished, he searched the glove compartment for a tape. He found a heavy metal selection and put it on, loud. Perfect.

He had left the Northumberland cottage shortly after ten. The roads were clear almost all the way. He pulled into his parents' drive less than eight hours later, hands shaking, the tape deck still blasting. He did not set foot inside the house, but walked straight over to Marshwood instead, where he was confronted with a surreal vision, as far from the atrocities that had crowded his head since hearing the news bulletin as he could have imagined.

The main lawn was strewn with Persian carpets. Beaten free of their habitual coating of dust, they had recovered some of their original jewel colours and were proving irresistible to Isla's children, who island-hopped from rug to rug engrossed in a game. Isla lay on the largest rug in the middle of the lawn, the rose-patterned one from the drawing-room. The kitten, Leo, sprawled contentedly in the sun beside her.

A perfect day, and hot. They did not notice his approach. He saw the children run towards her and fling themselves to the ground beside her, the cat leap up in disgust at the interruption. He looked on as Isla and her children lay on their backs, shading their eyes from the light. Marcus pointed. Jack followed the direction of his finger and almost smiled at the sight of the swifts, back for the summer and flying high. This then was Isla, he thought. Not the girl he remembered, tearful and passionate, but this pretty woman without a care in the world, lying on a Persian carpet in the middle of an English country garden with two children and a cat, her dress riding up to expose slim brown thighs as she stretched a bare foot up towards the sun. One of the children must have said something funny, because they all laughed. Beth rolled on top of her mother and began to rain kisses down onto her face. Jack clenched his fists.

Once, on the road with Elena, he had stopped their Jeep beside a meadow.

'Don't tell me we have run out of gas.' He had grown used to her phlegmatic approach to danger and was surprised by the anxiety in her voice. 'Bandit country,' she told him. 'I would not want to be stranded here.'

'We have spare gas anyway,' he said. 'But that's not why I stopped. This field. It's so beautiful.'

And it was. The heavy rain which over the past days had turned the roads and the surrounding country to mud had brought boon to the meadow. A weak sun had come out, lighting the snowcapped peaks of the distant mountains and sparkling off the countless droplets caught in grass which shone with a verdant lushness, a lushness that seemed to cock a snook at the war and its attendant trail of destruction.

'I want to photograph it.'

Elena gave a shout of laughter. 'Oh my God! Always the photographer. He sees something beautiful and he must take a picture.' She brought her fingers up to her face, making a square over her right eye. 'Snap, snap, snap. Make sure you do not miss anything.'

He moved around the Jeep for a different view. 'What do you want me to do with it?'

'Run in it. Roll. Make love. Fuck, Jack, I don't know. *Live.*'

'Nope.' He put down the camera and grinned at her. 'I don't know what you mean.'

'I'll show you.'

And before he could stop her she was off, dancing through the swaying grass.

'You mad bitch!' he shouted after her. 'Elena, *mines!*' He watched her with his heart in his mouth. *Any minute now . . . any minute now a landmine could go off and Elena, sexy, crazy, adventure-hungry Elena . . .*

She was back, panting, laughing, happy. 'You see what I mean?' Her face was flushed, her eyes sparkling. '*Live.*'

Marcus had spotted him. They were all looking at him, Isla tugging down her dress. He walked slowly over to meet them.

'We're spring-cleaning,' she laughed, waving to indicate the rugs. 'You can't imagine the dust. How was Scotland?'

'It was Northumberland.'

'Was it lovely?'

'Very lovely.' He needed to get her children out of the

way. He needed to ask her if she had seen the news. He needed her to take him in her arms and make him forget what he had heard today, and seen the year before.

'Why were you watching us?' asked Beth.

'I was thinking what a beautiful composition you made, all of you on the rug. Madonna and children. With cat.'

'Kitten.'

'Is it really still a kitten?'

'He.'

'I'm sorry, is *he* still a kitten? He looks enormous.'

'What's a madonna?' asked Marcus.

'Traditionally, the mother of Jesus,' said Jack.

'Who *is* Jesus, exactly?' asked Beth.

Isla coughed. 'I'm afraid their religious education hasn't really taken off yet. Much as I try to instil some sort of awareness in them.'

The children wandered off, Beth stalking Leo, Marcus clutching binoculars.

'There's a pair of kestrels in the wood,' explained Isla. 'It's his most burning desire to see them, but he hasn't yet.'

'Talk to me more about religious awareness.'

'Excuse me?'

'You said, *much as I try to instil some sort of awareness in them*. I just wondered . . .' Oh Christ. How had he got on to that? His mind was so full of her bare legs, of the swell of her breasts against her flimsy cotton dress. He knew he had been right to come back. Just the sight of her was almost enough. 'You know, in Bosnia, it was so much . . . cultural clashes, religious . . .'

'Oh!' She nodded, in the wise, understanding way people who knew nothing of the war did whenever it was mentioned, in the hazy belief that religion must be at the heart of everything. 'Of course.'

'Are you . . . do you go to church?' *This conversation*. It was risible, really.

'A bit. I think since having children I understand better what it's all about – God, Jesus, the notion of sacrifice. The idea that we contribute to something greater than ourselves. Love.'

'Ah, love,' he said without thinking, and she blushed.

'I know it sounds stupid.'

'No! No, it doesn't sound stupid. I'm not a believer, that's all. Seen too much.'

'Yes, of course,' she repeated, and he was suddenly filled with a violent, insane desire to shake her. *Of course!* Eight thousand men and boys shot while the world watched, a city pounded by mortars while its inhabitants starved, twenty five thousand refugees. *Of course!*

'Have you seen the news?'

'The news?'

'Srebrenica. The massacre. Were there pictures? I've seen nothing. There was nothing, where I was, I didn't know. I heard it on the radio.' He rubbed his eyes wearily. 'I didn't know,' he repeated.

'Oh my God, Jack!' So *she* did know. She knew, and yet she still lay with her children on a rug on a lawn with a cat watching swifts in the sun . . . She knew, and she had forgotten. He swayed. She took him by the arm, marched him to the kitchen and poured him a whisky.

'And I bet you haven't eaten,' she said. 'I'm going to make you a sandwich.'

'A sandwich.'

'Trust me, you'll like it.'

She stood over him while he ate. 'What's wrong with that bit?' she asked when he left half on his plate.

'I'm not hungry any more.'

She sat down opposite him. 'Do you mind if I ask you a question?'

She had been right to feed him, and right to bring him here. The kitchen was cool but its windows were open wide onto the garden bright with evening sunlight, there were flowers on the table and the smell of a roasting chicken in the air. Isla had put a plate containing half a fruitcake before him, and he leaned forward to pick at the raisins which had gathered around its base. She sat across the table from him, and his earlier feelings of desire and anger gave way, with this sense of well-being at her hands – full belly, quenched thirst, pleasant room – to tenderness.

He could forget what he had heard on the radio this morning, and the hellish months in Bosnia, Sarajevo, the trip, Elena.

'What's your question?' he asked.

'What is war like?'

'What is it *like*?'

'Granna's been dictating her memoirs again. There's a lot about the war, Grandpapa and . . . well, others. I wondered what it was like for you. In Bosnia. What made you go?'

What had made him go? A lifetime ago, what had made him turn down an easy shoot in the Serengeti and ask instead to replace one of his paper's outgoing war correspondents? He didn't want to think about it but Isla was looking at him, expecting answers.

'I guess,' he said slowly, 'for me it was about extremes of human behaviour. With *interest* in extremes of behaviour. I thought I'd seen it all, I'd covered so much – disasters, riots, famines, whatever – and to be blunt I was getting bored. And then this guy, the guy I replaced, he got back from Bosnia and he said he'd never seen anything like it.'

'And you, being you, just had to find out.'

'Something like that. I thought . . . somehow, I thought that being in a war zone, confronted with the bare essentials of the human condition, I would discover some fundamental truth about myself. About what it means to be human. Does that sound pompous?'

Isla shrugged. 'And were you? Confronted with fundamental truth?'

'No. Unless the fundamental truth is . . . well, I saw the extremes all right. And don't get me wrong, it was exciting. Addictive. You're there in your little world, running from story to story, hoping to get *the* picture, the one that'll make headlines, the one that'll make *you*. And then you get sick of it. Because however good your pictures are, that's all they are. Pictures. And all around you people are dying, and you're supposed to stay impartial, and you try to do what you can to help but here's the thing: unlike them, unlike the people you are shooting, *you can always get out*. And when you do, you realize that nobody gives a fuck, really, whether you stay or go. And you end up feeling profoundly dislocated from everything – their life, your life, life in general. You talked about Bella, Clement, the Second World War. Here's the difference: it was *their* war. Bosnia was no more my war than any of the other disasters I covered were my disasters. Maybe that's the truth I discovered. That I wasn't living *my* life.'

'Do you still feel that now?'

He looked straight at her as he answered. 'Most of the time.'

Isla dropped her gaze first.

'Can I ask you something else?'

'What?'

'Will you photograph Marcus and Beth for me?'

And now the mood was broken. He felt the colour drain from his face, and saw hers begin to register anxiety as he failed to answer. He swallowed and began to knead his hands together, a relatively new gesture which he dated back to his return from Bosnia.

'Jack, are you all right?'

'I have to go.'

And then somehow he was outside, striding towards home, leaving her behind. Back in the house he unpacked his old Leica and felt its familiar weight. He took the cap off the lens and polished it, he loaded a roll of film, taking his time over it, fighting to keep control of his shaking fingers. Ready at last, he took a couple of shots without looking through the lens, just to remind himself of the feel of the button. The clicks were normal, almost comforting. *I can do this*, he told himself firmly, and raised the camera to his eye.

Elena was there, as he had known she would be. He hurled the camera across the room. The lens shattered as it hit the opposite wall.

The sequence of small square windows in Clement's workshop threw pale distorted rectangles of light onto its dusty floor. Isla hopped deliberately from one rectangle to the next, pointing her toes and extending her leg to increase her chances of not stepping on the ground in between. It had been a childhood game and it formed an important part of her Marshwood rituals.

Bella had given away most of Clement's wardrobe to charity when he died, but his workshop was almost exactly as he had left it. 'What else would I do with the space?' she shrugged when people suggested she clear it. To Isla, she confided that she liked to think he would have somewhere to go that was his, if ever he came back.

'If he comes back?'

Bella looked disappointed at Isla's incomprehension.

'You mean his *ghost*?'

'Well he *might*!'

Isla came into the workshop once a year to clean it, and her cleaning always followed the same pattern. First she swept the floor, then she dusted the shelves, then she polished Clement's wood-turning instruments – the parting tools, chisels and turning gouges which she always put back in order of size. And then she always hopped, from one rectangle of light to the next, making a wish every time she landed.

Her wishes this year were confused, being mostly about Jack, but partly also about Richard and Marshwood. *Make me love Richard again. Make us not have to sell Marshwood. Make Jack go away.* She had not seen him since his abrupt departure the day before. *Actually, make him stay. Make him stop playing games with me. Make him . . .*

'Still playing the old game, I see.'

Isla wavered mid-hop, lost her balance and fell. Jack

stood in the entrance to Clement's workshop, one shoulder resting against the doorframe, both hands in his pockets.

'You made me fall,' she said. 'Now I'll have to start again.'

She was on her feet and moving away from him before he could step forward to help her.

'I was just thinking about Grandpapa. And . . . well, you know . . .'

Her hands fluttered towards the workbench. This was the effect Jack had on her, this irritating reduction of her power of speech. He stepped across to the bench and picked up the larger chisel. Isla swallowed and stepped away. This too was how things were, a dance in which the space between them was forever being reduced and expanded again.

'Did you want something?'

'I came to apologize for yesterday. Leaving so suddenly, I don't know what came over me.'

'That's OK.' She stood looking at him awkwardly. 'I didn't mean to . . . That is, you were upset, I didn't realize how much. I'm sorry.'

There was a complicated pause, during which Isla resumed her dusting of the instruments she had already cleaned.

'Granna's been telling me about her lover in the war,' she offered, then blushed.

Jack arched an eyebrow. 'Bella had a lover?'

'Yes. No. Not a lover, as such. Someone she loved. It troubles me. Because of Grampsy.'

Why was she even talking about this? She opened her mouth and words poured out, filling the space between them as if they were her only defence against the magnetic pull of his presence.

'What . . .' His voice was gravelly, lower than usual. His mouth still curved in an amused smirk but his eyes did not quite meet hers. 'What, do you think Clement might not be . . .'

'My grandfather?' Isla almost laughed. 'No, that's not what troubles me.'

'What then?'

She didn't answer but stepped back again as he moved towards her. He stopped and turned back to the door.

'It's a beautiful day,' he said. 'I came to see if you'd like a walk.'

'I can't.'

He arched an eyebrow. 'Can't?'

The voice was light. The eyes, visible now that he no longer stood with his back to the light, not so.

'I have things to do.'

'Things?'

Another step towards her. This time, with her back against the table, she could not move away.

'Please, Jack.'

'Please what?'

He was right beside her now. His shoulder brushed hers.

'Please what?' he murmured again.

'You know.'

'Tell me.'

She could actually remember how it felt to kiss him, the weight of his body on hers. She forced herself to think of Richard instead, but only the memory of their last painful love-making – when? two months ago already? – presented itself.

'I don't understand what you want.'

'I've told you. I came back for you.'

'You say that,' she whispered. 'But . . .'

'But what?'

'I'm *married*.'

Time, apparently, had stopped. An insect beat against a window, a wasp, its buzzing high and frantic. Dust danced in a dirty sunbeam. Sweat beaded on Isla's lip, but she did not wipe it off. Jack slid a finger between her collarbone and the neckline of her dress, edging it off her shoulder. She clenched her fists.

'I'm married,' she repeated.

'But you want me.'

'No.'

The finger was retracted. She shrugged her dress back into place.

'You're lying.'

'Maybe.'

'No. You *are* lying.' He was shaking. 'But you'll come. You'll see. You won't be able not to.'

It was lunchtime by the time Isla came out of the workshop. The children, whom she had left in Bella's care, were playing in the garden when she returned. Various dolls and teddies hung from the branches of the fig tree beneath which they had set up camp.

'They're being parachute jumpers caught in trees,' said Marcus cheerfully. 'Granna told us about them.'

'Granna told you about parachutists caught in trees?'

'She was sad, and Beth asked her why, and if somebody had died, and she said yes, someone long ago who flew planes in the war, and Beth asked why did people fly planes, and I said so that people could jump out with parachutes, and Granna sort of laughed and then she said sometimes parachute jumpers got caught in trees and it was horrible because they died a slow and painful death, but other people flew planes for different reasons and they also died.'

There seemed no obvious response to this. 'I'll get lunch then,' said Isla.

'We've eaten. Granna said we could have a picnic.'

Isla noticed the remnants of a large chocolate cake on a plate beneath the tree.

'Did you have anything else?'

'Granna said to help ourselves to anything we wanted. She went to lie down.'

'I love Granna,' said Beth. 'But I do feel a bit sick.'

'I'll get you some water,' said Isla.

Back in the house, she found Bella lying on her bed.

'Are you all right?' she asked.

'Why shouldn't I be?'

'You don't normally lie down in the afternoon.'

'So I'm showing my age.'

'I didn't say that. I'm just concerned.'

'No need.'

Isla sat on the end of the bed. 'You're being prickly,' she said. 'What's wrong?'

'I think the memoirs are a bad idea. I don't want to go on any more.'

'But . . .'

'I'm not going to change my mind. I don't know what I was thinking, telling you all those old stories to try to make you understand.'

'They've upset you.'

'As if talking about the past ever changed anything.' Bella raised herself painfully from her bed, indicating the end of her brief moment of weakness. 'Pass me my walking stick. Where were you?'

'In the workshop, tidying up. Sort of.'

'I don't know why you bother. No-one ever goes in there.'

'I like it. And I was talking to Jack.'

'And what did Jack have to say for himself?'

'Nothing, really. Granna, I . . .' She trailed off, because really, what could she say about Jack? *I don't know what to do? I don't know what I want?* 'I'd like to know how the story ended. With Louis.'

Bella waved her away. 'Better not.'

'But I really want to know.'

'I think you should make your own ending,' mused Bella.

'I don't understand.'

'Work it out.'

The sky clouded over towards the end of the day, and a light rain kept the children indoors. The brilliant countryside grew dull. The air temperature plummeted and with it the children's good moods. With the break in the weather the morning's interlude in Clement's workshop appeared distant, as if belonging to a different day altogether.

Richard called in the early evening. 'What time is it?' asked Isla. She felt rather than heard him sigh with irritation.

'Six hours' time difference, Isla. It's half-past one.'

'Aren't you at work?'

'It's also Saturday.'

'So it is. Oh look, here's Beth.'

She tried to picture Richard's face as Beth launched into a detailed account of the fate of Second World War paratroopers. Laughing, frowning, amused, disapproving? The last, she suspected from her daughter's thunderous expression. Beth hated an unreceptive audience.

'I really don't think your grandmother should talk to them about such things,' he said when Beth, growing bored, passed the receiver back to Isla. 'It'll give them nightmares.'

'Coming from the man who made them watch *Bridge over the River Kwai* last Christmas . . .'

'That's different.'

'Worse, surely, because of the pictures.'

'It's horrible here at the weekend.'

'Poor darling. Isn't there a pool or something?'

'I've done the pool.'

'Aren't your clients taking care of you?'

'There's some sort of barbecue thing this evening. I hate to say it but I think you were right not to come. It's so dull here. We're out in the middle of nowhere. I miss you all.'

'Is the work interesting? What's the rest of the team like?'

'Young. Keen. Trying to show off in front of me. Hustling to buy me a beer, as if it weren't all on expenses.'

'Price you pay for being the boss.'

'I guess.'

What I should be feeling, thought Isla later, *is sorry for my husband. And I do. But . . .*

But what?

But pity was a poor substitute for desire.

But all the time she spoke to him she thought of Jack.

But later that night while Richard, feigning bonhomie, congregated with team and clients around a Dallas patio, his wife sat on her window ledge scanning the night sky for a sign from the man she was about to take as her lover.

Because he would become her lover. She knew, when she watched out for him all afternoon, that it would be soon. He had not left her thoughts. He was too close. *I think you should make your own ending.* Blessing, dare, dismissal – she explored all the possible significances Bella could have given the words before settling on their meaning, independent of Bella's intentions. *Make your own ending.* Her decision. Her will. Her choice.

His light came on, as she had known it would. She knelt on the window-seat with the light behind her. Jack's light flickered on and off, three times. An invitation.

Isla crept carefully down Marshwood's creaking staircase and slipped out of the house into the sleeping garden.

The first time was quick, almost frantic. She followed him silently upstairs and stood before him in his bedroom and they stared at each other as if unable to believe what they knew was about to happen. And then he grabbed her to him, and without understanding how she was lying beneath him, and he was tugging at her top, and she was pushing him away again in order to pull it off and unhook her bra before fumbling at the fastening of his jeans, and then her hands were under his shirt stroking his back, and his hands were at the waistband of her knickers, her own jeans were stuck around her knees, and they were laughing and panting and moaning as their mouths sought each other with short hot kisses, their entwined bodies trembling until finally, naked and free, he entered her and she cried out and immediately they were still. Afterwards, whenever she thought about him and the first time they were together, she always came back to this moment of stillness, which seemed to contain everything she was, and ever had been, and could ever hope to be again. And then Jack began to move inside her, and she moved with him, all conscious thought flown, aware only of this force, this powerful energy which was neither hers nor his but the result of their bodies together, until she saw stars and wept into his shoulder as he held her tightly against him.

It was still dark when she left. He walked her home along the lane rather than cutting across the lawn damp with dew. A barn owl hooted on Pater Noster and Jack's arm tightened around her shoulders.

'It's only an owl out hunting,' she laughed.

'It startled me.' He turned towards her. His face was hard to read in the darkness. 'I wish you'd stay.'

She cupped his cheek. 'I'll come back tomorrow,' she said.

'Tomorrow.'

'It's already today.' She leaned against him and laughed again.

'What is it?'

'I was just thinking.'

'What?'

'I feel happy.'

It surprised her, the lack of guilt. She kissed him goodbye at the front door and considered making love to him again right there on the step, except that exhaustion overpowered her, sweet and immediate, and there would always be tomorrow, tomorrow that was already today. She slipped out of his arms, smiling, and she was still smiling as she slipped under her covers, and as she drifted immediately to sleep, and when she woke in the morning.

The sun was back the following day, the blue sky stripped of clouds, the temperature already warm at breakfast time.

'Beach weather,' declared Bella.

Beth screeched and began to run around the table.

'Why are you doing that?' Marcus wandered into the kitchen and eyed her curiously.

'We're going to the beach.'

'Oh, *cool*.'

'I didn't say . . . I never said . . .' Isla stopped protesting. Why not go to the beach? She loved the beach. *Get a grip*, she told herself when she realized that she did not want to leave the house in case it meant missing a chance of seeing Jack. 'I'll make a picnic,' she said. 'It's ages since we went anywhere.'

'Can't we have lunch at the café?' Beth, a notoriously fussy eater, was partial to the crab sandwiches served at the beach café, a fact which always astonished anyone who knew her.

'Even better.'

'And can we have an ice-cream?' asked Marcus quickly.

'Of course.' Isla began to laugh. The children whooped, their excitement too big for the crowded kitchen. They spilled out into the garden, running in circles towards the paddock, straight into Jack coming the other way.

Isla's heart skipped a beat. Beth was talking to him now. She was asking for something, Isla could tell from the way she tugged at his sleeve as she spoke. Jack laughed. In the kitchen, Bella coughed pointedly. Isla blushed as she realized that she had been staring straight at him, lost to everything but the sight of him, and that she had not heard a word her grandmother had spoken.

'I said I won't come with you. My ankle.'

'No. I mean, fine. You don't mind us going?'

'Why would I mind?'

'You might want company.'

'I have just as little company when you're not here, you know. And the others will be over later.'

The children burst back into the kitchen, followed by Jack. Beth looked petulant, Marcus disappointed.

'He won't come!' said the little girl crossly.

'Good morning, Jack,' said Bella.

'I can't,' explained Jack. 'I have work to do. Otherwise I'd have loved to come with you.'

His eyes wouldn't meet hers. *It's happening again*, she thought wildly. *It's going to be like last time, when we were kids. He wishes it had never happened. He's never mentioned work before.* Beth and Marcus were both talking at once. Bella was telling them to stop shouting. Jack was still laughing. Isla picked up the bucket of vegetable peelings from the side of the sink.

'I'm going to the compost heap,' she announced.

She walked in a daze. The damp morning grass chilled her sandalled feet but she barely noticed it. She fought through the blurred fog of her mind to regain an intelligent level of consciousness, but all she could think was that the mere sight of him had reduced her to this, an incoherent automaton.

He was waiting for her behind the barn as she returned with her empty bucket.

'Hello.'

216

She toyed with the idea of marching straight past him but the temptation to stay was too great.

'You don't have to be nice,' she said stiffly.

'Excuse me?'

'If you don't want to. If you don't want to talk to me, I mean. I mean, if last night was just . . .'

'Just what?' he asked quietly.

She scuffed the ground with the end of her sandal. 'You know. A one-off.'

'Is that what you think? That that's what it was?'

She faltered. 'Well, you clearly don't want to spend time with me.'

'Does this have anything to do with me not coming to the beach with you?'

'Of course not!' she lied. Too quickly though.

'Isla,' he said. Too softly. He was standing very close to her. Too close. She looked around wildly, but she stood between him and the wall and escape was difficult. 'Did it ever occur to you,' he murmured, 'that if I went to the beach with you today, after what happened between us last night, I would have to spend the whole day lying face down in the sand?'

Now it was she who was staring. He gazed back, his expression at once solemn, quizzical and salacious, and she burst out laughing. Her back was right up against the wall now, and Jack was pressed against her. 'Isla,' he repeated in a murmur as his lips skimmed her collar bone.

'You didn't talk to me,' she whispered.

'You didn't talk to me either.'

'I couldn't.'

'Neither could I.'

She could feel his hard-on through his jeans and the thin fabric of her dress. She reached down to stroke him. He moaned. She bit his lip. 'Do you like that?'

'Touch me.'

'Like this?' She slid her hand along the flat of his belly into his shorts, and he gasped.

'Be careful,' he said hoarsely.

'Do you want me to stop?'

'Yes. No. I'll tell you what I want.' She took her hand away but kept it close to her on his hip as he spilled secret fantasies into her ear.

Somewhere in the real world a cuckoo called. A black-bird sang. A tractor revved its engine, a dog barked, a child shouted. The moment ended.

'I have to go,' said Isla.

'Tonight?'

'Oh God yes.' She did not hesitate. Not for a moment. 'Tonight.'

She thought about him all day. On the beach, as she watched Marcus build a castle of pebbles and sand, and in the café where Beth ordered an extravagant lobster with a side order of chips. After lunch, when they walked with their ice-cream cones up onto the cliffs, trying to decide which flavour they liked best. She inhaled the smell so peculiar to the English coast, of sea and fresh grass and cows, and she thought of how often she had been here with him, when they were Beth's age, and Marcus's, and as teenagers, and how she would like to return here with him soon. She found that thoughts of Jack, rather than distract her from her children, somehow crystallized her feelings for them, so that they appeared before her in all their magnificence, two hard, precious diamonds glittering in the intoxicating light on the edge of the cliff. Their ice-creams eaten, she ran with them, caught them, tickled them until they fell laughing to the ground. They lay there, partially concealed by the waving grass, caught between the pale blue of the sky and the dark blue of the sea. The children briefly rested their heads against her, and even as she was filled with fierce, blinding love for them, so she wondered at the fact that she still thought of *him*. As they walked back down to the beach, the three musketeers as Marcus pronounced them, a skylark rose unexpectedly before them, bursting with song, making them laugh with sheer pleasure.

'How,' asked Marcus, 'can such a small thing make so much noise?'

'Because he's happy,' said Beth.

The second time, he made her wait. He undressed her himself, then laid her on his bed, pushing her back when she tried to touch him. Forehead, eyes, nose, mouth. Neck, collarbone, shoulders. Down, down he went. Breasts, stomach, hips. His tongue moved down her legs, thighs, knees, calves. He turned her over and licked the soles of her feet before beginning another journey up her body. He raised her onto her hands and knees and slid his tongue between her legs.

'Now,' she moaned. 'Now. Please.'

'Beg,' he whispered. He slid his cock between her thighs. She gasped and turned to face him, falling hungrily onto him, and he watched her take him in her mouth. She whimpered as he pulled out, then groaned as he turned her over again and plunged into her from behind. 'Beg,' he said.

She screamed as he climaxed with her.

'You've drugged me,' she told him afterwards. 'It's the only explanation. I feel completely stoned. Stoned on sex with you.'

He laughed, folded her hand in his, kissed each finger in turn before taking her index in his mouth and sucking it slowly. She caught her breath.

'You see?' she said. 'I could do it again. Right now.'

'Come here then.'

'Oh no you don't.' She flipped onto all fours and straddled him, pinning him to the bed, dishevelled hair falling into eyes bright with laughter. 'Now it's my turn.'

*   *   *

'That was intense,' he said on the way home.

'Hmmm.'

It was warmer than the previous night. She had tied her cardigan around her waist so as to feel the night air on her bare skin. She walked pressed tightly against him with his arm around her, trying to match her steps to his, skipping every few to keep up with his longer stride. He changed his step deliberately to confuse her, making them sometimes longer, sometimes shorter. She tripped, giggled and turned to face him. Lifting her arms to his neck, she placed each of her feet on his. 'There,' she said. 'Now walk.'

He clasped her to him and began to waltz slowly down the lane. 'Do you remember, this is how my mum once tried to teach us to dance? *Boom, tick tick. Boom, tick tick.*'

Isla crowed with laughter. *'Boom, tick tick?'*

'It's what she always said!' He turned faster, lifting her off his feet, humming. Isla laughed louder, beating his shoulders with her fists.

'You're crazy,' she said.

'About you.'

'Come. There's something I want to show you.'

He put her down. They had reached Marshwood now, and she took his hand to lead him round the back of the house towards the orchard. It was darker here with the trees all around them. She sensed him tense and tugged him on.

An old quince tree, gnarled and misshapen, stood alone at the far side of the orchard. Curtains of wild jasmine fell from two of its higher branches. Isla pushed the nearer one aside. The ground at the foot of the tree was soft and springy with moss, its roots forming a horseshoe hollow into which Isla dropped, pulling Jack down after her.

'Look,' she pointed.

From where they sat, they had a perfect view down the moonlit valley, hunched in darkness beneath a floating band of white mist.

'Isn't it perfect? I found it the other day when I was looking for Leo.'

'Come here.'

She lay beside him, resting in the crook of his arm.

'I knew it would be like this between us,' he said. 'I always knew it couldn't end like it did.'

'Your fault,' she murmured against his chest. He poked her ribs gently with a finger and she chuckled. 'Deny it.'

'I never stopped thinking about you, Isla. All those years.'

'All those women.'

'There weren't so many. And you were always the one. I knew it. I knew I'd find my way back to you. Isla? Isla, are you *asleep*?'

'No.'

'You know, I meant it earlier. What I said. I'm crazy about you.'

It didn't matter about anything else. Richard, her marriage, the woman he had only half told her about. There *was* nothing else. Just the naked truth which belonged to that moment.

'Yeah,' said Isla. 'Me too.'

Her existence took on a schizophrenic quality, sharpened by the exhaustion of short nights and constant dissimulation. By day she was mother and granddaughter, doing the things she always did, preparing meals, settling disputes, suggesting games. She devoted if anything more time to the others than usual, to make up for her nights. She found that hours could fly by if she let herself think about him, hours which saw her staring vacantly into space, outwardly still while emotions raged inside her. She tried not to put a name to her feelings. She knew only that she longed for him always, that the mere touch of his hand on hers made her melt and at the same time brought her unimaginable peace, that the sight of his face on a pillow beside hers filled her with joy too painful to contain. In weaker moments she told herself that he was the other half she had always sought, the other half which completed her and without which she would forever be lonely, the other half she was born to be with. But on the whole she fought against thoughts of this nature, just as she resisted the occasional feeble whispering of her married woman's conscience, telling herself that as long as she didn't give voice to her feelings – as long as she did not admit to actual *love* – then this strange thing she was doing, this unexpected, wonderful, extraordinary thing could remain light, an adventure, a moment of suspended time in which anything was possible and which had no bearing on the reality of her life.

He was afraid of the dark. He had been as a child, and she guessed early on that he was again. His alarm at the sound of the hooting owl, his moment of tension following her into the orchard were followed by other tell-tale signs: a squaring of the shoulders every time he left her, a passing look of panic if she wandered away from him when he walked her home before sunrise. She raised the subject with him one night in bed, asking him directly if her hunch was right.

'It's not the dark so much,' he mused, 'as the trees.'

'The trees?'

'The sound they make. Rustling, whispering. It's fine during the day but at night . . . they sound human. Is that mad?'

'A bit. Is this to do with Bosnia?'

'A bit.'

'Tell me.'

'Do you really want to know?'

'No, I'm just pretending.' She nudged him. 'Go on. What happened?'

'Nothing. Really, nothing,' he repeated. Isla rolled her eyes. 'We visited these woods once. That's all.'

'You and her. Elena.'

'And a bunch of UN soldiers.'

'And nothing happened.'

He shrugged. 'We saw stuff. It was horrible.'

'I wish you'd talk to me about it.'

'It would spoil things though, wouldn't it? You never talk to me about Richard, do you? Real life. It just gets in the way.'

How bleak he looked, thought Isla. How bleak, and how lost. She came to sit beside him and laid her head on his shoulder. He took her hand and wound his fingers through hers.

'Afterwards,' he said. 'After the forest . . . incident, Elena just said *this is war*, this is what you came to photograph. She said the world needed to know what I had seen.'

'She was right, wasn't she? Jack?'

'I don't know. I just know that trees freak me out.'

They sat together a while longer, holding hands. And now a memory – her mother, Bella, Clement, arguing over Isla's fate as a little girl. Two children hiding in the bushes, their fingers interlaced. The feeling that all would be well as long as she did not let go.

'Jack, do you trust me?'

'Trust you?'

'Will you do something for me if I ask?'

'Not if you don't tell me what it is.'

'It'll be good. I promise it'll be good. But you have to trust me.'

'Put your shoes on,' she said when she came to the coach house the following night. 'We're going for a walk.'

'Isla . . .'

'You said you trusted me.'

They walked side by side to the gate leading onto Pater Noster, but had to go into single file as the path narrowed up the initial steep climb. This would be the hardest part for him, she knew. She had brought a torch. Its pale beam swept the ground before her, picking out the tangle of hazel and stunted oaks which formed a low arch above them. He knew the walk. He knew that this would end, and that soon they would come out onto the open hillside. She could hear him right behind her, breathing steadily. She squeezed his hand.

'OK?'

'OK.'

They emerged from their tunnel and glanced back down the hill behind them. Tall ferns covered the ground here, waist high, brushing against them as they passed.

'Isla?'

'What?'

'Just so you know, the ferns aren't much better than the trees.'

She made him stop at the top, where the squat rounded side of the hill narrowed to the ridge which led to the old Roman remains half a mile away.

'Look around,' ordered Isla. 'Take it all in.'

She stood behind him, holding him by the arms to turn him slowly in a complete circle. Obediently, he looked. Down the hill to Chapel St Mary, where only the occasional light flickered. Westwards to St Ann's, a crouching shadow in the light of the half-moon. Behind them towards Bambridge, dimly aglow. Back down to Marshwood, hidden behind its trees.

'Got it,' he said.

'Now close your eyes.'

'No.'

'Remember, you know what's around you. Try to visualize it. I'll tell you when you can open your eyes.'

He looked so helpless and exposed, standing on top of the hill with his eyes shut, so blindly trusting. She stepped forward to kiss him, then thought better of it, turned her back to him and began to run. She stopped at the stile over the wire that bisected the ridge and looked back to where he still stood, his position unchanged. Her heart filled with tenderness. She was mad. These last ten days were nothing compared to what she was about to do. She had definitely lost it now.

Isla undressed quickly, pulling her jeans and knickers off over her trainers – which she kept on – and placing them in a bundle with her T-shirt, bra and sweater

227

beneath the stile. Then she walked a few paces back towards him. Her body tingled as the night air lifted her curls and caressed her naked skin. She laughed out loud.

'You can't catch me!' she yelled. Jack, a quarter of a mile away, looked up. She waved her arms over her head and danced a jig then turned on her heels and raced ahead of him towards the old fort, her purpose giving her wings. By the time he caught up with her, she was already standing on the highest ledge of the encampment, her pale naked body glinting in the moonlight. He ran towards her.

'Isla, you mad—'

She held out a commanding hand.

'You must disrobe in order to enter the magic circle!' He hesitated, then began to undress.

'I'd keep your shoes on if I were you,' she hissed in a theatrical aside. 'Sharp stones and all that.'

He shed the last of his clothes and she nodded towards the ledge adjacent to hers.

'Now what?' he asked.

She had no idea. She hadn't planned this far, having assumed he would catch her well before the fort. She threw her shoulders back, assumed a warrior's stance and improvised.

'My name is Isla!' she shouted into the night. 'I am named for a Scottish river. I banish you Romans back to the land whence you came!'

He took his cue from her. 'I am Jack,' he bellowed, 'which means . . .'

Isla cackled. 'Not a lot you can do with Jack.'

He pulled a face at her. 'I am Jack, which comes from John, which means "the Lord is gracious". Return to your heathen gods!'

'Begone!' cried Isla.

'Begone!' he echoed.

He flew down the almost vertical side of his own ledge up onto hers and they collapsed together on the ground, helpless with laughter.

'You are completely deranged,' he gasped at last.

She leaned back into his arms. 'Look,' she said. 'Trees, all around. But we're above them all. Do you see, Jack? You're above the trees. And there's nothing to be afraid of.'

The noise – mournful, deathly, above all *loud* – made them both jump. They clutched each other. At the far end of the ruins, a solitary white shape was moving, soon joined by others which closed ranks with it, advancing towards them in a ghostly mass.

Bleating.

'Sheep,' breathed Isla. Jack began to laugh again. He laughed until he wept, and he only stopped when Isla laid her body gently over his and silenced him with her mouth.

Afterwards he gave her his sweater and they lay on their backs in the grass, counting stars.

'This is how it's meant to be,' he told her. 'You and me. This is how it's meant to be, always.'

She took his hand, turned it and kissed his palm. Then, still holding it, she led him back down the hillside.

'Don't leave tomorrow.' Jack and Isla lay on their side looking at each other on the night before she was due to leave. A breeze blew in through the open window. Isla shivered. He drew up the sheet to cover her naked body. His hand on her waist felt warm through the thin fabric.

'I have to. You know I was supposed to go tonight. I can't keep extending my stay. We're meant to be going to Corsica on Friday.'

'The family holiday.' He sounded bitter and resisted her attempt to kiss him. She turned away from him and lay on her back.

'What will happen to us, Jack?'

'We carry on, I suppose,' he said.

She smiled and slid her hand between his legs. He placed his hand over hers to stop her, then changed his mind. She carried on stroking him gently.

'Do you think we can?'

'Why not? You want to, don't you?'

She pressed herself more tightly against him, and he laughed. 'Well then,' he said. 'I will be your other life. Your secret life.'

230

She stayed with him longer that night. They lay together talking in whispers, planning their future together, their future which would be lived, they were not quite sure how, in parallel to their current existence. A future of meetings at Marshwood, of assignations in London. They would find a hotel. He would rent a flat, where he would write – he fancied becoming a writer – and wait for her. They would meet during the day when her children were at school. 'Maybe,' she whispered with a mischievous grin, 'I won't go back to work after all.' And then they made love again happily, buoyed by this picture they had painted together of a double life which would belong to nobody but themselves, a world inhabited only by Isla and Jack, selfish, loving and alive. She had always resisted falling asleep beside him, but tonight she could not leave him. Her last conscious thought, before sleep overwhelmed her, was that the sensation was more delicious even than any of the sex, and that she wanted to do it again, and often.

Your secret life. She walked home alone at dawn, leaving him asleep, his beautiful body sprawled across the bed. She took the short cut across the wet grass which soaked through her canvas shoes, breathing in the pure sweet morning air. Mist still cloaked the valley, a thick white blanket against which the emerging trees appeared almost black. The animals were stirring in the fields beneath Marshwood. Cows lowed, sheep bleated, a blackbird filled the air with his full-throated song.

Isla froze as a fox crossed her path, returning from a night's hunting. He stopped too and stared back at her. He was magnificent, his coat a gleaming dark red, his brush held high, white tip pointing to the sky as he sniffed the air between them before departing again at a trot towards Pater Noster. Isla bit her lip and hugged herself. *A secret life*, she repeated to herself. Yes, it could work. Right then, Isla felt that she had never been more certain of anything. A secret life with Jack would solve everything.

Her mood shattered as soon as she crept into her room. Beth was lying in her bed, and she was wide awake.

'I never told you what happened to Elena.'

'No.'

'And you never asked.'

'I figured you'd talk when you wanted to.'

Isla and Jack leaned against the counter tops of his parents' kitchen, not touching, not even close. Their arms were folded, their eyes evasive. This was not what they had chosen. This was not what they had agreed.

'I never wanted to.'

Three feet between his side of the kitchen and hers, three feet which might as well have been three miles, three cities, three continents. She had come to tell him about Beth. Beth who had been waiting for her that morning. Beth to whom she had lied. *I couldn't sleep, I went out for a walk, there was a fox and a blackbird.* Beth who had climbed out of her mother's bed to look at the dawn, who had made her a necklace of nuzzled kisses, Beth who trusted her. *Next time, can I go with you to look for the fox?*

Jack's voice, low and rapid. He was talking, at last, about Bosnia. She should listen. She must listen. She owed it to him after what she had just told him. Coming back when they had decided that last night was to be their goodbye, seeing the light flare in his eyes at the sight of her then die when he heard what she had to say. *I can't, we mustn't, we have to stop* . . . Beth, Marcus, Richard, the sudden realization – at last! – of what she was doing to them, of what her behaviour could do to them.

Listen to Jack. There had been a road trip, Elena's idea. They had slept together in his room at the Holiday Inn, with a chair under the doorknob to keep his room-mates out, and afterwards she had told him he had to get out of Sarajevo.

'It is terrible here,' she said, 'but it is only a part of the story. Like many cities, this is a melting-pot, you know? I will take you to places where people think differently. I will be your interpreter. We will go to Jezero, my grandfather's village. There you can photograph the real Bosnia.'

Richard would be back soon, he would wonder where she was. She had to go *now*. There was no time for this, this story of Jack's life which did not involve her.

Isla let herself slide to the floor until she sat with her back against a cabinet. Jack followed suit. They were closer now, their legs crossed at the ankles in mirror poses, stretched out in front of them, almost touching across the small kitchen. Almost.

'She had all this money in a belt, over five thousand dollars. Crazy. Like she didn't care what happened to it . . . It was for her grandfather, to get him out, to her parents in Italy. He hadn't wanted to leave with them, and she was worried about him. She made me promise to take it to him, to help him if anything happened to her.'

Listen. Don't think about Richard, the children, the time. You owe Jack. You owe him. Now that he's talking about it at last, you have to listen.

Rape, pillage, ethnic cleansing. Warring brothers, murderous friends. Bosnians, Muslims, Serbs. Saviours, snitches, saints and spies. Orphans and bandits, soldiers and thieves. Pockmarked roads and shelled villages, singing rivers and snowcapped mountains, forests dark with bloody secrets. Elena had promised him the real Bosnia, and she gave it to him. They met a Bosnian who had killed his best friend because he was a Muslim, and a Muslim woman who had given shelter to her Serbian neighbours. They spoke to a man who had been made to give up his daughter in exchange for his hostaged son, and a girl who had been raped by boys she knew from childhood. They met children who had lost both their parents and parents who had lost all their children, people who had lost limbs, eyes, hands, feet, their savings, their livestock, their livelihoods, their lives. They met people whose eyes were dead from seeing so much suffering and people of boundless generosity, people who could not talk and others who could not stop talking, people who threatened them and people who welcomed them without question into their homes. Militiamen who bragged about the numbers they had killed, hollow-eyed British soldiers who dreamed of keeping peace, an optimistic Swedish officer who still thought he could make a difference and an American journalist high on heroin who told them he had gone to war to get away from his wife. People spoke to them of prison camps and mass rapes, of genocide and targeted killing, of NATO bombs and Serbian soldiers, of extortion rackets and hunger. They saw villages where the ground was still damp with blood, they hid under tables as gun battles blazed around them, they walked with UN soldiers through a forest of human bones, and two months after leaving Sarajevo they were not much closer to Elena's grandfather's village.

'So did you make it?' Isla had given up looking at the clock. It was very quiet in the coach house's kitchen. Jack, silent now, carefully balanced the heel of his left foot on the big toe of his right. He wore odd socks. The sight made her carefully tender.

'I'm going to buy bread.'

'Excuse me?'

'They were the last words she said to me. *I'm going to buy bread.*'

Until that morning he had allowed himself to believe in the permanence of summer, but that day there was no mistaking the chill in the air when they stepped outside their inn. Jack shivered, bouncing on the balls of his feet for warmth.

'You see?' She had been warning him for days now that the season was changing. Late September, heading into the mountains – there was not much time left before the first snow joined forces with the ever present blockades to make the roads impassable. 'We have to press on now. There's a woman opposite who sells bread. You get the Jeep ready. There's no time any more for distractions.'

'Distractions?'

'Stories. Photographs.' She flashed him a teasing grin. 'You'll see,' she said. 'It is very beautiful where my grandfather lives. All year round you can see snow on the mountains, and there is a big lake where in summer we swim. He has the biggest house in the village, with a courtyard and a Jeep and horses you can ride. You will like it there very much.'

'Elena . . .'

She raised a finger to his mouth. 'Don't you know? My grandfather's village is still standing.' She dropped her voice and he leaned closer to catch her whisper. 'This is because I am a witch, in case you hadn't realized, and I have cast a spell on it.'

Bitterness and laughter, the essence of Elena. Jack chuckled. She gave his arm an approving squeeze. 'You get the Jeep ready,' she said. 'I'm going to buy bread.'

He followed her through the lens of his camera as she crossed the road, depressing the shutter at the precise moment when, still smiling, she turned to wave to him. Which was also the moment when the sniper who had been watching her, the sniper who possibly resented her involvement with a foreign journalist, or fancied her, or was simply bored, the sniper who thought nothing of stopping a life in its tracks on a beautiful morning in early autumn when people's breath turned to mist in the air, the sniper in short who took Elena's life cocked his rifle, took aim and fired.

'I caught it on film. At least I think I did. I never had it developed. And I haven't touched a camera since.'

And what could Isla say to that? In the hall, a clock struck ten. Isla, briefly, thought of Richard arriving at Heathrow, before turning her gaze to Jack. He sat with his head tipped back and his eyes closed, and she saw where tears had gathered, quivering and solitary, awaiting deliverance. She crossed the floor to straddle him, knees hugging his thighs, and gently kissed them away.

'Don't go,' he whispered.

'I have to, soon.'

One arm circled her waist. Fingers pressed painfully into the back of her neck as he drew her closer.

'You mustn't.'

She pressed her head to his shoulder to escape the grip of his fingers. She felt his heartbeat beneath her cheek, saw it throbbing in his throat. *How easy if this was all it came to. Two heartbeats. A pulse.*

A sigh as his lips sought hers.

'Jack . . .'

'Please.'

'Jack, no.'

Shadows shortened and the morning pressed on. At Marshwood, Bella stopped Beth and Marcus from diving through the hedge to find their mother. In London, a bleary-eyed Richard emerged from his plane to join the long shuffle through Heathrow to reclaim his luggage. In the old coach house, Isla tried to detach herself from Jack but found she couldn't leave him yet. Instead, she asked questions.

'Who shot her?'

'I don't know.'

'But why?'

'I don't know.'

'And what happened to the money?'

'I have the money.'

'And her grandfather?'

'I don't know.'

His memories of what happened after Elena was shot were unclear. He had cried. At some point he had thrown up, and then he had slept. He had been picked up by some British soldiers, put in a lorry bound for Split. From there he had flown back to London, where he stayed in the flat of a friend, another photographer on a shoot in Arizona. Eventually, he had made his way to Marshwood. To Marshwood and to Isla.

'You have to find out.'

'He's probably dead.'

'You have to go back and find out.'

Tears. Anger. Recriminations. A sobbing farewell, professions of love. It was past eleven by the time Isla left, the children squabbling cheerfully in the back, Jack's words ringing in her ears.

I can't go back.

I can't stay.

You don't know what it's like, you don't get it, what a place like that does to you. You with your perfectly comfortable little life, your lovely little life you are so dissatisfied with but that you run back to the moment it's threatened.

I'm going now, Jack.

Isla!

His face as she walked away . . . She had turned back once and almost faltered. *Stories need endings, Jack. And we're not it. We're not each other's endings.* He came to see

239

them off, and she thought that he would cry again, but instead he had submitted almost like a child when she pressed her lips to his forehead. And now it was over, and their separate lives could resume again. He with his demons, and she with hers.

'I can't wait to see Daddy,' announced Beth from the back seat. 'It will be so utterly delightful to be all together again.'

Isla, despite herself, snorted out loud at her daughter's solemn pomposity. She caught Marcus' eye in the rearview mirror and grinned at him. *When did they grow up so quickly?* The question seared through her mind, and with it the knowledge that nothing in her life was more important than her children. She had a vivid flashback to Marcus' birth, so different to how she had imagined it, the long hard labour culminating in the humiliation of stirrups and the brutality of forceps, the briskness of the obstetrician, the comforting tone of the midwives barely masking their anxiety, Richard white as a sheet bravely holding her as she screamed. And then the atmosphere changing, everybody laughing as the newborn Marcus bawled with indignation. Richard's tears as he cradled his son before placing him on her breast. The three of them alone at last, Marcus lying cleaned and swaddled in his cot, she pale and exhausted against her pillows, Richard still holding her hand, beaming, radiating pride, for once at a loss for words. They had become a family that day, something greater than Isla and Richard, something worth fighting for.

You are more yourself with me than at any other time. Jack had thrown this at her towards the end of their quarrel when he realized that she would not share the burden of his pain and that nothing he could say would make her stay. *You can't keep sacrificing who you are.* She had almost believed him, but on that drive home, buoyed by memories which did not involve Jack, she staved off the pain of leaving him with thoughts of what she was *really* going back to. Not just routine and sacrifice but the satisfaction of a life's work, a striving for constancy and tolerance and, yes, love, which the myriad tiny elements that constituted daily life smothered but had not killed, love which lay dormant but just needed to be rekindled. She would make it work with Richard. For all their sakes.

But by the time she reached home, Richard had spoken to Bella, and Bella had told him everything. And three days later, Isla rides a Spanish bus with her children, watching the dusk close in over the Alpujarras, running to the mother she hardly knows because she has nowhere left to go to hide her battered face.

PART II

SUMMER INTO AUTUMN

And now Bella is alone, and Marshwood is very quiet without its summer visitors. Her foot better, she is busy curbing her garden's sprint for the wild. Today she is working on a laurel hedge choked with bindweed. Her mother, she remembers clearly, had her own solution to the problem of bindweed. *How strange*, she thinks as she heads to the house to fetch it, *that I should be older now than I ever knew her.* She tries to remember her mother as she was towards the end of her life, but finds that she can picture her only as a young woman, worn down by her three boys, brushing impatiently but not unkindly at the little girl clinging to her legs. *Mother.* Vague and exhausted, living in the shadow of the moral high ground occupied by her pious husband, to the point that she even followed him to the grave within months of his own demise. Bella closes her eyes, and it seems to her that she can *smell* her childhood, just out of reach, the sweaty, boisterous warmth of her brothers, the soapy lavender of her weary mother, the stiff forbidding cloth of her father's suits. A confused time, even then. What would her mother have made of Louis, or of Isla and Jack? Had she ever yearned for more than life had given her, longed to walk in the moonlight in an evening dress and borrowed boots, to sit hand in hand by a lake with a man she loved? Sometimes it seems to Bella that she is there still, by the lake, waiting to be kissed.

She begins to tug away at the bindweed, wrapping her fingers around the base of the long sinewy stems and pulling them carefully upwards in order to draw out the roots before pouring hydrochloric acid into the holes they have left behind. When Marshwood became overrun with soldiers, shortly after Louis left, the young private who came to help in the garden laughed at her use of acid against the problem of bindweed.

'It kills the roots!' she had protested.

'I should say it does.'

Isla knows, of course, that Marshwood was turned into a convalescent home in the later stages of the war. There are photographs, a whole album of them, of damaged men in uniform here – men on crutches or leaning on sticks, with bandaged heads or arms, men strolling in the grounds or lying on the sofa. There are pictures of ambulances in the drive, motorcycles and Jeeps, nurses in uniform, the Italian POWs sent up from the prison camp in Bambridge to work in the vegetable garden. Perhaps, if she told her about that time, Isla would understand why Bella spoke to Richard. As it is, she wonders if her granddaughter will ever forgive her.

When had Clement guessed? She had been lying on the sofa in the dark when he returned from a local land-owners' meeting. She claimed a headache. Then, when he asked after Louis, she began to cry.

'I'm just worried about him,' she hiccuped into his handkerchief. 'In case . . . in case . . .'

'Of course you are.' He poured out two careful measures of brandy and handed one to her. 'Drink up. It'll help.'

She drank, pulled a face, sniffed. He watched her, his muddy eyes half closed in thought.

'I'm sorry,' she said. 'He's just so young.'

Clement continued to look at her in silence. 'I'm sorry,' she repeated uncertainly.

'He's young,' said Clement at last. 'But he knows how to take care of himself. Didn't I once tell you there's something of the angel about him? You'll see. He'll turn out to be indestructible.'

'Are you sure?'

'Oh Belle.' He smiled sadly. 'Who can ever be sure? But yes, if it makes you happy: Louis is indestructible. You mustn't worry about him.'

Had he known then? Or did he only guess later on, the night of the plane crash, when Bella – cool, calm Bella – briefly lost control?

You mustn't worry about him . . . Easier said than done. That night, the night of the plane crash, her first thoughts were for him. Her first thoughts, and the thoughts after that, and after that . . . She was jolted from sleep by the sound of rattling windows and a low rumbling which grew steadily louder as it drew closer. Later she would say the noise had come from directly above, though when they retraced the plane's trajectory she realized this would not have been possible. She ran from her room, down the stairs to the door of the terrace. She was vaguely aware of Clement shouting at her to stop but she did not listen, erupting onto the terrace to see the huge body of an injured bomber silhouetted against the night sky, close enough for her to make out the sound of rattling metal and the puttering of an engine in distress. It was flying low, straight towards the dark mass of St Ann's. She held her breath, willing it higher. For a moment she thought it was going to make it. Then it hit the side of the hill and, a few seconds later, exploded.

Bella began to giggle. She would feel bad about that when she discovered how many people had died in the crash, four German airmen who would be buried in a communal grave in Bambridge: four young men who carried mascots and letters, who had inflated their life rafts in the hope of bailing out over the sea and instead had lost their lives crashing improbably into an old Dorsetshire manor house. She would tell herself that she had been confused by her rough awakening, even that she had been slightly crazy. But at the time she could only giggle, and then laugh outright, hugging herself closely, because even though she had always known that it could not have been him, the relief on recognizing the plane as a German bomber rather than a British fighter was too much.

From the dark hills came the sound of car engines revving and voices shouting. Inside, the telephone began to ring. She heard Clement answer it but made no move to go inside. Her knees were shaking. She sat down on the steps leading from the terrace to the lawn.

Clement appeared from the house and crouched awkwardly before her.

'That was Nancy,' he said. 'The bomber actually crashed into the Pinkertons' place. We have to go up there. They'll need stuff – blankets, tea, supplies, anything we can bring.'

The Pinkertons' spacious house had been turned into a nursing home for convalescent officers at the beginning of the war, when he had taken up a job in the War Office and she had taken her children to stay with her sister.

'I'm going to pick Nancy up on the way. Come on, hurry up and get dressed. I'm not leaving you here alone.'

The fire was roaring by the time they arrived. A motley crowd had gathered on the Pinkertons' lawn, consisting of men in pyjamas with blankets over their shoulders, nurses in hastily pulled on uniforms, the local Home Guard, the police and people from the village.

'Look,' said Nancy. 'There's Kitty! I tried to call her too, but she must have already left. Yoo-hoo, KitKat!'

Kitty hurried over bearing a thermos. 'Isn't it too awful?' she asked breathlessly. 'The poor Pinkertons! They called the Fire Service, but by the time they get here . . .'

'Is everybody out?' asked Nancy.

'They're still doing a head count.'

Bella gazed at the house, a fine example of early Georgian architecture, once as graceful and well pro-portioned as Marshwood was square and heavy, now belching flames and smoke into the night sky. Half the west wing had collapsed, and the dark fuselage of a plane stuck surreally out of what she knew had been the library.

'No wings,' she observed.

'They were ripped off as it went through the orchard,' said Kitty. 'Look.'

She pointed towards the apple orchard, a source of forbidden pleasure to generations of scrumping village

250

boys. Half the trees had been decapitated. Two had been uprooted. Scattered amongst them were large sheets of jagged metal.

Louis, Louis, Louis . . . Standing on the Pinkertons' lawn with the crowd milling behind her in the shadows and the house blazing before her, her own life suddenly appeared before her eyes and she knew with absolute certainty what she must do. She must write to Louis as soon as she got home to tell him she had changed her mind. They would meet at his suggested hotel and they would be together, and afterwards they would walk hand in hand in its grounds or in the countryside, and she would put her head on his shoulder, and he would hold her, and they would be happy. Yes, they would be happy. They would have no need for words, there would be no plans. Just a moment outside time and a place belonged only to them. If he died – her eyes watered at the thought – at least they would have had this. And if he lived . . .

'What happened to the crew?' she asked suddenly.

Kitty pulled a face and pointed at the fire. Bella shook her head.

'No.' Somebody was screaming. She registered with surprise that it was herself. She was screaming and running towards the house. Kitty tried to hold her back but let go with a cry of pain when Bella pushed her out of the way. She ran as she had never run in her life, until she felt the heat of the burning house in her lungs and red floating cinders singed her hair. And now strong arms were holding her, a rough voice was speaking to her, a uniformed chest stayed hard beneath her flailing fists. *Get her out of here! Get this woman out of here!*

Louis would not die. She would not let him. Because if Louis lived, who knew what would happen? Life. Love. Adventure. All hers for the taking, if only she had the courage to grab them. If only he lived. A blanket around her shoulders, a mug of sweet tea in her shaking hands, a kindly arm about her. Dry, painful sobs. Nancy's voice. *What were you thinking, Belle?* Turning towards her, giving in to the warmth of those familiar friendly arms. *I don't want Louis to die.*

Was that when Clement had guessed? Had he realized, even then, that she had already made her choice, that however much she longed for Louis the pull of Marshwood was too great? Did he know, as she did, that already her life was inscribed on the curve of every one of its paths, in the soft earth of the garden she tended, in the walls she painted and repaired? He had not questioned her as she stood weeping in Nancy's embrace, nor at any time afterwards. Nancy had brought her home and put her to bed. He had come up to see her a few hours later, and gently – how gently, and yet how absolutely! – laid the problem of Louis to rest by telling her about his offer to the Army of Marshwood as an alternative to the Pinkertons' place.

'They're already bringing people down,' he told her.

'The nurses are opening up the spare rooms. I think it's right, Belle, don't you? I hope you don't mind.'

'No.' She tried to smile. 'Of course I don't mind.'

'We'll have to move out. The head nurse made that very clear.' He smiled faintly. 'Esther Higgins. Nurse Higgins to me, I'm told. You wouldn't want to mess with her. I said we could move to the housekeeper's cottage as soon as you're strong enough.'

'I'm fine, really. I can go tonight if they need us to.'

'Tomorrow will do. Even the day after. Belle, I don't know how long they'll stay. Will it be all right? I just thought it was time, you know. Time to do our bit. I think, if it doesn't sound quite mad, that the house would like that.'

'It doesn't sound mad.' Clement looked relieved and Bella managed a small laugh. 'Well, maybe a bit.'

'We shan't be able to have visitors for a while,' he said slowly.

Bella bit her lip. 'I don't suppose we shall.'

'Though of course if you wanted to go visiting yourself . . .'

If you wanted to go visiting yourself . . . What was he saying? She looked up at him, but he would not meet her gaze. 'If that is what you want,' he repeated with an effort.

If Clement had not been so generous, if he had not made it so easy for her, would she have gone? He sat by her bed, neither touching nor looking at her, holding out

253

his understanding like a gift, and Bella was terrified.

'It's not what I want,' she said in a low voice. 'What I want is . . .'

'What?'

Four children, two girls and two boys whom she would love equally, who would go to local schools for as long as possible. Windows thrown open to the sweet Dorset air, carpets and cushions and paintings and clutter . . . Her tears began to fall again. Clement said nothing but after a while his hand crept over the counterpane to take hers, and he held it as she cried.

Once the wounded officers and their carers were installed, it made sense to keep them where they were. A month after the fire, Marshwood's status was regularized and the house was officially requisitioned. Marshwood was transformed at bewildering speed: objects of value were removed, along with Bella and Clement's clothes and personal items, and either taken to the cottage or put into storage in Clement's workshop, the pantries were turned into storerooms, the attics into extra bedrooms. The courtyard was filled with army vehicles, trucks, cars and motorcycles. Everywhere Bella looked there were strangers – strangers working in her kitchen, sitting in her chairs, walking in her garden. In uniform, in dressing-gowns, in slings and on crutches. The house even smelt different, a combination of iodine and tobacco.

'You'll want to keep out of our way,' Esther told her. 'In due course. Just let us get on with things.'

Bella was growing used to Esther's blunt ways. 'I really don't mind about the house,' she said, 'because it was so empty before. I'm glad to see it put to good use. But I'm blowed if I'll let that excuse for a gardener ruin my kitchen garden.'

William, the private sent by the Army to tend the garden, had grown up in Tooting and informed them in cheerful tones on arrival that he wouldn't know a hoe from a trowel or the back end of a bus.

'They're sending up some POWs from Bambridge to help. Italians.'

'Even worse,' said Bella. 'No, you shall just have to put up with my presence in your midst. I'm not letting all that effort go to waste. And besides, we all need the food.'

They needed the food and she needed activity – any activity – to take her mind off Louis. Six months passed. Six months of working with William and the Italian POWs in the garden for as long as the weather permitted, sorting through its produce with Marshwood's new cook to decide what to keep and what to sell at market. Six months during which, when winter truly closed in, she hung up her gardening clothes and volunteered to help in the overflowing infant school. Six months of obsessively listening to the radio every evening with the patients in Marshwood's

255

drawing-room, six months of reading out loud to those who were too unwell to read to themselves, six months which saw her relationship with Clement recover a degree of forced intimacy in their cramped twin-bedded room and which brought no news of Louis. In February, they heard news of the German defeat at Stalingrad; in early March, of their withdrawal from Tunisia. Bella learned from one of the patients that Free French pilots flying in Britain were being sent to North Africa. He had said he would not write and he stayed true to his word, but as more time went by with no news of him she began to think that perhaps Clement was right. Perhaps he was indestructible, and if this was the case then perhaps he would return. She allowed herself occasional daydreams in which she liked to picture him in the Egyptian desert, or to imagine their meeting again after the war. In Paris perhaps – or better, in Avignon or Aix or one of the southern towns she had once driven through with Clement. There would be no reason to meet there other than the sun, the lazy promise of afternoons heavy with heat. She would wear a white dress. He would wear . . . her fantasies always petered out. She did not know what he would wear, or whether he would even agree to meet her.

'I was just coming to find you.' On a sunny morning at the end of March, Esther called out across the courtyard towards the barn which was the market garden's new HQ. Bella, in boots, Barbour and gardening belt, watched her come with an affectionate smile. The season was on the turn again, the days still cold but longer, the sun brighter, the damp earth full of new fragrance. Winter was over. It felt good.

'There's a package for you.'

Over the months she had stopped expecting the worst with every post. She took the package, a slim manila envelope, and turned it to look at the sender's address. RAF. Not Louis' handwriting.

'Is it bad news?'

Bad news before the war had meant a number of things, from failing a piano exam to the announcement of a death. Bad news now carried only one significance.

'Are you all right?'

'Fine. I'm fine.'

She returned to the cottage to open the package. It contained a diary, her own letters and one from his commanding officer which she had to read several times before the words ceased to swim before her eyes.

He had disappeared over the ocean. They had been under attack, had lost several planes, and in the mêlée nobody had seen or heard what happened to him. They had tried to reconstruct events afterwards by means of the other pilots' photographs, but nobody had managed to capture Louis' last moments. With no witnesses he was reported missing, believed dead. This had happened two weeks ago. There was little cause for hope. As his next of kin – it was the next-of-kin reference which broke her down – his belongings would be sent on to them, but in the meantime he thought they would like to receive his private papers. Louis Duchesne had been a true Frenchman, a fine pilot and a good friend. He would be sorely missed.

He had evidently been an erratic keeper of diaries. The first entry, dated in July 1940, made her smile through her tears as she deciphered it in her schoolgirl French. *We are in England! And have had such an adventure* . . . There followed what she recognized as a description of his escape as he had told her about it on their first meeting, the stolen plane, the flight to Gibraltar. *I have decided to record everything, for my parents and for myself, so that I do not forget* . . . The next entry was dated six months later. He returned to the diary in spates, and she could not work out from what was written what drove such moments of assiduity. Much of what he wrote appeared to be accounts of flights, visibility, people he met. It was obvious he had little time or indeed inclination for writing. January 1942, and her own name appeared, followed by Clement, Nancy and others.

Her head hurt with the effort of deciphering him. She flicked to the end. The final section – everything following their last meeting – was written in English. She realized with a bittersweet stab of joy that many of the entries were addressed to her. She read them with brimming eyes, jumping from section to section, her heightened state of emotion rendering her incapable of consecutive reading.

If you are reading this, it means that I am dead. Or as we say in French, when we are trying to be polite about these things, that I am disappeared.

Did you believe I would not think of you? I hope you do not think me cruel by not writing. I want to, believe me. And yet I think that you and I have come to the end of our story and it is better for us to turn the page. Every storyteller knows that everything is in a good ending. Do you think it is the same with life? Can you measure a life by the manner of its death? I hope not . . . I think I have shown courage in life, but I doubt when the end comes that I shall go without protesting . . .

Your face when I told you of my desire to be a priest! A picture. You are so transparent to me, my lovely Bella, for all your very English reserve. I wish . . . but no. This is not to be a record of wishes. I have no wishes as to us. Only a desire for celebration at our having met.

That, of course, is a lie, or at least partly so . . .

Anglesey is all sand. Sand in my flying boots, sand in my eyes, sand in my sheets at night. After the war – ha! Do you still believe those words, 'after the war'? I do not. War has become our natural state of being – I shall never go on holiday to a beach again. Every summer I shall take my children to the mountains instead.

Today I have received a letter from Clement. It was nice

to hear from him, but it has unsettled me. Marshwood full of soldiers, other men in the room I think of as mine. And also, you. I realize that I like to imagine you just as I left you. Standing in the lane at the entrance to Marshwood, all quiet around you, your eyes huge in the early dusk. You are all mine in that image. But now Marshwood is overrun with soldiers. There is no room for me in that picture and I must find some other Eden . . .

A letter from Clement . . . Bella thumbed through the small raft of letters that had been returned with the diary until she recognized his handwriting. She pulled the letter out of its envelope and scanned it rapidly. Clement gave a brief account of the plane crash and the transformation of Marshwood before coming to what she guessed was its main objective. *A small bathroom, a tiny bedroom – only just big enough for the two of us, and a sitting-room cosy or small, depending on how you look at it. Of course, it is ridiculously small. I don't think either of us realized, when we offered the use of the house, how all consuming our makeshift hospital would become. We are unfortunately no longer in a position to welcome visitors.*

So Clement, for all his apparent generosity towards her, had written to Louis, quietly making sure he had no further impact on their lives. *No longer in a position to welcome visitors.* A cold, quiet fury swept through her as she re-read this.

Where else could she go but to the lake? She walked fast, ignoring her headache and her shortness of breath, stumbling through the tunnel formed by the beech trees, blind to the tiny buds curled on their naked branches. She dropped heavily to the ground when she arrived at the lake, sitting on the damp grass with her arms wrapped round her knees and no idea of what to do next.

She had come here to find him, she realized, in the mad hope that the fabric of time could somehow part so that she could step back into that moment when she had sat here with him last. She kept her eyes tightly shut to conjure up his face, his voice, his smell, his touch. She thought of his gold and hazel eyes, his olive skin, his mouth and too-wide grin. She lingered on the slim shoulders, the brand of American cigarettes he liked, his penchant for silly card games and his new love of Haydn. She knew details, so many details. He wolfed down tea and biscuits, he became mildly flirtatious when he danced, he loved England but missed his country. He adored flying but hated fighting, he enjoyed books and wished he could read faster, he was good with babies. He loved life. He was made to be happy.

Was that all there was to be between them? A few meetings, a half-kiss, the turned-away promise of something more? She spread her hand on the ground, willing the moss beneath her fingers to respond to her pressure, to become his hand, willing him back. The moss remained unchanged, damp and springy. Bella thumped the earth and howled.

Regret, loss, unhappiness. In time, she would feel all the attributes of grief, but right then her overwhelming emotion was rage. Rage against Clement for not trusting her, rage against Louis for dying, rage most of all against herself for not recognizing how short her moment with him was.

Night was already beginning to fall by the time she got home. Clement was waiting for her in their tiny lounge.

'Darling!' He rushed over to her, helped her remove her coat, led her to an armchair. 'I was so worried.'

'Louis is dead,' she said, and burst into tears.

Isla and Jack. Jack and Isla. How Bella had loved them! The looks exchanged when they thought she wasn't watching, their radiance, their endearing attempts at discretion . . . As if it were not obvious to anybody what was going on! The moonlight flits across the lawn, the midnight creaking of floorboards. She had watched them return once in the very early hours of the morning. In the still pallor of the day's first light they had seemed to belong to another world entirely, a place of magic and shadow. Oh yes, she had loved them with a passion and as she bore silent witness to their affair she spared not one thought for Richard, because there had been no place for him in that enchanted world.

A few days have passed now, and there is still no news of Isla. She has a nagging doubt that all may not be well, but she daren't call her. Richard will be at work, of course – but what if he isn't? She would not want to talk to him. She is pretty certain he would not want to talk to her, either . . .

She had not *meant* to tell him. Perhaps, if she and Isla had spoken about the affair, their conversation would have panned out differently. If Jack had not appeared just as Isla was leaving, if they had not stood in the exact spot where she last said goodbye to Louis, if Isla had not unconsciously mirrored Louis' last gesture and pressed her lips to Jack's forehead. If she had not brought Jack into the house to make him a cup of tea, if it had not been so obvious that he had been crying, if he had not answered the call from Richard telephoning to find out where his wife was . . .

Perhaps if she had understood all those years ago that she would have only one chance with Louis, or if she had admitted to Isla her regret at not having taken it . . . What had she said? *Regret is the sign of an overactive imagination.* How pompous. How false. How *wrong*. More and more as she grows older, it seems to Bella that life is not a linear process. This has never been more obvious to her than in these last few weeks. Of course she is not Isla, and Jack is not Louis, and Richard is *certainly* not Clement . . . but still. Patterns repeat themselves, and not necessarily for the best.

The last drops of acid spent, she begins to clear the hedge. She pulls cautiously at first so as not to damage the laurel bushes but her impatience soon gets the better of her, and she begins to rip at the sinuous tendrils coiled tightly around the branches. The laurels look naked without their blanket of weeds. They will need to be hacked back, trimmed into shape. Clement had been good at that. He was always an enthusiastic cutter of hedges.

Clement, who on the day after they learned of Louis' death came to her with a baby's rattle as a gift. A smooth gleaming object of polished walnut and simple beauty, sized for a baby's hand. The dried lentils which filled its hollowed head made a soft rustling sound when it was shaken, and he had carved an intricate garland of flowers around its diameter, and a bow above their intertwined initials. *I thought that maybe it was time.* A shy smile, sad but hopeful. Callie's father, Isla's grandfather. Her husband, with his marvellous workshop and his dreadful hats, his passion for literature and gardening. She sees him sometimes in Marcus' meticulous wildlife observations, in Callie's approach to her painting, in Isla's passion for the countryside around Marshwood. This has been her life, and she has loved it. And yet she knows that it has always had a sharper focus because of Louis. Sometimes she thinks that her precious life was his dying gift to her, but she has always wondered what would have happened if she had made a different choice. Or if he had lived . . .

She knows that she should not have said anything to Richard. But there, she had called out from the kitchen to tell Jack to answer the phone, and he had come in looking distraught to tell her that it was Richard on the line, and by the time she got to the phone herself Richard was getting impatient and asking where Isla was and how come she had left so late and wouldn't it have been better for her to come home last night, and she gave half-hearted responses because (a) she didn't like his tone of voice and, more importantly, (b) from where she stood in the hall she could see that Jack had already left and was walking back up the lane looking as if he carried the world upon his shoulders, and she thought how different he was right now from the naughty child they had all loved and how much she wished he and Isla had never fallen out, and then Richard was growing more and more irritated because she wasn't answering and saying he supposed he should go and prepare for the others' arrival and asking by the way, who was the bloke who answered the phone because he sounded like he knew who Richard was but he had no idea, and she sighed and told him that the bloke in question was Jack.

'Jack?'

'He is an old friend of Isla's.'

And if he hadn't had to have the last word as always,

if he hadn't sounded so arrogant, or dismissive, or so *knowing* or cynical, if, if, if, still she might not have said anything.

'Oh yes, she mentioned him,' said Richard. 'Hardly her friend, from what I heard. Bastard, by the sound of things.'

'They grew up together,' said Bella coldly.

'Whatever,' said Richard. 'I just hope she gets here soon.'

'There's no *whatever* about it,' insisted Bella. 'They were close.'

'OK, they were close! Big deal. I've got to go, Bella. Got to grab some shut-eye before the gang gets back.'

And if this last sentence had not irritated her so profoundly, if she had not sensed its underlying claim of ownership, she might not have made that first dangerous remark . . .

'They still are,' said Bella.

Richard sighed. 'Still are what?'

'Close. Jack and Isla. They are still close.'

A silence, in which she felt almost sorry for him. And then his question, 'Bella, what's going on?'

'Something that should have happened a very long time ago.'

She knows that she should not have meddled, she knows that she should have left it to Isla and Richard and Jack to sort things out amongst themselves, but in that moment she had had enough of dissimulation and it had all come out. Jack has gone now too, muttering something about unfinished business to attend to. She hopes that the unfinished business involves Isla. And on balance, she is still glad that she spoke to Richard.

What's going on?

Something that should have happened a very long time ago.

Such a disproportionate answer to such a little question. With Isla away in Spain, the events surrounding his return from Dallas have become an obsession for Richard. He still does not know what makes him more angry, his wife's faithlessness or Bella's whistle-blowing. The conversation had not lasted long. He had questioned her meaning. She had explained. He had hung up. This too had felt somehow disproportionate. Rage, tears, cursing would have been appropriate. Instead he had *thanked* her.

Until he found out, Richard had come to accept the dimming of Isla's passion as an inevitable consequence of marriage – its natural course. What glimpses he caught of her passion now were directed at the children rather than at himself, but he balanced the occasional stab of jealousy this gave him with the conviction that this usurping of her love was only natural and right. And in truth he also loved to see the way she caressed them when she thought nobody was watching, her tenderness when they were hurt, the dreaminess that came over her sometimes when she watched them play. It had never occurred to Richard that it could work any other way. Much as he enjoyed the pre-baby years – the freedom, the travelling, the fun and the parties – even at the time they had felt like an interlude. What Richard loved, what gave him *purpose*, was to belong to a family and what hurts – the real sense of betrayal – is the realization that this has not been enough for Isla. The truth is that out there in Dallas, once his anger towards her for not joining him had abated, distance and loneliness had afforded him a clearer picture of her. He remembered how the girl he married had been given to loud bursts of laughter, to frequent singing undaunted by the fact that she was always off key, to rapturous and impulsive love-making. He had taken her gradual withdrawal into herself as a sign of encroaching maturity but with time on his hands he began to see how much she had changed. Richard, never known for his imagination but driven to flights of fancy by the Texan heat and three weeks of lonely nights, even visualized a new person growing *inside* his wife, a person living her life far away from him and from her own physical confines, a person, he realized with something akin to panic, quite beyond his reach. He had come back determined to do something about it, and ready to talk again about this desire she kept bringing up of going back to work. And then – well. He is not proud of what happened then.

After talking to Bella, Richard had gone into Beth's room and stretched out as much as he could on her small pink bed. It had occurred to him that, other than for a few brief minutes fetching or looking for something, he had never been in this room without his daughter. Empty, it retained the feeling that its owner had only just stepped out and would come roaring back in at any moment. A large collage, the product of a series of rainy afternoons, lay on the trestle table along the wall awaiting completion, a marine landscape made up of glittering fish on dark blue cardboard, of pasta shells and tinfoil sharks and tissue-paper octopuses. On the floor, Beth's teddies sat aligned in order of height in front of her easel, on which was written, in Marcus' approximate spelling, *do not muve under pein of deeth*. Postcards, pebbles, treasures and toys jostled for space on shelves, and an old dress of Isla's, now presumably donated to the dressing-up box, lay over the back of the armchair by the bookcase. He had never been in a room whose occupant was so very present in her absence. It had the hushed, still atmosphere of time suspended in mid-flow, like a fairy-tale castle waiting for the moment when life would resume again at the exact point where it had stopped.

God! He was shattered. He pulled Beth's duvet up around him, breathed in her sweet, biscuity scent and remembered, with the curious sharp pain of sudden memory, that when she was a baby he used always to sleep with her on weekend mornings. He would lie on the sofa in the living room, Beth nestled against his chest like a kitten while Marcus watched TV with the volume turned low, longing for the moment when she would need feeding and he could take her back in to Isla and they would all pile into the big bed together. For a moment, as his eyelids began to close, he forgot the conversation with Bella. Then, remembering, he got up and resumed his prowl around the house, ending up in the kitchen.

Outside summer flourished, riotous and garish, but the room in which he sat was dark. Isla always said it was a room made for winter, for lights and candles and the smell of baking, but he had never realized until now how much its cheeriness relied upon her presence. The sun had put in its brief appearance, sweeping tentative beams half-way across the floor before sinking beneath the low windows. The afternoon was marching on, and still she was not back. He even wondered if she would come at all.

He was tired but could not summon the energy to rise from his chair. Instead, he hit his tightly clenched fist against the open palm of his other hand. He hit hard, over and again, but it never hurt enough for him to realize what he was doing.

He waited until the children were out of the way,

of course. Beth burst into the kitchen and threw her arms around his neck, with Marcus following more slowly, smiling shyly but clearly pleased to see him. Isla bustled in behind them, and did he detect or was he imagining something furtive about her behaviour? Beth was dispatched upstairs to fetch the bag of presents from America. Isla had stopped at the supermarket on the way home, and sandwiches were made, glasses of milk poured. The children ate ravenously, asking questions, giving news. The kitten, astonished at finding itself back in London after three weeks at Marshwood, mewed pitifully. The stairs were littered with belongings as Isla unpacked in the hall, throwing dirty laundry downstairs towards the kitchen and handing clean clothes to the children as she searched their bag for toothbrushes and essential toys. It felt like watching a film of his own life, a curiously enjoyable film which lulled him into a false sense of comfort, reassuring him that all was well while at the same time reminding him that his reality was a sham. The children's supper finished, he told himself he could take it no more.

'Bedtime, I think,' he said.

'But it's still early!'

'Bed,' he repeated firmly. 'Mummy and I need to talk.' And had she flinched at that point? Had she blushed and frozen, or again was it just his mind playing tricks?

'Come on,' she said cheerfully. 'I'll take you up.'

'No,' he said, because he couldn't wait any longer. 'Stay here.'

He heard her give instructions from a long distance away. *Start running a bath, I'll be up in a minute, get some clean jim-jams out of the drawer, don't forget to brush your teeth.*

'It's not fair!' complained Beth on her way upstairs, and Isla actually laughed before turning – and did she look apprehensive? – to face Richard.

'Well?' she asked. 'Was it a good trip?' He was short of breath by then, and felt light-headed. She was gathering up the children's tea things, loading the dishwasher, putting away food. For a moment he thought he must have imagined everything.

'Come here.' He spoke with difficulty.

She stepped over to him, her head cocked to one side, her expression quizzical. 'Rich? Are you all right? I'm sorry we weren't here when you arrived, we were held back leaving . . .'

'I spoke to Bella.'

'Granna?'

'She told me.'

'Told you what?'

'You bitch.'

He had not meant to hit her. He thought afterwards that he never would have if she had not looked at him like that, so innocent. Such a hypocrite. His fist flew of

272

its own accord, and once he had struck her he found he did not want to stop. He grabbed her by the shoulders and shook her, forced her back against the kitchen table, unclear of anything except an overwhelming desire to hurt her, to make her feel some of the humiliation he had suffered as Bella told him about the affair with Jack. He lifted her skirt and fumbled at his trousers, pulling her hair so that her neck arched painfully backwards. Her teeth sank into his wrist and he let her go, pushing her roughly so that she fell, crumpling slowly, slowly to the ground.

Into the silence that followed – the silence which was marked by his own weeping, and Isla's whimpering, and their ragged breathing, but which was silence nonetheless – the door swung open to reveal Marcus.

'What are you doing here?' He hated the sound of his own voice, harsh and accusatory where it should have been reassuring.

'I came to find Leo.' Marcus sounded close to tears. 'I was afraid he was lost. It's not good for cats to travel around.'

'I'll bring him to you.' Isla's voice was tight, its comforting tone too obviously fake.

'Mummy, are you OK?'

'I fell.' He still remembers, with something that surprises him by being close to admiration, that she even managed a smile. 'Aren't I silly? I slipped on the rug. After all the times I've told you and Beth to be careful . . .'

She left the kitchen with Marcus, and he heard them search for the kitten, their footsteps in the living-room above, then the sound of a bath being filled. She did not come back down, and he crumpled into a chair and thought, *is this really how it ends?* With two people once in love hurting each other, and a small boy watching them?

No, Richard is not proud of what he did. Secretly, he knows that no amount of provocation can justify his act of violence. He should have waited for the shock to wear off, given her the opportunity to speak. He should certainly not have acted on the basis of a conversation with an old woman who as far as he is concerned has long been going senile. But for now, he knows that he can't think like this. For now, the only way he can live with his conscience is to tell himself that the bitch had it coming to her.

Bella's betrayal. The violence of Richard's reaction. Jack's story and the sad reality of their separation. Isla came to Callie's house in Spain because she could think of nowhere else to go, and because from the depths of her misery she felt a long-buried tug of yearning for her mother's love to put it right.

She spent two nights with Richard between her return from Marshwood and her departure for Spain, two nights in which they neither slept nor spoke but lay in careful, untouching silence, each hating the other but preferring to share a bed rather than risk upsetting Marcus by sleeping in separate rooms.

'We're going to have to speak to each other on holiday,' she said at last in the early hours of their second morning. 'Or the kids'll notice.'

And then his announcement. 'I can't go on holiday with you.'

'But it's booked!'

'Too bad.'

'And the children . . .'

'I can't do it. I can't go and play at happy families on the beach, knowing what I know.'

'You'll have to try.'

'I can't.'

'Look at my face, Richard.' He glanced up quickly, then looked away. She took his chin in her hand and forced him to turn back to her. 'If I can make the effort, so the bloody hell can you.'

'I can't spend all that time with you.'

'But what are we going to tell the children?'

'Tell them I have to work.'

'We can't go *without* you!'

'Do what you like, Isla. Just not with me. I need time to think.'

Beth greeted the news of the cancelled holiday with a storm of angry tears. Marcus simply shrugged.

'Don't you mind?' asked Isla.

'Not really.' Isla looked at him closely. He had barely spoken since witnessing the row with Richard. She had tried to make light of the event, maintaining her lie about slipping and proffering assurances of love. She knew that he had not believed her about the first. He seemed indifferent to the second.

'But what are we going to *do* all holidays?' wailed Beth.

'We'll find things,' Isla assured her. 'There's loads to do in London in the summer.'

Richard, dressed for work, marched out of their bedroom just as Beth, unconvinced of London's summer attractions, announced that she wanted to go back to Marshwood. The front door slammed. The house shook. *Oh God*, thought Isla. *I can't do this either.*

'Daddy didn't even say goodbye!' Beth burst into tears again. Marcus, quite out of character, kicked a crate of toys. A plush elephant fell out, a veteran of her own toybox as a child, bald in parts and losing its straw stuffing. A memory: walking past a toyshop in Portobello, tugging on a sleeve. *That one. I want that one.* An adult voice, her mother, more indulgent than strict, *somebody forgot the magic word . . .* A man's laughter, a few minutes of panic as they waited in the shop – would earlier customers get to the elephant first? Would her parents change their minds? – then the elation of holding her new toy in her arms.

Whispering to it all the way home, the certainty that this inanimate object had a soul and that they belonged to each other. Callie laying out a dish of milk at the dinner table for the new elephant to drink from. Callie. Her mother.

She told Richard that night that they were going to Spain.

It doesn't take long to fill Callie in on what has happened. Her mother – blue-jeaned, sandalled, swept-up greying hair held in place by an ochre-splodged paintbrush – picks them up from the dusty village square in her ageing Seat. In keeping with firm instructions received on the phone, she does not question Isla's battered face. Instead she pelts the children with information about local wildlife and unsuitable lists of the activities on offer in the area – rafting, bullfighting, abseiling, rock-climbing. The children, exhausted and hungry, barely respond to this grandmother they hardly know. Once installed in her little whitewashed house, they nibble at the tuna sandwiches and hard-boiled eggs she has prepared, then fall into bed. Beth is asleep almost immediately, her tightly balled fists thrown over her head. Marcus takes longer and Isla lies beside him in the darkness, struggling to keep awake herself until his breathing becomes more regular and he no longer clutches as she tries to slip away. Leaving the door ajar, she pads barefoot across the red tiles of the kitchen floor to join Callie, who waits for her in one of the two wicker armchairs on her tiny terrace, a bottle of red wine and a plate of powdery almond biscuits on the low table beside her. And there, with the moon riding high over the mountains and a cool night breeze rustling through Callie's olive trees, she tells her mother everything.

What she wants more than anything is for Callie to tell her that everything will be all right. No. What she wants is for Callie to take her by the hand, like the little girl she once was, and to put her to bed as she has her own children. She wants to lie in the darkness as she used to with her bedroom door half open and she wants to know that her mother is just outside, listening out in case anything should happen to her in the night. She wants to be comforted by the smell of white spirit and oil paints, she wants the warmth of unconditional embraces, she wants to weep and not be asked why she is weeping, she wants to be loved for who she is, she wants to be understood.

Callie in many ways has been perfect since Isla's arrival with the children. As a rule she hates any disturbance to her painting routine, but she has accepted this unexpected visit without question. She has filled her normally bare pantry with pasta shells and biscuits, she has looked out clean sheets and made up beds and all through the evening, as Isla talks, she has poured wine and served snacks and made sympathetic cooing noises. She has listened to Isla and firmly ignored her fingers' itching for a paintbrush, but she knows that somehow, despite all this, she has not delivered what was wanted. Isla goes to bed, expressing gratitude which Callie reads correctly as a poor cover for disappointment.

He's gone, Callie. Think of the child. Her parents' voices, respectively distressed and disapproving, float back to her down the years. She sits out on the terrace long after Isla has gone to bed. The night air is cool up in the mountains and draws out scents from her garden which are obliterated by the heat during the day, oleander, rosemary and thyme. Callie knows the price she has had to pay for this life of hers – this garden, this freedom, the sightings of Africa from her terrace on a clear day. She has always known the price, and paid it willingly. How clear her choice had seemed to her! Daniel – her husband, her rock, the love of her life – was gone. Isla, the constant reminder of what she had lost, remained. She felt guilty for a long time that her love for the child appeared to have followed Daniel to the grave. In time, she grew to understand that it was not the love itself which had died, but her ability to express it. A subtle distinction though, and one that made little odds to their everyday life. People had told her Isla was grieving, but how was that possible when she continued to display such an appetite for life? She had heard her daughter laugh again within weeks of burying her father, and the sound had infuriated her. Everything had made Callie angry in the few years following his death, when she stormed from continent to continent, and demonstration to demonstration, and at one stage from man to man, searching for something, anything, anyone to fill the void of his absence. And then she had come here, on a painting course paid for by her father, and she had known that this was her place because here, for the first time since his death, she had *felt* Daniel's spirit around her. This spirit of his is at the root of the peace she has found here, in this pretty village on its rugged outcrop, and it has fuelled her painting for as long as she has been here – her *real* painting, not the bland pretty watercolours she sells to tourists to earn her living. For a long time she painted him – portraits based on memories and photographs, highly figurative at first but growing ever more abstract until she realized that what she wanted was no longer to paint Daniel himself but somehow to capture the essence of him, of what he was and meant to her. Warmth and light, the grandeur of life, the shadow of death . . . These have been her new obsessions over these past years, which have kept her bound to San Rafael. Friends, her home, the occasional lover – these count, but really, as long as she can paint, Callie is happy and she paints better here than anywhere else. At the moment, she is working on a giant canvas of the sun setting over the Alpujarras. Simple enough, and yet it isn't working for her. Callie has never been bound by false modesty and she knows that technically her work is excellent. She also knows that this particular painting lacks the magic that will satisfy her.

The dogs begin to howl as they always do at about half-past eleven, baying to each other across the valley. At midnight, she hears her seventy-six-year-old neighbour Aurelio stagger home from the village bar to receive his nightly telling off from his irate daughter. Paca is on fiery form tonight, and the whole hillside is treated to her opinion of her father's drinking habits. Aurelio responds with a series of meek *sí hija*s as they move indoors. Callie knows that even now Paca will be helping him to undress, that tomorrow morning she will cook eggs for his breakfast, and that he will sing her praises in the village as he does every day. She feels a stab of unfamiliar envy for Paca and Aurelio, caught in their eternal tug of war between love and rebellion, affection and duty. What disturbs Callie the most about Isla's story and her arrival here is the implicit assumption on her daughter's part that she will be able to help. Callie cannot see how, given their history – their lack of history – this might be possible. And yet here she is, that child whom she left so long ago, seeking her out. Sometimes of late Callie has wondered about her life, asked herself whether loneliness is not beginning to encroach on what once was merely solitude. Callie, a great believer in the workings of Fate, wonders even whether there may not be some greater purpose to Isla's unexpected visit.

She rises early the following day in the hope that morning will shed fresh light upon her painting, but the children appear as soon as she sets up her easel. They stand barefoot in their pyjamas, hand in hand.

'We're hungry,' says Marcus.

The painting will have to wait. *Damn*, Callie thinks, before reminding herself that her relationship with her grandchildren may also be a part of the designs of Destiny. 'I'll make you some hot chocolate.'

Breakfast is a silent affair. Marcus yawns over his cereal. Beth, taking her cue from her brother, chews and swallows vacantly. There is no sign of Isla. Once they have eaten, Callie takes the children for a walk up the road leading away from the village. They drag their feet in the dust, too listless even to complain in the heat which is already searing. Callie is beginning to worry that perhaps they are ill when they cross a herd of goats coming down the mountain and Beth falls instantly in love.

'Look at the babies! Can't we have one?'

'Imagine Leo with a baby goat!' Marcus gives a bark of sudden laughter.

'Baa! Baa!' Beth charges her brother, two fingers raised to her forehead in imitation of a goat's horns.

'Meeoww!' Marcus runs away, still laughing.

'Who's Leo?' asks Callie.

'He's our cat!'

'Oh!' says Callie. Then, with a flash of inspiration, 'I have a cat.'

'You do?' Beth looks surprised. 'Where is it?'

'She's not really mine,' admits Callie. 'She's a stray, but she comes round quite often when she's hungry. Maybe when we get home we can put some food out for her. She's all white, with a stripy ginger patch over her eye. I call her Gingernut.' She shrugs. 'It seems to suit her.'

'Gingernut,' says Marcus. Another bark of laughter. 'Gingernut!' he shouts.

Beth runs down the road after her brother, then back up the hill to Callie. 'Come on!' she orders. Callie looks down at the small, not very clean fingers tugging impatiently at her sleeve. Once, a lifetime ago, this was Isla.

'I'm coming,' she says gruffly, then surprises herself by breaking into a run.

Isla is up by the time they reach home, looking very young in a summer dress, her bruises hidden behind huge sunglasses. They spend the morning outside. Callie gardens, Isla pretends to read, the children play with the watering hose. They look, thinks Callie, rather enjoying the sensation, just like countless other families spending the summer together up in the mountains. In the heat of the afternoon, Callie – getting into the swing of this grandmother role – suggests that they all repair to the cool of her studio, where she donates a blank canvas to each of the children. These, she tells them, are to be their summer project and they are to think carefully about what they want to paint.

'Why do I have to *think*?' asks Beth. 'Why can't I just paint?'

'Because,' answers Callie, 'things generally work out better if you think about them first.'

'Ha!' laughs Marcus. 'Beth *never* thinks!'

Callie stifles a chuckle. 'What?' demands Marcus. 'It's *true*.'

Isla thinks that he looks better already, her little boy, the traces of anxiety left by those awful few days in London kissed away by a morning in the sun. She leaves them to their painting and wanders off by herself, following the creek that runs through Callie's garden upstream to where it widens into a natural pool. The natural hollow formed by the stream has been enhanced here by an ingenious makeshift dam, the enterprising creation of local boys idling away precious moments when they are not needed in the fields. This is a place much beloved of the inhabitants of San Rafael, but today it is deserted. Isla slips out of her cotton dress and into the pool. She winces as the cold water washes over her bruises, then relaxes when she realizes that it does not hurt.

Her body glows white in the dark green of the water. The bottom of the pool is said to be popular with snakes, but when she lies on her back with her head tilted behind her she hears only the rush of the creek in her ears. Above her, the clear blue of the southern sky pierces through the latticed brown and green of the overhanging sweet chestnuts. She floats, immobile, until gravity begins to take effect and she feels her limbs tugged gently downwards. For the first time in weeks – in months, perhaps – she feels quite peaceful. *How easy it would be to stay here.* She restrains the instinct urging her to move and her head sinks beneath the waterline. She opens her mouth, just a little, and tastes a trickle of earthy river water. *They say that drowning, once the fear is gone, is a pleasant way to go.* Who had said that?

The sound of voices reaches her, distorted through the water. People are coming. She turns onto her front and swims a few strokes underwater to the other side of the creek, using a tree root to haul herself out. The new arrivals wave. She waves back, picks up her towel and stretches out in the sun.

The afternoon passes, heavy with heat. She pushes aside thoughts of Bella and Marshwood, Richard and Jack, focusing instead on the pattern of light and shade on the grass around her, on the sound of other bathers laughing and the sharp taste of the wine Callie pours out when she wanders home in the late afternoon. Later she bathes the children in Callie's bathroom before letting them back out into the garden where they escape her, running naked to dry themselves. In the half-light of dusk they appear sprite-like and enchanted. Cut grass and dried earth stick to the soles of their feet as she finally herds them to bed, leaving a smudged trail behind them. She lingers with them over their bedtime story, squeezed into one small bed with Beth between her legs and Marcus against her shoulder, and once again she only leaves them when she knows that they are asleep.

Callie sits at her usual place on the terrace. Yesterday's half-full bottle of wine sits on the little table with some local ham, slices of cold tortilla, tomatoes, bread and cheese.

'A good day,' says Callie after a few minutes of silence.

'Yes.' Isla stops toying with the food on her plate and leans back in her chair, nursing her glass of wine.

'The children are terrific. We got along famously this afternoon. They seem so grown up, even Beth. Compared to the last time I saw them.'

'Yes, well,' says Isla. 'It's been a long time.'

The statement hovers between them, part accusation, part regret. Callie lights a cigarette, inhales, exhales slowly.

'What do you want exactly, Isla?'

'I don't know.' For a brief time, driving away from Jack, she had been so sure. It seems strange to her now, how determined she had been on that drive, determined and full of a sort of elation which stemmed from the conviction that what she had done had been right and, to an extent, noble. 'I really don't know what I want,' she says now to Callie. 'I think I just want to be left alone. I feel like my head is so full of other people's voices I can't hear my own. I want them to stop. I just want – it sounds stupid – to be me.'

'What I meant was, what do you want from *me*?'

'From you?' Isla looks thoughtful. Lost too, thinks her mother. 'To turn back time, perhaps?' She smiles sadly. Callie looks away. 'Solace, I suppose. Sanctuary. Do you remember the great moth funeral?'

'I don't think so . . .'

'Funny. It's one of my strongest memories of before. Before Daddy died, I mean.'

Winter. London a hushed monochrome, transformed by falling snowflakes. Snow on the ground not yet blackened by traffic. The crunch of footsteps, the shrill, excited cries of children. Isla bundled in layers of woollen clothing, many-stockinged feet tight and cold inside wellington boots, careful not to break through the thin icing sugar coating to the dirty stone of the pavement. And then, on the ground, just out of reach of the stamp of her small foot, the moth. Brown and orange tipped, hopeless, flapping its broken wing in tired circles in the unfamiliar snow.

'We took it home. You couldn't understand what it was doing there. You knew it was going to die but I couldn't bear to leave it. You wanted to go to the park, you said it would be so pretty in the snow, but we turned back and went home and spent the morning making a new home for the moth. It was dead by the end of the day. I cried, but then you organized the most perfect funeral. We baked a cake, and we had music and candles, and then when Daddy came home we buried the moth in the window-box. I was so happy.'

'Because of the moth?'

'Because of you. You and Daddy. My cosy life, so safe. You asked me what I want. I want that feeling back.'

'Oh, Isla . . .'

'I don't know what to do. I want you to tell me what to do . . . Because I am responsible for these two little people, and they are going to get hurt, and I don't want that.' She sighs. 'I want you to make it all go away. Because you are my mother, and that is what mothers do.'

'But you are an adult.' Isla raises her chin defiantly. 'Don't look at me like that. You know what I mean. I can't repair your relationships with Richard and Granna, I can't give you Jack. I can't even tell you I think you should *be* with Jack, if that's what you want. They're your actions, your choices.'

'All I ever wanted,' says Isla, her voice trembling dangerously, 'was a normal family. And when I had it . . .'

'It wasn't enough. I know.' If Callie had stayed, if she had raised her daughter herself, would she have taken her in her arms now? Isla's face is in shadow, but she is almost certainly crying. Callie clears her throat. 'You can stay as long as you want, you know. I can't turn back time, or take away what has happened, but I can give you a physical haven, at least, while you work out what you want to do. It's something, isn't it? Isla, isn't it?' she repeats when her daughter fails to respond.

'Yes,' says Isla. 'It is.'

That night, Callie does help Isla to bed, pulling back covers and closing shutters while Isla undresses.

'Stay and talk a bit?' asks Isla. She lies curled against her pillows and pats the mattress beside her.

'You should sleep,' says Callie, but she sits down anyway, pulling a spare blanket around her shoulders.

'Do you think Grandpapa knew about Louis?' asks Isla.

'I'm sure he did.'

'Did you?'

'I knew a bit.' She smiles at Isla's look of surprise. 'My godmother. Nancy. She took me out for a drink on my eighteenth birthday and ended up reminiscing.'

'What did she say?'

'Not a lot. Enough.'

'Did it feel strange?'

Callie shrugs. 'Mainly it felt – it *feels* – like something that happened a long time ago.'

'Do you think it was wrong, me and Jack? Really badly wrong, I mean?'

'*There is nothing good or bad, but thinking makes it so,*' quotes Callie.

'Mum . . .'

'I don't think right or wrong comes into it. I think it sounds marvellous, in a way. But rather devastating as well, no?'

'Why do you suppose Granna told Richard?'

Callie frowns. 'That's anybody's guess.'

They all telephone over the next few days. Callie fields the call from Bella.

'I'd forgotten how much she infuriates me,' she says afterwards.

'What did she say?'

'She couldn't understand why you were here. I said that you had nowhere else to go.'

'But did she say why she did it?'

'Not really. She came out with some mumbo-jumbo about how you weren't happy and how obnoxious Richard is and how she thought it was for the best. I told her I knew about Jack, and also about these memoirs of hers.'

'Oh!' Isla bites her lip. 'I don't know if those were meant to be confidential.'

'They're memoirs, aren't they?' says Callie irritably. 'She *wants* people to know. Either that or she hasn't thought them through. Which to be frank is highly likely. *Anyway,* she said that in that case if I knew all that then I would understand. She wouldn't say any more.'

'Did you tell her about Richard?'

Callie nods.

'What did she say?'

'Nothing at first. Then, when I elaborated, she cried.'

'Oh.' Isla has never seen Bella cry. She is shaken by the thought. Then, as if to remind herself, she touches her hand to her face. Remembers the last night she spent next to Richard, when everything hurt – her bruised pelvis, her grazed cheekbone, the dark bruise around her eye. The sense of betrayal. So Bella has cried, has she?

'Good,' says Isla.

The conversation with Richard when he calls later the same day is brief but draining.

'I need to know what you want to do.'

'About what?'

'What do you think?'

It has not occurred to Isla yet that she needs to *do* anything. So far, just coming here has felt like an end in itself.

'I need to get better,' she tells him.

'You're not sick.'

'We both need time to think.'

'I miss the children.'

For a moment, she feels sorry for him. Again, she reaches up to feel the swollen contour of her face.

'Maybe if you hadn't run away, we could have discussed this sensibly,' says Richard.

'Maybe if you hadn't hit me, I wouldn't have run away.'

'You provoked me.'

'You tried to rape me.'

'You're being melodramatic.'

'I hate it when you say that.'

'*I hate it when you say that.*'

'Fuck off.' She hangs up. He calls back immediately. She stares at the ringing phone until Callie comes in from the garden to pick it up.

'It's Richard,' says Callie. Isla shakes her head. Hears, as if in a dream, Callie tell Richard that now is not a good time. Callie calling the children. Beth chattering to her father. Marcus refusing to. *I should move. I should put on a show, tell Marcus to speak to his father, be a role model, an adult, a mother.* But when she tries to get off her chair, she finds that she can't move.

The call from Jack is the worst because just the sound of his voice sends her heart into orbit.

'I got your number from Bella,' he tells her.

'Where are you?'

'London. I couldn't stay in Dorset.' He sounds strained. 'What happened to the family holiday?'

'Richard had to work.' The lie rolls out automatically. She crushes the telephone against her ear to feel closer to him. 'We came here instead.'

Silence, followed by a soft laugh. 'You could have come back to Marshwood.'

'We could have.' She tries to smile.

'I wanted to let you know I'm going back to Bosnia. And to say I'm sorry, for when we parted, for the things I said.'

'It doesn't matter.' Her voice feels thick. Her hands on the receiver shake. 'That's good, Jack. That you're going back to Bosnia, I mean.'

'I could change my flight . . .'

'Don't . . .'

'If you want me to. I could come out and . . .'

'Good luck, Jack.' She only just manages to squeeze out the words before hanging up. And then she bursts into tears.

She had not anticipated the pain of being without him. Now that he has gone her rebellious mind, scorning any notion of worthwhile sacrifice, throws up a kaleidoscope of memories – the shadows in Clement's workshop, dancing naked on Pater Noster, his hand on the small of her back as he slept, the feeling she had when she was with him of being gloriously, exuberantly alive. In the short time they were together she never envisaged a real future with him, but now her imagination takes off on flights of fancy she does little to control and presents her with visions too tempting to resist. Jack by her side in Callie's garden, Jack walking with her in the mountains, Jack in her bed. Jack and Isla with time for each other, nights spent in each other's arms, days lying together with no reason to get up, years living together, growing old together, Jack as her lover, Jack as her husband, Jack as the father of a future child . . . The visions – they are stronger than daydreams – provide their own kind of happiness. Sometimes she imagines him now in Bosnia, picking up the trail of Elena's grandfather, and she dislikes herself for the stab of jealousy she feels for the dead woman. Easier to ignore the fact that she has no future with him, that he has demons to face alone, that she has decisions to take which she cannot allow him to affect. Easier to let her visions seduce her, and to let her imagination rule.

The children have adapted quickly to their new setting. For the first few days after their arrival, undeterred by local custom or change of climate, more for her own sake than for theirs, she tried to keep a close watch on them, insisting that they follow the same routine as at home, punctuating their days with an implacable succession of feeding and dressing, grooming and washing which helped her keep the illusion of control. Gradually, though, she has given up and the sweet wildness of summer in the mountains has claimed them. They live half naked, their bodies turning nut brown in the sun, their hair bleached white, their sandalled feet permanently black with earth and dust. Just a month ago, she thinks, she walked with them on the beach in

Dorset and thought of them as her glittering jewels. Now even their beauty does not touch her. She goes through the motions of mothering, distributes affection, reads and listens to stories, organizes walks and expeditions, but feels nothing but an overwhelming urge to weep which is surpassed only by her need to sleep.

Callie, growing impatient, suggests outings to break the monotony of their days.

'We could drive down to the Alhambra,' she says a week into their stay. 'Make a day of it.'

'We're fine here, aren't we?'

'Maybe the children would like to do something different.'

'Maybe . . .' Isla tries to muster interest in the idea. 'It's an awfully long way.'

'But you can't just keep on doing *nothing*!' pleads Callie. 'Darling, I know . . . I mean I don't *know* but I think I can understand what you're going through. When your father died . . .'

'Really, Mum, I'm fine. I just need a little time to think.'

'That's the problem. Thinking isn't going to help you. You can think your whole life away. You have to *do* something.'

'I will.' Isla's mind is already wandering, away from this conversation and back to Jack. They do not go to the Alhambra, or the coast, or even down to the next village. The days succeed each other, uniformly blue.

Isla's bruises fade, her cuts and grazes heal. Richard's telephone calls grow more frequent and more pressing. Callie, after her first burst of enthusiasm for her new grandmotherly status, begins to show signs of wanting to get back to her painting. Even the children grow bored with their mountain idyll. Isla knows that she cannot hide for ever, that she has a life in England waiting to be picked up, but she also fears that to move forward will mean to let go of Jack, and she is not ready for this yet.

Sleep is best for finding him. Awake, she is alarmed to note that her memories of him are already unclear, but asleep they are physical. On another perfect afternoon in the last week of August, with the air shimmering in the heat, Isla sits in a deckchair in the shade and lets conscious thought abandon her. His lips on hers, the warmth of his body, his smell . . . If she focuses hard enough, she can *feel* them . . . A soft breeze picks up, carrying the scent of lavender from the bushes massed behind her chair. Honey-bees swarm over its flower heads, their steady humming pleasant and soporific. The sensations of the afternoon are melting into impressions of Jack, his body warm beside hers, his breath caressing her bare skin. As she gives in to sleep, he rushes to meet her and her face relaxes into a smile.

'Marcus caught a baby lizard.'

Her brain gropes wildly for an anchor as Beth's voice jolts her from sleep.

'He says he wants to keep it but I don't think he should.'

Beth is glaring at her through a tangled mass of hair. In plastic flip-flops, her brother's cast-off shorts and a grubby crocheted bikini top bought at a local market, she looks mildly neglected but adorable.

'Wake *up*,' she insists.

Isla heaves herself out of her chair. Her head swims as she stands up. She remembers that she has not yet eaten today, and puts a hand out to steady herself before following Beth across the parched yellow grass towards the corner of shade where Marcus sits cross-legged on the ground.

The lizard turns out to be exquisite, with scales of silvery blue and eyes the colour of amber. It sits stock still in the palm of Marcus' hand, the rapidly beating pulse at its throat the only indication that it is alive. Isla crouches down beside Marcus to admire it.

'I caught it,' whispers Marcus. His eyes are shining. 'You can't get the big ones, they're too clever and too quick. I'm going to keep it in a box and feed it flies.'

The lizard, perhaps sensing distraction, makes a hasty bid for freedom, but Marcus is ready and catches it as it leaps from his palm. Isla can just make it out, twitching helpless between his cupped hands. A lump rises to her throat at the sight.

'That'll be nice,' she nods. 'How will you catch the flies?'

'I've thought of that. I'm going to pick them off the sticky fly-catcher in the kitchen.'

'Gross.' Beth pouts in disgust.

'Don't you think,' asks Isla, 'that the lizard would prefer live flies?'

'Some of them are still moving on that sticky thing, you know,' says Marcus. 'It's a very slow death.'

'But they wouldn't be whole, would they?' persists Isla. 'If you peeled them off the sticky thing. Their wings might come off or something.' She is overcome by an unexpected desire to giggle and bites the inside of her cheeks to maintain her composure.

'You think I should release it,' says Marcus glumly.

'If you love something . . .' begins Isla.

'. . . set it free,' he finishes with a mournful sigh.

'It's scared,' declares Beth. 'Also, you're kind of squashing it.'

'When you've released it,' says Isla, 'we can walk down to the bar and I'll buy you a Coke and some cakes to celebrate.'

'Coke?' says Beth. 'Really?'

Even Marcus is won over by the prospect of forbidden treats. He opens his cupped hands on the ground. The trembling lizard raises its miniature head, blinks once then vanishes. The children cheer it on. Isla, to her surprise, finds herself joining in.

They take their time over their drinks, seated beneath the ancient chestnut trees which spread their shade over the tables set outside the village bar. When the last sip has been drunk and the last crumbs eaten, they make their way slowly back up the hill. The late afternoon sun is merciless, and they pause in the shade of a whitewashed wall to catch their breath. From where they stand they have a perfect view of the valley and the mountains. The sky is still a bright cerulean blue, the scent of thyme wafts towards them from the nearby scrub, the valley glints silver in the shade. In the distance they can just make out snow on the higher peaks.

'It's just like Marshwood,' says Beth.

Marcus snorts. 'It's so *not* like Marshwood,' he says.

'Yes it is.' Beth turns to Isla. 'Isn't it?'

'I know what you mean,' smiles Isla. 'Like on the terrace. The same feeling.'

'Exactly.'

'I'd like to go home soon,' says Beth. 'I love it here, but I miss Daddy.'

Marcus has squatted by the road to examine the flattened remains of a foolhardy toad. 'Look,' he says. 'You can see its webbed feet and everything. Can I keep it? It *is* dead.'

'But still kind of yucky, don't you think?' asks Isla. Marcus' mouth sets in a mutinous line. 'I'm not even sure you could scrape it off the tarmac.'

'I thought Dad might like to see it.'

'Your father?' Why is it so surreal to hear Richard

referred to in this context? Surely it is a normal thing for a small boy to want to do, to share an interesting – if disgusting, she thinks with a grimace – discovery with his father? She realizes with sadness that the unreality of the remark stems from the fact that this is the first time she has heard Marcus mention his father since they arrived here. 'Do you miss Daddy too?' she asks softly.

Marcus, it turns out, has not finished surprising her today. 'No, I don't,' he says vehemently. 'I hate him.'

Isla catches him as he bursts into tears, his head buried in her neck. 'I don't mean it,' he cries. 'I do hate him, but I love him too.'

Old MacDonald had a toad,
  ee i ee i o.
They need her. This is the point, thinks Isla, singing silly made-up songs on the walk back to Callie's along the dusty road. Her children need her, and it's time to go home.
  And the toad went splat, carols Beth.
  The toad went splat,
  Here a splat, there a splat, everywhere a splat splat.
Even Marcus laughs. They spill into Callie's garden arm in arm, pushing and shoving through the gate, and Isla wonders, with something like amazement, whether things may not, after all, be all right.

Callie is excited this evening. She sloped off to her

studio after lunch and stayed there until Isla called out as they left for the bar, at which point she moved to the terrace. No easel today but a sketchbook in which she has been drawing furiously all afternoon. She can sense the change in Isla as soon as she and the children return from the bar. She is leaving, of course. Callie feels a pinch of sadness even as she tells herself that this is a good thing. No more trying to find time to paint. No more interruptions. Life back to normal, just as she has carefully constructed it.

The children decide to go in search of their baby lizard again. Isla throws herself into her armchair on the terrace.

'So,' says Callie. 'You've decided to leave.'

'How did you know?'

'I could tell from your footsteps.'

'I don't know what I'm going to do. I don't know if Richard and I can stay together, but I guess we have to try, right? And the children want to go home.'

Callie's fingers, itching for a pencil, drum against her sketchbook. Isla does not notice. *This is not about you,* thinks Callie. *This is about Isla. Only Isla.*

'I mean, I know I did wrong, but do you think I should forgive him?'

'I think,' says Callie absently, 'that forgiveness is really a matter of personal choice.' She can't contain herself any longer. 'I've had some ideas for a new painting.'

'Mum . . .'

'Look.'

Isla looks and sees, roughly drawn out in pencil, a familiar scene. In the bottom left-hand corner stand the chairs and table of the terrace, looking out onto the walled garden where two scantily clad children play, crouched with a watering-can over a bed of flowers. Beyond the garden the mountains loom, kissed by the setting sun. They still dominate the picture, but the furniture, the children, the flowers will temper it, imbue it with an intimacy against which the landscape will look all the more dramatic.

Callie explains what she has been trying to capture. It has to do, she says, with grace. 'These evenings are full of it, I think. Time stands still, and yet the moment is so transitory. I realize now that that is exactly what I have been wanting to paint, but until now I've not known how to. I hope it works.'

Isla hands back the sketch-pad. 'I think it'll be beautiful, Mum.'

'Ah, well . . .' Callie sighs fatalistically as she puts the pad away, but she looks pleased. 'If it works, I have plans for a whole series – four, I think. Morning, noon, afternoon and dusk. But do you see? This fortnight, you here, the children . . . I knew there was a reason for you coming.'

Isla tries to ignore the hurt of this remark, which Callie follows with a disarming kiss, cheerfully pronouncing the words Isla longed to hear on the night she arrived and which she now almost believes. 'It will be all right, you'll see. Everything will be all right.'

The children's game has turned to tears, and routine calmly takes over from conversation. Isla gathers Beth in her arms, Callie takes Marcus by the hand, and together they make their way back into the house. A sore knee is kissed, a dispute settled. Outside, the sky explodes again in its nightly routine, bathing the mountains in colour before donning its mantle of indigo. A herd of goats descends from higher pastures towards the village, where tourists are ordering their first drinks of the evening. Inside the house, supper is prepared in the kitchen and cool sheets folded back on beds. There are no illusions. Soon Isla will leave and this brief interlude in their so separate lives may never be repeated. But for now teeth are brushed, stories told. As lamps are lit against the falling of night, something very like love, serene and unperturbed, fills the house with peace.

'Nowhere else to go.' A month after speaking to Callie, this is still what hurts Bella the most.

Today she is attacking the forest of nettles which has advanced, unnoticed and unchecked, on the ruins of the old summerhouse. *You have given me a haven.* That was what Louis said. She can hear him now, his voice ringing with sincerity, sitting on the terrace on one of those balmy evenings. *A haven.* All that Clement ever wanted, his life's work, building a home, a place of safety. Somewhere to live at ease, to bring up children, to assemble friends. A place to reflect its owner, stability, permanence. *Nowhere.*

She hacks at the nettles with a pair of giant secateurs, cuts them right down to the ground and rakes them into a big pile. She fetches the wheelbarrow and begins to heap it with dead nettles. Her back hurts from the exertion, her head aches but still she carries on, gathering them in her gloved hands before throwing them into the barrow.

She removes her gloves when she has finished in order to push back the strands of hair which have escaped their clasps and cling to the sweat of her forehead. A lone nettle is shaken loose as she begins to wheel the barrow up the path, tumbling in a slow, graceful arc towards the ground. Bella's reaction is automatic. Forgetting her discarded gloves, she lets go the barrow and lunges forward to catch the nettle as it falls. For a short moment, she feels no pain. Then her closed palm begins to burn. She drops the short green stem and starts to cry.

It is Kitty who finds her sobbing by the summer-house, holding a can of paraffin with which she douses the offending nettle patch. She takes her old friend by the shoulders and leads her gently back to the terrace where she sits her down before returning indoors to fetch cushions for her back and vinegar for her hand.

Dear Kitty. With her gaggle of children and grandchildren and her peaceful contented life, never questioning, often overlooked, always giving. She returns from the kitchen again, this time with mugs of hot sweet tea. Bella, shaken by her unaccustomed tears, tells her about Isla, Jack and the conversation with Richard.

'I didn't tell you before because I'm worried that I may have gone slightly mad,' she admits.

'I prefer the word *confused*,' says Kitty with inhabitual wryness. 'It happens to the best of us. In fact I was going to ask you when I arrived. What *were* you doing with that paraffin?'

'I was going to burn the nettle patch.'

'Are you sure, dear, that that is altogether wise?'

'I don't know.' Bella raises her hands in a gesture of defeat. 'I mean, look.'

Kitty looks.

'The wilderness is taking over. A sort of *blitzkrieg*. I shall have to take on a gardener, but who?' She pushes her hair back angrily. 'The last one spent his whole time drinking tea and whining about his wife. She left him for her chiropractor. I didn't know we *had* chiropractors, but apparently there are *two*. In the village!'

'I should think chiropractors would be jolly useful for a gardener,' says Kitty brightly, then adds quickly, 'though I can absolutely see why yours might not be so keen.'

305

'None of them know what they're doing any more, *and* they charge a fortune. Really, it's too bad!' Bella casts a petulant glare over the terrace.

The truth – she has known it for some time, even if she will only now admit it – is that a gardener, even a miraculously competent one, unchallenged by a wandering wife and the light hands of the improbable chiropractors, would be hard pushed to know where to start. Months of full-time work are needed here. She does a mental check of her land: the orchard, where plum and apple trees are rotting, unpruned and diseased, yielding less fruit every year. The kitchen garden, once so bountiful, where mint and lemon balm have triumphed over every other species. Her mind wanders to disused flowerbeds now home to nettles and brambles, and to tangled, gloomy hedges, before returning to the terrace which lies before her now. The beds that border it contain only a few valiant rose bushes, struggling with the end of summer. She surveys the paving stones, searching for one which is not cracked or slippery with weed and moss, but there are none. Behind her, one of the uninsurable windows slams, caught in a sudden gust of wind. Bella turns to look at it, and suddenly she knows exactly what she has to do.

She tells the others what she has decided over bridge at Kitty's later that afternoon.

'You can't surely mean that. Selling Marshwood

because of a patch of nettles. After everything you've put up with until now. Made *us* put up with.'

'Esther dear, it's not really because of the nettles. I think we should consider the nettles a metaphor. Or a catalyst,' adds Nancy hurriedly, not quite sure herself which they are. 'I think it's marvellous news.'

'Yes, well. Seen sense at last,' snorts Esther, though it strikes all her friends that there is a little less swagger in her manner, a little more gentleness than in the past.

'But are you sure, dear? Are you really sure you're sure?' asks Kitty. 'I know how you felt this morning, but do you think, perhaps, you need a little more time . . .'

'Darling, you're not helping,' cuts in Nancy. 'We have to be practical. Now, Esther, is that little cottage of yours still for sale? The one Jack and Isla liked which caused all that trouble?'

'Rub it in, why don't you,' grumbles Esther. 'No, it isn't. It's been sold.'

'Bugger!'

'Nancy!'

'I'm sorry, Kitty, but really, bugger! It sounded *perfect*. Esther, why are you grinning like that, like a demented gibbon?'

'Because,' beams Esther, '*that* cottage has been sold, but as luck would have it, old Mrs Williams across the courtyard died last week. And her cottage is an awful lot nicer!'

'Esther!'

'Kitty, darling, you must try not to be so easily shocked. At your age, it's a little contrived. This is splendid news. Mrs Williams' cottage sounds like just the thing. When is it going up for sale?'

Bella sits back and allows Nancy to take control, turning her spur-of-the-moment decision into reality. Nancy has always been a natural organizer, and she swings into action once again, bringing out the local telephone directory to compile a list of estate agents. The exhilaration Bella has felt all day since making her decision, is beginning to give way to worry that she might be making a mistake. She is seized with the irrational fear that once she sells the house, she herself will disintegrate and there will be nothing left.

'I'm frightened,' she admits later when she drives Nancy home. It is, for Bella, an admission on the scale of a confession. 'Nothing felt more appealing this morning than making a fresh start, but now I'm frightened I can't do it, that if I do this I am just going to disappear.'

Nancy considers her gravely for a moment, then shakes her head. 'No you won't. We won't let you. Come on, Belle. At our age? We *know* it can only get better.' She smiles wryly at her friend and then, before they get sucked into conversation, reaches out, list in hand, to start on her round of calls to estate agents.

Callie telephones to give Isla the news.

'She was nervous about telling you herself. I said I

would. I can't believe you haven't actually spoken to her since you got back.'

'I can't believe she's actually selling.'

'Only if we give our consent.'

'And did you?'

'Of course.'

'Don't you *care*?'

'A twinge.'

'No more than that?'

'Darling, my life is here.'

'Hmm.' A pause, as Isla digests this.

'I was thinking you ought to go down and see her. Make sure everything's going to plan. I mean I'd love to go myself but I'm so busy . . .'

'I can't go to Marshwood now. Richard would kill me.'

'How *is* Richard?' Callie's voice drops a conspiratorial octave.

A muted shuffle from the door behind Isla reveals that Richard is listening.

'Fine,' declares Isla. 'Everything's fine. I have to go.'

Isla has been back for over a fortnight now and Richard and she have yet to have a proper conversation. They have perfected the art of circling around each other, contriving – by working late, by a devotion to superfluous housework, above all by paying excessive attention to the children – never to be alone together.

As long as they do not mention what has happened, as long as they do not actually talk to each other, there is a possibility that everything will indeed be *fine*. But Callie's telephone call has coincided with an unforeseen event. Minutes before their conversation, neighbours have called round on their way to the park, their own children and a new puppy in tow. Would Marcus and Beth like to join them on the puppy's first walk? Marcus and Beth did not hesitate. By the time Isla hangs up, the children have gone and with them the absolute safeguard of their parents' civility.

'Granna wants to sell Marshwood.'

They sit opposite each other at the kitchen table, the remains of the interrupted family lunch between them, and she tears a slice of bread into ever smaller pieces, trying to focus on what this sentence means to her. Selling Marshwood – it should signify so much, and yet confused fragments of other issues cloud her mind. Callie's indifference, Bella's nervousness. The fact that Richard sits before her, his face closed but his chin jutting forward as it always does when he is spoiling for a fight.

'Presumably you need to consent?'

'Yes. Though I can't see how I can object. Not if . . .'

'What?'

'I was going to say, not if we can't afford to keep it.'

'Is that some sort of dig?'

And there it is, the first crack in the ice of their politeness. Isla tries, feebly, to ignore it.

'Of course not.'

'Only I don't see why, on top of everything else, I should subsidize your rendezvous with your lover.'

'Richard . . .'

'I heard what you said to your mother. *Richard'll kill me if I go to Marshwood.*'

'I didn't mean . . .'

'Do you know what gets me?' He leans forward, his guarded position the mirror image of her own, his face and voice tight with a control which his words belie. 'What gets me is how you could do it to the children.'

'The children knew nothing about it. They still know nothing about it.'

'No, but they could have. I don't suppose it entered your head that they might have guessed what was going on, might have *caught you at it.*'

'No,' she admits. 'It didn't.'

'I don't suppose you thought for a minute what a betrayal it was of them, of me, of everything we stand for.'

'I didn't,' she repeats evenly. 'I thought about me. Just for once, I did what *I* wanted to do.'

'Selfish bitch.'

'What did you call me?'

'You heard.'

She is shaking. She hates herself for shaking. She takes a deep breath to steady herself. 'I'm going upstairs,' she says.

'Afraid of what I might say?'

'Afraid of what you might *do*.'

'What's that supposed to mean?'

He looks so angry, standing before her now, his fists balled up like Marcus' when he is trying not to cry. Angry, and uncertain.

'Let's drop it, Richard.'

She flinches as he steps forward to block her way out of the kitchen, but she meets his eyes with a steely look.

'If you hit me again . . .' He lets her pass, but roars up the stairs as she climbs away from the kitchen towards the living-room, giving up all pretence of control. 'That's right, run away, Isla. Run away to your lover and his big dick and forget about the rest of us.'

And now something snaps in Isla too.

'I've never forgotten about the children!' she yells. 'Ever! Why do you think I finished it? Why do you think I told him to leave, to go back to Bosnia to find his dead girlfriend's grandfather? It wasn't for you, you bloody . . . you bloody *psychopath*!'

Oh God this isn't me. This monstrous woman hurling abuse at her husband. This is not me . . . Richard is still shouting, on and on, and all she can think is how angry he is, how hurt, and all because of her.

'. . . it's such a fucking cliché, that's what gets me. Husband goes on business trip, bored housewife jumps on first available male . . .'

Is it worse for him? My bruises have faded and somewhere I understand his reaction. Whereas I don't think he understands, I don't think he understands at all . . .

'Oh Richard, I'm so unhappy. Richard, I'm so lonely! And all the time treating me like some sort of leper in bed while you're giving it out somewhere else. It makes me sick.'

But then he never tried to understand. Not once, when I tried to explain. Oh God, he's so bitter . . .

'I have to go to Marshwood . . . Poor Granna . . . I wouldn't be surprised if you'd planned it. You and the witch. You got her to tell me, because you were too afraid to do it yourself. Yes, that's right. And your mother too . . .'

. . . what have I done? Oh God, oh God, what have I done? Guilt, hitherto held in abeyance by the memory of his violence, hits her like whiplash, and at this moment she knows that there is no going back.

'. . . *do you read Pepys? You mean you actually go out and earn money? Why then you can pay for my crumbling fucking medieval lifestyle . . .*'

A chasm has opened at her feet, pulling her down, and she knows that everything she has endured so far – the slow choking of the last few years, the pain of losing Marshwood, leaving Jack – are nothing compared to the imminent disintegration of her marriage.

'There's nothing left, is there?' she asks when Richard finally stops. 'Nothing but hurt and mistrust and years of living alongside each other not knowing what's going on inside.'

'What do you mean?'

'That's all there is between us. The children, like some sort of smokescreen, but other than them . . . there's nothing left, is there?'

She doesn't want to say it, but the words are waiting, fully formed, pushing against her lips, demanding to be spoken. She tries to swallow them. They burst through unheeding.

'I think we should split up.'

'What?'

'You heard.'

His face crumples. In the few seconds before he speaks, she lets herself believe that the words, after all, may be retrievable.

'You're just saying that.'

'Richard.' She speaks gently, as if he were a child. 'Have you heard yourself? You hit me and you haven't even apologized. You're ranting at me but I don't think you've even stopped to ask yourself what drove me to do what I did. I'm not trying to blame you. But it's like you're not even trying. I don't think either of us is.'

'But I don't want . . . that's not what I wanted.'

'What do you want?'

Silence. A sigh. The impression that somehow every bone in his body has collapsed on itself as he grows visibly smaller before her eyes. 'I don't know,' he admits.

So. No more pretending. Tonight Richard sleeps in the spare room. Tomorrow they begin to unfold the logistics of their separation, the framework of which, they have wearily agreed, will be *whatever is best for the children*. They both know that in the short term this will mean Marcus and Beth remaining in the house with their mother, and they also recognize how unfair this is on Richard. They can neither of them see any other solution.

She looks in on him on her way up to bed. He lies fully clothed in the middle of the pristine spare room bed.

'It always did feel like a hotel room,' she says sadly.

'Spare rooms always do, however hard you try.' He does not sound as hostile as before. He speaks his next words to the ceiling and she has to crane forward to hear what he says.

'What I did, Isla . . . I didn't know I could do something like that. It scared me.'

Isla comes to sit on the end of the bed. She would like to lie beside him, but surely given what they have just decided this would not be right? Instead she lays an awkward hand upon his ankle, a part of his body she realizes curiously she has never held before.

'I didn't think I could either,' she says soberly. 'Somewhere I never thought it *was* me doing it, even though I felt more myself than I have done for years. I wanted it to be something different. Outside reality and time, you know? Something that existed only of itself, something without consequences. An isolated act.'

He turns onto his side with his back to her, and when he sighs she feels the last remnants of his attachment to her leave his body with his breath.

'There's no such thing as an isolated act, Isla. Everything we do has consequences. Everything.'

'Even when they don't seem real?'

'Even then.'

On the night he leaves home, she cannot bring herself to lie in their old bed. Instead, she curls up on the sofa in the study, then jumps up again when she remembers how in the early days of their marriage they used to make love there. He is present everywhere, and yet all around her there are signs of his absence, empty spaces on bookshelves, in wardrobes, on the bathroom shelf. She goes from room to room, stalked by Richard's reproachful shadow. She can almost hear him saying *look, remember? We were happy* . . . She escapes him eventually in the kitchen – *her* room, warm, messy, crammed with memories of children's meals and sticky fingers, of afternoons baking cakes and painting pictures. She sits at the table until dawn, when she finally creeps up to bed, too shattered to care any more, to be woken what feels like minutes later by Marcus informing her that it is time for school.

'We've had breakfast,' he says. 'Me and Beth have both

had Rice Krispies, but now Beth is saying she wants you to do her hair. Also, we're late.'

It is a quarter to nine. *Great*, thinks Isla. *My first day on my own, and already I can't cope.* She hauls herself out of bed, pulls on yesterday's clothes and stumbles downstairs to the hall where Beth stands waiting for her, wearing an approximation of her school uniform, attempting to drag a brush through her tangled mop of hair.

'Where's Daddy?' she asks brightly.

This, then, is their new reality. Gaps in the fabric of the house, half-empty closets, a less cluttered bathroom, a depleted CD collection. Beth, sturdy in the daytime but in Isla's bed every night. Marcus in an angry sulk again, this time with his mother, his father's status having been elevated by his departure, punishing her by refusing to eat the meals she prepares, by withholding good-night kisses and information about his school day. She grows used to the constant close companionship of the guilt which helps her keep up a stream of mad, bright chatter with her bewildered children, manically cooking and arranging activities after school, swimming, playdates, picnics, anything to keep them out of the house, anything really to avoid having to sit still and actually *think*. One night a week and every other weekend she hands them over to their father almost with relief, the sorrow she feels at their parting her penance for their smashed lives.

And during these absences, as during the school day, she works.

This work is the only positive to have come out of the mess of their lives, and it has been brought about improbably by the children's school PTA committee. Isla's bruised face, Richard's departure, the cancelled holiday in Corsica . . . all, somehow – how? – is widely known.

'We girls must stick together!' Hilda Robertson, the matronly Chair of the committee, swept down on Isla on the first day of school.

'No, really,' protested Isla from the depths of her self-flagellation. 'In a way, it was all my fault.'

Hilda swept aside all notion of Isla's blame with an extravagant sweep of the hand.

'Playground!' she barked, getting excited. 'Pergola, nursery, swings! New space! Architect!'

'Right,' said Isla cautiously.

'Said you'd do it,' concluded Hilda. 'Saw what you did with your own house, jolly impressive. Thought you might enjoy the work.'

The PTA's championing of Isla's affairs has not ended with this first project, the (unpaid) planning of a new play area in a previously under-used part of the school's grounds. A few weeks into term, a timid parent approached her about a complete house renovation.

'I can't afford a real architect,' she admitted. 'But Hilda said you were good.'

'I'll do it,' said Isla. 'We can work on a payment schedule later.'

These projects are a far cry from her early dreams of splendour, but as soon as she sits down to work, the rest of the world slips away. Suddenly her days are filled: she has to test playground equipment, assess the shock absorbency of rubber surfacing, source eco-friendly wooden flooring, battle with planners, negotiate with builders. At the heart of this, a new excitement grows, the realization that she can *do* this, that she is good at it, that she can build on these two projects to find more work. The pleasure she finds in it is marred only by the thought that perhaps she ought to feel more guilty about this too – deriving happiness from something so external to the people she loves.

She has spoken to Bella only once since returning from Spain, a strained, most unBella-like conversation in which her grandmother asked her directly for her permission to sell Marshwood.

'Isla? Are you still there?' Bella's voice was uncharacteristically timid.

The only way Isla can cope, aside from telling herself she has brought this on herself, aside from working every hour she can and obsessively pretending nothing is wrong, is not to let anything touch her.

She stood at the kitchen counter, telephone wedged between shoulder and chin, still wielding the knife with which she had been chopping onions for supper as jumbled images crashed through her mind. A collection of hideous gardening hats, a dog leaping for a stick, two children running wild, a fox's muzzle twitching in the early morning, a sea of paper-thin letters . . . It took a physical effort to push them away. She gritted her teeth and hit the palm of her hand, hard, on the solid beech worktop.

'Isla?'

Onwards and upwards. No man is an island. Stiff upper lip. Truisms poured into Isla's mind, blocking out the need for rational thought and bringing with them an inappropriate propulsion towards hysterical laughter.

'Isla?'

'I'm here.'

'Will you come down soon?' This tone of voice, hesitant and a little afraid, was one Isla would learn to recognize – as though she frightened people, or as if they were afraid of hurting her. 'Only it's been ages.'

Half a day: morning dew, a blackbird singing, the tangled hair of a wakeful child, a broken camera – countless broken hearts – the furious breath of her husband against her cheek, the discovery of a betrayal still unexplained. Less than a day. Twelve hours which changed the course of her life. Twelve hours to set against a marriage and the years to come. Go down to Marshwood? *Talk?* Isla's tremendous guilt ebbed just enough to remind her that she was also angry, and that much of her anger was still directed at Bella.

'I think,' Bella battled on bravely, 'that perhaps I need to explain myself, why I acted as I did.'

'I can't for now,' replied Isla shortly. 'I'm very busy. I'll come when things have settled down.'

Her curtness towards Bella – confused, frailer than she thinks, maddening Bella – has taken its place high on the list of things Isla reproaches herself for. Every morning since this conversation she tells herself that this will be the day when she calls her. She tells herself that she will drop the children off at school and that then, as her morning coffee is brewing, before she sits down at her new architect's table – an extravagance, but a necessary one, symbolic of her re-entry into the world of work – she will telephone Bella, and she will tell her . . . what? That she misses her? That she forgives her? The first is true, the second not. Better then, on the whole, to live as she is now, every day adding a new layer to her eggshell of protection, waiting for the rawness of her nerves to calm, trying to extract herself from the clutches of what has happened and turn towards the uncertain future.

The anxieties pushed back during the day assail her in the hours of darkness. Isla worries about the children and the effect of the separation on them, about Jack chasing demons in Bosnia, about Bella and Marshwood. She worries also – and this confuses her – about Richard, who has grown too thin and looks always drained and somehow grey. His invisible contributions have come to the surface, a series of chores which bore her and which she previously took for granted, involving insurance premium renewals and the taking out of dustbins, hooks to be driven into walls and lights to be put out at night. She is surprised by how much she misses him. Sometimes, as an exercise, she pitches the two against each other: memories of Jack against memories of Richard. Her lover is shadowy, a recollection of brightness turned dim by the sourness of subsequent events. Her husband . . . In the weeks that follow their separation, her mind stretches further and further back, so that the reality of the man Richard has become is replaced by the ghost of the boy she married. It is not enough, she chides herself as she collapses into bed, the memory of a few years of passion, of a shared love for children and a life built together. Putting aside her guilt, she tries to remind herself of her unhappiness before meeting Jack, the times she cried herself to sleep and he did not notice, the times he dismissed all notion of her going back to work or having a life which did not directly involve him or the children. She tells herself that marriage cannot be reduced to this, a handful of good memories and a question of who does what around the house. And yet . . . she misses him.

Time drags and yet the year pushes relentlessly on. The clocks go back. Richard appears on her doorstep one evening to discuss plans for half-term.

'Half-term?'

'That would be the holiday between the summer and Christmas?' He half smiles.

'I know what half-term is.' Is he teasing her? What has happened in his life to make him so jolly?

'Then why ask? Look, are you going to keep me on the doorstep, or can I come in? Only it is still sort of my house too, and I'm cold.'

'Oh. Come in.' He bundles past her, blowing on his hands. She kicks the door shut, then feels childish and wishes she hadn't.

'I'll come straight to the point.' Their discussion takes place in the living-room. They are standing, avoiding the implications which sitting down might give of intimacy or a desire for a prolonged visit. 'I'd like to take them down to the New Forest.'

'What, for the whole time?'

'Yup.' Again, that little upbeat note. Why?

'But what about work?'

'What about it? I've got masses of holiday left to take. Summer didn't really happen for me this year, if you remember.'

Aha! The bitterness is back. Isla feels uncharitably relieved.

'I thought you'd be pleased. You're always saying how much work you have these days.'

'But for a whole week?'

'It's what happens, Isla, when parents divorce.' He

323

looks more than bitter now. Bleak. No . . . sort of *empty*, she decides.

'Divorce?'

'Isn't that where we're heading?'

'I . . .' She has not wanted to think about divorce. Divorce, with its lawyers and its intrusiveness, with its expense and carving up of lives, with its dictates and its finality. 'It's a big word,' she says at last.

'Isla.' He takes a step towards her and she, as if partnering him in a dance, takes a step back. She does not want him close to her, not with this expression he is now wearing. Not bleak, not weary but worse. *Hopeful*.

'You could come too.'

'No.'

His expression hardens.

'Whatever. I thought for the kids . . .'

'It would only confuse them.'

'Sure.'

'Also, you're right, I've got too much work,' she says crisply. 'And I agree, it's time we moved on and formalized things. I'll find a lawyer tomorrow.'

The last leaves have fallen from the lime trees in the street, and the geraniums in the window-boxes have shed their lingering flowers. Alone in her big house, Isla works on the revised plans for the house renovation. When they are as good as she thinks she can make them, she calls her client, only to discover that she too has gone away for half-term. And then, with no

324

work to do and no children to tend, with a steady rain falling outside, Isla unplugs all the telephones, takes to her bed and sleeps. She sleeps through Tuesday night until late on Wednesday morning, eats a bowl of children's cereal and goes back to bed, waking late in the afternoon, when she drinks two cups of tea in front of the television before going to bed again. She barely sees daylight for the whole week the children are away, but stays in her room with the curtains drawn, only getting up to go to the bathroom and to feed the cat when his protestations grow too loud. She does not read or listen to the radio. She only sleeps or waits for sleep.

At the beginning of the week, the thought of going out seemed undesirable. By the end it is terrifying. Now that Hallowe'en is over, London is gearing up for Christmas. It is a time of year Isla normally loves, a time for hearty cooking and planning parties, for new winter coats and buying chestnuts on the way home from school, not to eat – none of them enjoy the dry texture of roasted chestnuts – but because of the smell and the warmth which spreads from their paper bags through their woollen gloves. A time for hidden presents and white lies, for country walks at Marshwood and in the New Forest, pink cheeks and damp hair, roaring fires and endless cups of tea. As Isla sinks further into misery, she tells herself that Christmas without Marshwood is unthinkable: no bringing down of dusty boxes of decorations from the attic, no swearing at the Coven as she tries single-handedly to manoeuvre a giant tree into its traditional alcove under their contradictory directions, no drunken preparation of roast goose in the crumbling kitchen or random opening of Bella's unmarked presents on Christmas morning, no traditional post-lunch walk on Pater Noster, racing to the top to beat the falling dusk and catch a view of the valley, the village chimneys puffing contentedly, the sea a shimmer of silver, the moon already showing its pale face in the midwinter sky. No Richard, who was, she has to admit, always good about Christmas at Marshwood, never rising to the little barbed digs Bella could not resist shooting at him, the perfect guest, charming, urbane, even though the rest of the year they were at daggers drawn. Christmas without Richard will be strange as well. And without the children . . . No, that is not possible. Perhaps they can spend Christmas together, pretend. Perhaps for Christmas she will make an exception to her newly imposed rule of no holidays together and go to the New Forest, and perhaps afterwards she will take the children to Marshwood. Perhaps Bella will have organized a tree, and Callie will come too, and all the Coven will be there, cosily sipping sherry or whisky and ginger by a roaring fire. Perhaps Marshwood will be as she remembers it from her childhood, a blaze of lights, a muddle of dogs, Clement asleep in front of the fire, Jack's parents dropping in for a drink on Christmas Eve and Jack dragging her off for a surreptitious cigarette in the garden. Perhaps . . . She drifts back to sleep.

Jack is sitting on an outcrop of rock, tearing into a loaf of hard Spanish bread, the mountains behind him a blaze of gold and scarlet in the setting sun. She runs joyously towards him. Marcus and Beth are playing on the ground at the foot of his rock, and he drops them occasional crumbs which they feed to a giant lizard. She keeps running, and now she is calling out to them all, but nobody hears her and she realizes that she is no closer to them than when she started out. Even the lizard ignores her, which is all wrong, because shouldn't it already have fled? And then Jack looks up, and she breathes a sigh of relief as he stares straight at her, a sigh which becomes a scream when she sees the blood running from the perfect round bullet hole in his forehead. But now a plane is swooping down from the sky, and a young man wearing a red scarf stands on the wing and shouts down to Jack, inviting him to join him. And the children are scrambling up, begging to come too, but the young man laughs and says didn't they know? Only the dead are allowed to fly planes. And then they are all gone, even the lizard, and Richard is sitting on the rock, and at first she thinks his smile is one of triumph, but then she realizes that it is sad. He holds out his hand and says in Bella's voice, *let's go home.*

She is dragged from sleep by an insistent ringing but it takes her several minutes to realize that there is somebody at the front door. Her head spins when she stands. She pulls the curtains. It is still raining. She sighs, looks back at her bed. White sheets, duvet, pillows beckon temptingly. She turns away, glances at the ugly digital clock Richard has left behind and gasps with dismay when she realizes that it is past midday, and also that it is Friday.

The doorbell continues to ring.

'I'm *coming!*' she yells.

There's something wrong with me, she thinks as she runs down to the front door. *How could I lose a week?* A hysterical Leo almost trips her up at the foot of the stairs, twining reproachfully around her legs as she struggles with the keys.

'At bloody last!' Nancy, in impeccable vintage Burberry, marches into the hall, shaking a dripping umbrella. Kitty follows on her heels, looking outdated in heather-mix tweeds.

'I was sure you must be in,' she says as she kisses Isla. 'Because of the cat.'

'Did the taxi leave?' demands Nancy.

'Oh yes, dear. As soon as Isla opened the door.'

'Thank heavens for that. Thief. I won't tell you how much he charged us. Isla dear, may I use your loo?'

'On the landing,' says Isla faintly. 'First door on the right.'

'You're in pyjamas.' Kitty's smile is as kind as ever. 'You must be ill.'

'If you don't mind, I'll just run up and dress.'

She comes back down fifteen minutes later, showered and dressed, to find Nancy stretched out on the living-room sofa and no sign of Kitty.

'She went out to buy cat food,' says Nancy. 'And something for us. There was nothing to eat in the kitchen. No wonder you're so thin.'

'What are you doing here?'

'We've come to fetch you down to Marshwood, of course.'

'Why didn't you call?'

Nancy stares pointedly at the telephone socket. 'Oh.' Isla blushes. 'I unplugged it.'

'Belle's been calling you for days.'

'I've been ill.'

'As long as you're better now.'

Nancy glares at her. Isla looks down at her feet, feeling uncomfortably like a scolded schoolgirl.

'It's all she needs, to be worried about you. Have you any idea what she's going through at the moment?' demands Nancy. 'She's devastated at having to sell Marshwood.'

'Yes, well.' Isla scuffs the carpet with the end of her shoe. 'It's for the best in the long run.'

'That's as may be, but it's not the long run yet. And as if that weren't bad enough, now she *can't* sell.'

'Why not?'

'Because of the state of the house, what do you think? She's only had one real expression of interest so far, an American from Maine. He said the climate was just like home, but nobody's heard from him in weeks. Everyone else has run a mile. The estate agent is extremely pessimistic.'

'Can't she get a more cheerful one?'

'That's not the point. Things are bad, Isla. She was almost crying last night. All this rain . . . It's the roof, you see. That's when we decided. Kitty and I came up on the train, and Esther stayed to look after her. Oh look,' she points out of the window. 'Here comes Kitty now.'

Isla sighs and goes to open the door. Kitty bustles in, beaming. 'I found a dear little shop! Arabic. I've bought falafels, and hummus, and sweet little stuffed vine leaves, and tabbouleh and aubergines, and some lovely baklava for pudding. Isla, dear, have you packed? Oh and my goodness, we forgot the children! What are we going to do about them?'

'They're away,' says Isla with gritted teeth.

'Oh, what a relief! Then we can leave straight after lunch.'

Nancy smirks at Isla's look of silent mutiny. 'We'll take your car.'

'London's not what it used to be,' sighs Kitty less than an hour later as they negotiate their way through early rush hour traffic. 'It used to be so glamorous.'

'You used to think that *suit* was glamorous, darling,' drawls Nancy. 'Just because you had it made off Bond Street. London's always been seedy.'

'Actually,' says Isla, 'this is considered a very nice area.'

'Is it really?' Nancy peers through the misted-up window at the Chiswick roundabout. 'It looks terribly ugly.'

They have reached the motorway at last, and Isla frowns at the speedometer as she negotiates her way into the fast lane. 'Forty-five miles an hour,' she sighs. 'This is going to take hours.'

'We'd better call Belle,' says Kitty. 'Do you have a mobile telephone?'

'Sorry.'

'I thought all young people had them,' muses Nancy.

'Well, not me. We'll stop at a service station. I need to talk to Richard too.'

'When did you last speak to your grandmother?'

'Really, Nancy,' says Kitty. 'I don't think it's any of your business.'

'Not for a while.'

'And what did you talk about?'

'I rather agree with Kitty. I don't know that it's any of your business.'

'She won't talk about it either. So you haven't sorted things out.'

'No.' She has spoken curtly, in the efficient hard voice she hates but which has proven so useful at fending off unwanted questions. And then, because suddenly she feels angry, she carries on talking. 'We *didn't* talk about Richard. *Or* Jack. *Or* my grandfather, or Louis, or her insane behaviour last summer. I didn't want to talk about them, or it, and I still don't. So don't try to make me.'

'I wasn't going to.'

'Yes, you were.'

The road has cleared at last. Isla puts her foot down on the accelerator. In the passenger seat beside her, Nancy stares out of the window as they leave the last of the city behind. There are still streetlights here, each lamp a halo of muted orange which provides a brief illumination of the rain as they pass.

'All the same,' says Nancy. 'You really ought to talk about it.'

'I knew it. I knew you'd try to make me!'

'I think she's right,' says Kitty in a small voice from the back of the car. 'I mean, I know it's none of our business, but it might make you feel better to talk.'

'It's a grieving process, the end of an affair,' says Nancy, a touch too cosily for Isla's liking. 'And the end of a marriage too, of course. It's like a death. Actually, in your case, *two* deaths.'

332

'If you don't shut up,' says Isla in the voice she normally reserves for the children, 'I am going to stop the car and leave you by the side of the road.'

'You can't say that to me!'

'Give me one good reason.'

'We're *old*!'

'Not good enough.'

'You wouldn't dare,' grumbles Nancy.

'Watch me,' says Isla.

They stop at a service station and repair to the public telephones, where Nancy fails to get hold of Bella and Isla calls Richard from a pay phone.

'I don't know what time I'll be back on Sunday,' she says. 'I've been kidnapped by the Coven.'

'Excuse me?'

'Don't ask. It's to do with the sale.'

'The sale?'

'Of Marshwood.'

'Of course.'

She bristles at the note of tension in his voice. 'Don't be snide,' she says.

'I'm not!'

'Yes, you are.'

'No I'm not. I was going to say, I'm sorry. About Marshwood, having to sell and all that. I know how much it means to you.'

'Oh.' She does not know how to respond to this

unexpected bout of sympathy. 'Thanks,' she says with an attempt at graciousness.

'I'm sure you understand, I can't keep on indefinitely . . . especially the way things are now . . . well, I can't keep writing cheques. But I really *am* sorry. Isla?'

He always was kind, before. Before things went wrong, when we were happy.

'Isla?'

'I have to go,' she says. 'I just wanted to ask, can you maybe hang onto the children a little longer on Sunday till I get back?'

'No problem. Isla, we need to talk. I've been worried. You didn't answer my calls. The children were upset, they wanted to talk to you.'

Oh God, the children! She realizes that she has barely spared them a thought throughout this whole miserable week. 'Can I speak to them?'

'They're at home. I came out to get some shopping for Mum.'

'I've been ill,' says Isla weakly. 'I was in bed, I took the phone off the hook.'

'Are you feeling OK now?'

Stop this! she wants to scream. *Be a bastard, be selfish, be all the things I need you to be. If you're nice, I'll cry.*

'Fine,' she snaps. 'I'll call you on Sunday.'

*　　*　　*

Richard throws his mobile and Elizabeth's groceries onto the passenger seat, slides behind the wheel and drives, lost in thought.

He first brought Isla to the New Forest when the rhododendrons were out. He had just got the Triumph back from the garage and she had been gratifyingly impressed, especially when he put the roof down.

'I never saw the point until now,' she told him.

'The point of what?'

'Roofless cars. I thought it was just fumes and wind and very bad hair. But now . . .'

'Now what?'

'It's amazing.'

They had driven down this lane when it was a tunnel of bright pink flowers, and she had pushed her seat right back to look up at them.

'They're so gaudy, it's almost obscene,' she said. 'Painted ladies. But glorious.'

'They're a pest,' he said. 'A blight to other plants. They're not indigenous.'

She had turned huge reproachful eyes on him. 'Don't spoil it,' she had said, then in a mock pompous voice repeated, 'they're not indigenous', and burst into an infectious gale of laughter.

Why is he thinking about that now? Memories such as this are unfair. Had he really been as stuffy as her teasing implied? The thought that he might have been – that he probably was – is hurtful, but not as hurtful as the thought of Isla in his car with the wind in her hair and her hand in his lap. She had stopped laughing very suddenly to ask if he thought his parents would like her. He had raised her hand to his lips and said, with all the vehemence she brought out in him in those days, that they would love her.

There are no flowers now. Richard drives his VW Golf through a lugubrious canopy of green, and puts an angry foot down when he realizes that he is scanning them in the hope of spotting one stray bloom.

'Isla called,' he says shortly when he arrives home. He dumps his shopping bag on the kitchen counter. 'She's gone to Marshwood. Some emergency to do with the never-ending sale.'

'I don't understand,' complains Hugh. '*Why* does Isla never come down any more? I miss her.'

'Richard's explained all that, dear.'

Elizabeth slams five plates onto the table. They are sitting in the kitchen, a room Richard has always associated with his mother but where Hugh, since his retirement, has become a frequent and not always welcome visitor.

'Well,' says Hugh, opening the fridge. 'It seems very moot to me, all this separation business. In our day we just got on with it, didn't we old girl? Eh?'

Elizabeth, Richard notices, is wearing her rare but unmistakable pinched look. 'Some of us did, I suppose,' she says. Her voice has the same quality as the look.

'Gallivanting about all summer on different continents,' grumbles Hugh.

'Spain's hardly a different continent,' says Elizabeth.

'And I was hardly gallivanting,' protests Richard. 'I was working.'

'Yes well,' says his mother – snappishly, he thinks. 'You work too hard. Hugh, what *are* you doing?'

Hugh is emptying the fridge of its contents and laying them carefully on the kitchen table. 'I thought I'd rearrange them,' he says. 'There was a pot of cream in there which tasted funny.'

'It's soured cream,' says Elizabeth. 'It's supposed to taste like that. Go and pull me some leeks for supper.'

'I'll go,' offers Richard.

'No, no. Your father will enjoy the fresh air. He's driving me mad,' she says as she begins to refill the fridge. 'Hanging around all the time. Good works, that's what he needs. I shall have to find him some.'

She removes the paper wrapping from five pork chops and beats them hard with a rolling pin.

'That bad?' asks Richard.

'It's not just him,' answers his mother. 'It's you, too. When are you going to tell me what's really going on?'

He has been bracing himself for a question of this sort, and yet now that it has come he does not know how to answer. He has offered no explanation for his separation from Isla other than a bland *we've not been getting on and thought this was for the best.* He has longed to confide in his mother and yet how can he? Tell her that Isla had been unhappy for years without him noticing, that she had an affair, that she had left him after he hit her, almost raped her, that she had taken the children and fled to Spain with a swollen face and a black eye, that Marcus had witnessed part of this, that he spends his days shuttling from home to work and back again like a ghost, wondering how life has come to this, that he has cried himself to sleep more than once in his empty flat and in his old bedroom in this house, that he wants to cry now, from shame at his own behaviour and hurt at his wife's.

'My poor darling,' says Elizabeth. She hands him a cup of tea and sits down opposite him at the kitchen table.

'She wasn't happy,' he says.

'I know.'

'She wanted to go back to work. She said she was bored.'

'Of course she was.'

'And I gave her everything, Mum. I really did.'

'Everything?'

It occurs to him that the conversation is not going exactly as he would like it to. He looks up to meet his mother's gaze and finds it frank, compassionate and yet curiously challenging.

'Everything I could,' he says.

'Tell me what actually happened.'

He is irritated and a little injured by the matter-of-factness of her tone. His story, so long suppressed, bubbles out of him, but he retains just enough control to edit out the parts he does not want to tell. It does not take long: Isla's alleged unhappiness, her infidelity, the telephone call from her witch of a grandmother (Elizabeth does not smile at this description of Bella), Isla's flight – even as he speaks he despises himself for the plaintiveness of his tone.

Elizabeth shakes her head and he relaxes in anticipation of her sympathy.

'It doesn't make sense,' she says.

'What doesn't?'

'This man, this Jack – is it still going on?'

'She says not. She says he's gone to Bosnia.'

'To Bosnia?'

'Something about a dead girlfriend.'

'Isla's lover has gone to Bosnia because of his dead girlfriend?'

'Something like that. He's some kind of journalist. Mum, she had an *affair*.'

'So you said.' Elizabeth sounds distracted. Her gaze wanders through the open window to the vegetable patch. The heavy rain has brought out armies of slugs. An enthusiastic Hugh, flanked by his umbrella-toting grandchildren, is showing them how to use garden secateurs to cut them in half. Elizabeth winces.

'Mum!' roars Richard.

'Sorry, darling.' She returns to her usual brisk self. 'So what are you doing to get her back?'

'What?'

'Isla. How are you going to woo her? To convince her? To win her back?'

'Win her back? Mum, this isn't a sort of . . . medieval contest.'

'Don't you want her back?' Elizabeth's eyes are kind now but her expression is pitying. He does not like this either.

'I . . .' He thinks of Isla, not as she was at the end, tearful and accusing, or increasingly distant over the past years, but of how she was before things went wrong between them, before – he can see it now – they drifted apart, chasing different goals, living different lives. He thinks of Isla coming here when the children were little, of taking them together to look at the wild ponies in the forest, feeding them at this table, laughing when she found Marcus asleep with the dogs in their basket. Isla at their wedding, glowing and beautiful, Isla beaming as she received her professional awards, Isla pregnant, Isla besotted with the babies and with him, Isla growing sadder and more extinguished, Isla whose unhappiness he refused to acknowledge, Isla who fell in love but who came back to him, Isla who has gone. 'Yes,' he says in a small tight voice. 'I do.'

'I'm not saying what she did was right,' muses Elizabeth. 'Just that I know Isla, and it won't have happened lightly.'

'No.' Now that the fight has gone out of him, Richard slumps against the table feeling defeated.

'You'll have to think of something. Something to show her how much you love her. How much she means to you.'

'A gift, you mean?'

'A gift. A gesture. Something mad and grand and over the top.'

'But what if it doesn't work?' His voice comes out very small, and he hopes his mother does not notice it shaking. Past experience has shown him that his mother is usually right, but he is not at all sure that he is capable of mad, grand, over-the-top gestures, or even if such a gesture would be appropriate. It occurs to him that his mother is behaving very out of character, yet when he looks at her he sees that there is a strength to her, an assertive determination which suits her.

'Then you'll know that it's over,' she says.

'But I don't know what to do!' he cries.

Elizabeth laughs and jumps to her feet. 'You'll think of something,' she says as she bends over his chair to hug him. 'My darling boy. You'll think of something, I know you will. And really, if you just stop to think about it, the answer's staring you in the face.'

*   *   *

This is surreal, thinks Isla as she drives slowly down the dark village street. No streetlamps here, only pitch darkness broken by lights in cottage windows, and all around them the looming black of the hills. She swings the car up the steep lane which leads from the village to Marshwood. Her passengers, both asleep, stir fitfully, disturbed by the change of gear. *To think once Marshwood is sold I shan't do this any more.* She reminds herself firmly of the sensibleness of Bella's decision, and tells herself that the end of Marshwood will not mean the end of Chapel St Mary, nor Bambridge and its surrounding hills. When Bella is installed in her cottage and she and Isla are reconciled, as they surely must be, there will still be weekends and holidays in Dorset. She will tramp the same paths with the children, watch them race over the same hills, hunt for bluebells with them in the shade of the same trees. This is surely the right approach, to look on the bright side. She drives past the entrance to Jack's house. *At least I shan't have to look at that, I shan't have to remember every time I go past.* Marshwood itself appears in the glare of the headlights. *At least the buyer, whenever we find one, will take care of the place . . .*

It is raining heavily again. Isla steps out of the car straight into an ankle-deep puddle in the drive and stands for a moment with her face turned to the sky. The wind rushes to meet her like a long-lost friend, stronger up here than in the valley, its voice in the leafless trees more a roar than a whisper, its cold breath laden with rain. She hears creaking from the woods beyond the paddock, and the insistent knocking of a gate not properly closed. *I'm home.* An unexpected surge of elation, followed by sadness and regret.

Kitty's hand slips into hers. 'It doesn't seem real, does it?' she murmurs. Isla shakes her head. Unreal, not to walk again through the dark garden with the wind and rain in her hair; not to sleep in her childhood bedroom with its views of Pater Noster and the corner of Jack's house; not to lie on the lawn on a summer's day counting swifts and listening to the cows lowing in the fields; not to watch Marcus line up woodlice on the drawing-room floor; not to—

The front door bursts open, casting a pool of light onto the sodden courtyard. Into it steps Bella, in galoshes and an ancient canary-yellow mac with a matching sou'wester pulled firmly over her head.

'At last!' she cries as Isla, Nancy and Kitty puddle-hop their way towards the front door. 'You have to hurry! You really have to hurry!'

There is no time for greetings, no time to wonder at this strange flapping Bella who scurries ahead of them down the flagstoned hallway. 'Two of your boys were here this afternoon, KitKat,' she gasps as she reaches the foot of the stairs. 'But of course they had to go home. Their wives were getting quite annoyed. And Esther and I simply can't cope alone. I was so worried you wouldn't come!'

'Honestly!' declares Nancy. 'You and Isla. Life would be so much simpler if you just answered the telephone.'

'What's going on?' asks Isla in a tiny voice.

'You'll see soon enough,' pants Bella. 'Esther's upstairs.' She has started her ascent towards the first floor. Isla notices with distress that she climbs with both hands on the banisters. She looks worn out. She thinks about running up to offer help, but decides against it in the face of what she recognizes as Bella's most stubborn expression.

Once, when they were very small, Isla and Jack fell asleep on these stairs. Bella and Clement were entertaining. It was a Christmas party and the drawing-room was full of guests. Jack was to stay the night, as he often did, on a mattress in Isla's room. The children had crept out of bed to spy on the grown-ups through the gap in the heavy velvet curtains pulled across the bottom step. Jack, ever ready, had produced a bar of chocolate. They had stayed long after the game had grown dull, refusing to admit to being sleepy, until they drifted off curled around each other like puppies, not waking until the following morning, each in their own bed. Isla knows exactly where they slept. If she shuts her eyes, she can see them, the rosebud motif on her nightdress, the tear in his pyjama pocket, their four skinny bare feet. She closes her right hand into a fist and gently strokes the fine white scar which runs across her palm. *Do you want to be blood brothers?* She is so tired. What she wants to do now, more than anything, is lie down on the stairs and sleep for another week.

'Isla!' Nancy is calling her urgently. 'You have to see this.'

The sound greets her before she rounds the final flight of stairs up to the landing, a symphony of different plops and splashes, dull, sharp, metallic, gentle, all different and all equally ominous. As Isla reaches the final step, Kitty seizes her arm and points, wordless, down the corridor which leads to Bella's room – the corridor which has all but disappeared beneath a sea of receptacles, washing-up bowls and an old baby bath, plastic buckets and Great-Aunt Mathilda's saucepans, all full to overflowing from the rain which pours in through the sodden ceiling.

'Bloody hell,' says Isla. She remains rooted to the spot, standing beside Kitty who has still not let go of her arm. 'Fuck,' she adds, to underline her point.

'Quite,' says Nancy.

'Never mind all that!' Isla notices Esther for the first time. Clad in blue workman's overalls and a head-scarf, she is emptying the largest cauldron with a bucket. 'We have to empty them! Now! Before they overflow!'

Bella leans over and tugs ineffectually at a copper cauldron. 'I *knew* it was too big!' she complains. 'I told them, but they wouldn't listen. Oh!' A small tidal wave sploshes out of the cauldron onto Bella's galoshes. She staggers and rights herself, but not before the cauldron, finally dislodged, empties half its contents down her sleeve.

'Granna!' As Isla darts forward to help, her trainer makes a loud squelching sound on the waterlogged carpet. She slips and trips over the baby bath. Her yell is lost in a sudden crash of thunder.

Kitty screams. And then the lights go out.

For a few seconds, Isla hears nothing but the steady drip of water. Then out of the darkness comes a new sound. It begins with short, breathless gasps, quickly escalates to a squeak to become something more like a sob. It is not until it reaches the shrieking stage that Isla realizes Nancy is laughing.

'It's not *funny* . . .'

And now other sounds again, more frail and yet equally rich, a low chuckle, a nervous giggle, a dry chortle.

'Granna! Kitty! Esther!'

As the storm rages outside, as the water falls ever faster into the aligned basins on the floor, as the wind whips up to a greater frenzy, the four members of the Coven clutch each other, rocking with laughter. Isla is not sure when she started to cry. She knows only that a hand – whose? – is extended towards her and pulls her down to the floor where the four old women she has known all her life cluck and coo over her as though she were still a child.

*   *   *

Isla has become rather frightening, thinks Bella when they disband later that evening. *Extinguished*. Even last April, when all this started – and by *all this*, Bella means Jack, the memoirs, putting the house up for sale, everything really that has happened since the abortive theft of the Edwardian silver – even last April, sitting in her bedroom unconvincingly going through all the reasons why Bella should move, she had seemed more alive. Bella had hoped – rather unrealistically, but there you had it – that Isla's new-found independence would suit her. She had wanted to believe, through the long months since her granddaughter's last visit, that Isla was blossoming thanks to her liberation from the shackles of an unsatisfactory marriage. She had not been prepared for the Isla she has seen today, thin and haggard looking in too big jeans and no make-up. She had expected her to take charge as usual, but once the lights were back on and her uncontrollable laughter had been spent, it was Nancy who had risen to the situation like the Girl Guide she had once improbably been, issuing crisp orders and generally, Bella suspected, enjoying herself tremendously. Under her instructions they had formed chains using buckets to empty out the larger containers until these were light enough to carry. Then they had wrung out the sodden towels and laid them on radiators to dry before using new ones to mop up the carpets.

'Just as well you never throw anything away,' Esther

had panted. 'We've enough towels here to soak up Noah's Flood.'

Bella had been too preoccupied with her own flood at first to notice Isla's silence. It was only when they sat down to dinner, with the pails emptied and the rain abating, that she realized how absent her granddaughter was. They washed down sardines on toast with a dubious bottle of claret, followed by black tea and chocolate biscuits, and as they ate and drank they talked in sober terms about the future.

'How much do you think Bella needs to spend, Isla,' asked Esther, 'to get the house into a reasonable condition?'

'It depends on what you mean by reasonable.'

'Waterproof would be good for a start.' Nancy chuckled. Even Bella managed a smile. Isla sighed.

'I'll need to measure up in the morning. I'm too sleepy for this right now. I'm going to bed.'

Very irritable, mouthed Nancy across the kitchen table as Isla left the room.

'So sad and lost,' said the more charitable Kitty.

'Have you given her the letter from Jack yet?' asked Esther.

Nancy raided the cellar once Isla went to bed, and they all got a little tipsy on the bottle of port she brought back, a relic from last Christmas, after which a surprised Esther announced that she was far too drunk to drive home.

They are all asleep now in the two spare rooms unaffected by the leaking roof. Back in her own bedroom, the temporary buoyancy afforded by wine and company leaves Bella. She sits down at her dressing-table feeling discouraged. Jack's letter to Isla sits just where she placed it when it arrived at the beginning of the week, propped up against her looking-glass. In all the commotion with the flood she has forgotten to give it to Isla, and yet it was the arrival of the letter which prompted her to call Isla in the first place. She had not wanted to forward it without giving her some warning. What if it set everything off again? She is not even sure what she means by *everything*, but what if Isla should suddenly take it into her head to run off to Bosnia? Or what if Richard should get wind of the fact that Jack was writing to Isla? Or if Isla and Richard should be on the point of being reconciled, and a letter threw this off course? Esther had accused her of meddling. A letter had been written, and must be read. *That*, Esther said, *is what letters are for*. But Bella had hummed and dallied, and then the rain had started, and the roof, until she was in such a state of general anxiety about everything – that word again! – that Nancy had declared she was off to London to fetch Isla, and Kitty, a little nervously, had announced that she would go too. *Time the child came home*, said Nancy. *You two have too much to talk about.* But still, perhaps it *will* be better for her not to give the

letter. Perhaps Isla is better off without Jack. Perhaps
. . . She catches sight of her reflection in the mirror.
Her face is still smudged from the day's exertions
and strands of grey hair are escaping their half-dozen
controlling pins. 'You look deranged,' she tells herself
as she begins to apply cold cream to her face. 'In fact,
I think you probably *are* deranged. Meddlesome old
witch.'

The last of the cream removed, she tightens her
dressing-gown belt and wanders over to the window.
The rain, she is relieved to note, has stopped at last,
and the clouds have even cleared sufficiently to reveal
a sliver of moon.

You would like children? She smiles. Louis. He always
comes. Whenever she stands here to watch the night
with her forehead pressed against the glass, his ghost
slips in beside her.

'They're all grown up now,' she tells him. 'Callie and
Isla. All grown up, and living their own lives. And me
. . .' She sighs. 'I'm all alone again. Except for you of
course. Though a fat lot of use you are.'

She leaves the window and returns to her dressing-
table. Louis' letters sit beside Jack's, gathered into a neat
pile beneath a Venetian glass paperweight. 'Of course it
was all your fault, you know.' He has gone, as he always
does when she leaves the window, but she enjoys talking to him. 'You and your bloody letters. I hope you're
satisfied.'

His diary is tucked beneath the letters. She pulls it out and opens it at the entry she loves the most, the final one.

Do you know, I think I have forgotten what life was before. I remember there was a town by the sea, with an old harbour guarded by two splendid towers, where fishing boats moored in the early mornings and respectable ladies haggled with fishwives. There was a beach and a promenade and a casino, and a house with a tangled garden full of raspberries in summer. There was a boy who called this home. But this was long ago, in a different life.

Today I remembered why I love flying. We are in Scotland now, in the Orkneys. Life is very quiet, very welcome after the hectic pace of the bases in the south and the awful sandy grind of Anglesey. This morning I went up alone as the sun was rising. A reconnaissance flight, routine. I had the sky to myself. In situations like this, alone up there with no other plane in sight, you can believe yourself to be one with the sky. And when a morning is as perfect as this one . . . Now my prose will grow florid and you will laugh at me, as you did when I described so perfectly the priory where I plan to live. But really, I wish I were a poet. Perhaps then I could describe better what I saw. Beneath me sleepy islands, purple as heather, stretching through the last of night to the open sea. Above me, the gold beckoning of sunrise. I flew towards it through the half-darkness, rising with the gathering light of day, and I was that sun and sea and sky. It was in itself a perfect moment. A holy moment, even. But nothing compared to what happened next.

Another plane came into view, a German fighter. In those seconds, it all came back – the fear, the loathing, the unhappiness. Henry, Xavier, so many others. He dipped his wings. That was all. He dipped his wings, and I dipped mine back. We passed each other in the empty sky, the enemy and I, sharing the beauty of being alive under the rising sun. But as I flew on, I felt that I had never before had such a connection with anyone. For what could bind two beings more closely than having together 'danced the skies . . . And touched the face of God'?

I pondered this thought. Of course I have felt close to other people, people I have loved. My sisters – there is something about the shared experiences of childhood. My parents, on occasion. You. But this moment this morning in the sky – it was illuminated. And what is life, if it does not contain such moments of illumination?

I would have made a good priest, don't you think? Ah, you are laughing at me again! And yet I know that you understand me . . .

And then the startling final line: *I know now that I shan't survive this war. But after today, I am not afraid to die.*

Yes, this was the point. *Moments of illumination.* It had not been fair to Isla, to leave the story unfinished. Stories must have endings, whether happy or not. She will give the diary to Isla, she decides, along with Jack's letter. Surely, once she has read them, everything will fall into place.

Isla is in bed but not asleep. She leans against her headboard with her arms clasped about her knees and watches in silence as her grandmother, looking like a startled ghost in her long nightgown with her hair down her back, advances into the room.

Bella stops a small distance from the bed and holds out a faded grey notebook. Isla closes her eyes.

'Not now.' *Other people's emotions. This is why I didn't want to come back. I can barely cope with my own.* 'Maybe tomorrow, when we've sorted the roof and everything.'

'I'd like you to read them *now*,' says Bella. 'They're important.'

'They?'

'There's a letter here from Jack.'

'Oh God.'

'I know that you are angry with me, and I'm sorry for the part I played in your husband's appalling behaviour . . .'

'The part you played!' Isla stares at her grandmother in disbelief. 'Granna, you . . .'

'I think I helped him reveal his true colours.'

'That's not fair! You provoked him, he would never have . . .' *Why am I even defending him?* 'Fine,' she glowers, and holds out her hand. 'I'll read them. *Alone*.'

Bella hands over Louis' diary with unbecoming meekness. The letter from Jack is tucked into its pages. 'The last entry is the most important. If you don't have time for the rest.'

'Thank you.' Isla's tone makes it clear the visit is over. Bella, to the best of her ability, scampers from the room.

Whom should she read first – Louis, or Jack? Isla slips out of bed and takes Bella's offerings to her window-seat where she sits for a long time staring out at the storm. She drops her face into her hands when she realizes that she has been looking towards Jack's house in the hope of seeing a flicker of light. Jack then, or Louis? On balance, she is more afraid of reading Jack. 'OK,' she says out loud. 'Let's get it over with.'

Sarajevo, 15 November 1995

Isla,

I've wanted to write for a while but until now haven't known what to say. Are you well, happy, moving on? Are you working again, do you still come down to Marshwood, is Bella still dictating her memoirs, is she still thinking of selling up?

I am back in Sarajevo after more than three months on the road. What with the usual faffing about in Sarajevo before setting out to get supplies and permits, endless roadblocks, detours, pigheaded soldiers etc. etc., we – my

354

interpreter Milan and I – didn't reach Jezero until late
October. We've been lucky – winter's been late this year
and the roads were still clear of snow. Jezero was in ruins,
of course. Difficult, if you have never seen a village in
ruins, to understand what this means. Windows without
glass. Houses without roofs. Fields without livestock,
streets without people, cars without wheels. Not a living
soul about, but you could see how the place must have
been beautiful, just as Elena described it – the lake,
the mountains, the big house with the courtyard. It was
burned, of course. In a grim sort of way I was glad she
wasn't with us.

'There is nothing here,' said Milan. He pulled his anorak
around his slight frame and shivered as he lit a cigarette.
'You will not find the old man. I am sorry, my friend.'

Jack contemplated the charred remains of Elena's
grandfather's house. Only the stable block was still
standing, to the left of the gravelled courtyard. Leaving
Milan, he walked over to peer inside, saw stalls, a few
strands of hay in the mangers, dirty floors. The small
adjoining tack room had been sacked, of course, though
a faint smell of leather still hung in the air. Something
caught his eye in the darkest corner and he bent down
to retrieve a red plastic curry comb. *'He has the biggest*
house in the village, with a courtyard and a Jeep and horses
you can ride.'

'Jack.' Milan leaned against the frame of the stable

door. 'Truly, I am sorry. But if we want to be anywhere at all by nightfall, we must leave now. I have heard there is a convent not far, where the nuns will give us shelter. Trust me, we do not want to sleep in this place.'

'You're right.' Speaking took some effort but made him feel better. 'Let's go.'

It was pitch dark by the time they reached the convent. Their approach had been noticed. The sliding panel in the heavy reinforced door set in the high stone wall slid open before they even pulled the bell chain. Milan explained their presence in rapid Bosnian and the door swung open to reveal an elderly nun wearing a military jacket over a grubby grey habit, heavy men's walking boots and an assault rifle over her shoulder.

'They can put us up for the night,' said Milan as they followed her through the dark grounds of the convent. 'She is taking us to our room, where we can eat.'

'She's carrying a Kalashnikov.' Jack felt a hysterical urge to giggle. 'That's got to be against her religion.'

Milan snorted. 'I think God will forgive her.'

Their room contained two plain cot beds, two chairs and a table. The first nun left and another came bearing a tray laden with bread, dried meat, pickled cabbage and bottled fruit. They washed down their food with glasses of plum brandy from the bottle Milan pulled from his rucksack, their conversation growing coarser and more maudlin as they drank. When they had finished eating, Milan produced a pack of cards.

'Will you play?'

'Not tonight.' Jack poured out another glass. 'Can't face you beating me again.'

Milan peered at him through the low light of the gas lantern the last nun had left behind. 'You are thinking of Jezero, your girlfriend and her grandfather.'

He drained his glass. 'I don't know how you stand it, Milan.'

The interpreter shrugged. 'You get used to things. One day peace will come – soon, if these talks in America work out – and we will all go back to our real lives and sometimes I think that will be the most difficult thing of all.'

'I'm still carrying around all this bloody money. What am I going to do with it if the old man's dead?'

'Give it to me,' grinned Milan. 'Then fuck off back to your country. Forget this mess. Have a happy life.' He reached into his pocket and brought out a small brown bottle from which he shook two pills. 'One each,' he said. 'Take it with another shot of *sljivovica*. It is not what the doctor recommends, but with this you will sleep. Without it, my friend, I guarantee you will spend the night awake after the day you have had.'

Elena, their trip, her murder, Jezero. Isla, Marshwood, the flight of summer swifts. The sound of the wind outside, an icy draught, the possibility of snow . . . Jack pulled up the hood of his sleeping-bag and passed out.

He woke to a throbbing hangover and the unexpected

sound of children's laughter. Milan was still snoring gently. They had both slept in their clothes. Jack staggered to his feet, pulled on his boots and jacket and crept outside. The low building which housed their bedroom gave onto a large high-walled courtyard, in which twenty or so children ran screaming after a football. Jack watched them, dazed by the contrast between this and Jezero.

'The resilience of children.' A middle-aged nun with a kindly face came to stand beside him. He noted with relief that she carried a flask and two tin mugs. 'I am Sister Agnes. I always drink my morning coffee here. Will you join me?'

She was the mother superior and had lived in this convent for fifteen years. 'Strictly speaking, ours is a contemplative order. We work in the community, but we do not run orphanages. Times change, however, and we adapt. More coffee?'

'Thank you. It's excellent.'

'People are kind to us,' she smiled. 'We are very lucky.'

'Where do the children come from?'

'Some are orphans. Others have become separated from their families. They are victims of what your media call ethnic cleansing. When the peace comes, we will try to reunite them with their families. It will take a long time. Tell me what you are doing in Bosnia.'

He told her everything. Elena, the way she was killed,

the search for her grandfather, the money he carried as she had in a belt around his waist. His feelings for Isla, about the war, about his inability to work. He lingered on this, describing his block vis-à-vis his camera as a form of impotence which stunted him.

'So now you are wondering what to do,' she said when he fell silent at last. 'Because, I imagine, life has little meaning. Your friend died over a year ago and since then she has fuelled you with purpose – mourning her, trying to forget her, returning here. And because of her you cannot even practise your profession. I can see that this must be terrible for you. You know the parable of the talents?'

'Vaguely. From school . . .'

'It is a difficult parable, open to many interpretations. But in essence . . . God has given us talents, which it is sinful to waste. Jack, I think I can help you.'

'You have already, so much.'

Sister Agnes waved her hand. 'Food, shelter, this is nothing. I can help you to reclaim yourself. Photograph the children for me. I need a portrait of each of them. This will help us to trace their families.'

'I can't do that.'

'I think you can. You have a camera. I am sure you have film. Why can you not do it?'

'You don't understand, I've tried before, I really can't . . .'

'Tut.' She pressed his arm. '*Can't* is not a word.'

'What are you *doing*?' groaned Milan when Jack returned to the room. 'I can't believe we got wasted in a convent. My grandmother would kill me.'

'I'm looking for my camera. The nuns want me to shoot a bunch of kids.'

'For real?' Milan, who knew much of Jack's story, propped himself up on his elbow to look at him.

'I haven't done it yet.'

'But still, you want to try. It's a miracle! A miracle in the house of God. I'm proud of you.'

'Fuck off, Milan. And by the way, if this works, I'm going to give the money to them.'

'I might have known,' sighed Milan. 'Nuns. They're worse than the bloody Mafia.'

Jack's head swam as he stepped into the yard, his old Leica with its repaired lens swinging from a strap around his neck. The temperature had dropped. His gloveless fingers were freezing but his palms were sweating. *I can do this.* Elena's face swam before his eyes. *I'm going to buy bread.* Jack wanted to cry. No, he wanted to scream and bawl his eyes out, and then he wanted to go and find Milan and get wasted again.

The game of football had ended and the children had all gone inside. What was he supposed to do now? He could leave – grab Milan and their gear and just hot-foot it in the Jeep. Then, out of the corner of his eye, he caught a movement.

A boy and a girl, aged around eight and six. Brother and sister, judging by the way they appeared to be quarrelling. The boy ran off and the little girl bellowed after him. Inside Jack, another memory stirred. Isla's children, his first glimpse of Beth yelling *it's not fair* across the lawn at Marshwood. And now it was Isla's face he remembered, and Isla's voice on Pater Noster. *There's nothing to be afraid of.* The boy was coming back for his sister, dragging his feet as he went. He stopped a short distance away and called out to her. The girl lifted her tear-stained face and beamed. Jack raised the camera to his eye and depressed the shutter.

I don't know when I'll be back. With all this talk of peace going on, I'm thinking I ought to hang around a little longer. And then – well there's still a whole world out there to photograph. Life goes on, eh? My parents want to sell the coach house. It makes sense, I suppose. So I guess I'll see you around . . .

She re-reads the letter carefully several times, searching for hidden meanings. Does he miss her? He had talked about her with Sister Agnes but did that mean he still loved her? And *I'll see you around*? She rubs her eyes, frowning. Then crumples Jack's letter, throws it across the room at the waste-paper basket and, with a sigh, picks up Louis' notebook.

* * *

How can I describe the tedium of these Atlantic convoys?

She finds it disturbing to read his diary, more so than his letters. These for the most part had retained a careful quality, a respect for convention and his reader. The diary is too immediate, too open. *Did you believe I would not think of you? If you are reading this, it means that I am dead* . . . A soft sigh escapes her lips as she comes to the end of the final entry. A sheet of paper flutters to the floor and she leans over the bed to pick it up. It is the letter from his Flight Commander. She frowns as she reads it. A kind letter, apparently heartfelt but unsatisfying. *Disappeared.* This word in particular stands out for her. The more she looks at it, the less meaning it holds for her because surely, *surely* it is not possible for people simply to vanish, like white doves in a conjuring trick? Surely they have to go *somewhere*. Where then did Louis go? Was he taken by fire, or swallowed by waves? There is no mention of either in the letter, but someone must have seen something – mustn't they? She thinks back to Louis' descriptions of his friends' deaths. He had heard Henry on the radio, seen a plane spiralling towards the sea, witnessed Xavier's crash. Had Louis gone down with his plane? Could he in fact have jumped unseen and parachuted to a watery grave? The only certainty appeared to be that he had vanished over the sea.

Perhaps he hadn't been hit at all. Isla closes her eyes and pictures a small brave plane with sun glinting off its wings, soaring in the sunlit silence. Perhaps, weary of living, he had simply broken away, flying against all dictates into the light until he could go no further. Yes, this could be a way of disappearing, melting gradually into the sheltering sky. In Isla's imagination the aircraft grows smaller, a small shining cross gradually engulfed by the burning sun.

There is a hollow half-way down her mattress made by the imprint of her own body over the decades. She curls into it now and surveys her bedroom. It has changed little since her adolescence. Bella's one concession to Isla's married status had been to install a second bed, separated from her own by a white painted table. Her old books still line the same bookcase shelves, old clothes fill her chest of drawers, her collection of Clement's hand-carved mice – one for every birthday – sits on the mantelpiece in decreasing order of size. *Nothing changes*, she thinks. *Except that we grow more weary and battered. But what difference do they make, this weariness, this battering? What do we learn?* After this past week, she understands perfectly how a disappearance such as Louis' could come about. It is after all what she herself has wished for.

She craves sleep but it does not come. Instead she lies on her side with her cheek resting on her hands and her eyes wide open, staring straight ahead. Outside, the rain has stopped but the clouds have parted, making a path for the shaft of moonlight which shines through the billowing curtains. *Pretty*, thinks Isla. *Though wrong* . . . She sits up slowly. Why, with the window tightly shut, should the curtains flutter so?

Her mind must be playing tricks on her. She blinks slowly and looks again. The curtains hang still now, not quite meeting in the middle. Yes, a trick, the play of moonlight and shadow on weary imagination. Sleep is coming now, stealing up weary limbs. As her eyes close, another small movement by the window catches her eye. The shadow of a man leaning with his forehead against the pane. She sees – or thinks she sees – a brief smile as he turns towards her. The moon goes in, and he is gone. Isla sighs and falls asleep.

She wakes late the following morning. The glacial temperature of her bedroom puts paid to anything more than a cursory wash. She runs the bathroom taps for several minutes before accepting that there will be no hot water this morning. Either Bella has forgotten to put the heating on or the ancient boiler, in sympathy with the rest of the house, has decided to throw in the towel. She dresses quickly in jeans, her warmest sweater and two pairs of socks, then wraps a thick woollen shawl around her shoulders for good measure. She peers at herself in the mirror. She looks *swaddled*.

On the landing, solitary drops of rust-coloured water continue to drip mournfully from the ceiling on which an efflorescence of interwoven brown rings has mushroomed overnight. Isla heaves several of the smaller pans to the bathroom where she empties them into the tub, then makes her way downstairs. Bella and Nancy, both wearing trenchcoats and gumboots, are seated at the kitchen table, glumly nursing cups of tea. Nancy is smoking, an old habit to which she only reverts under extreme duress.

'What's happened?' asks Isla. Bella sighs. Nancy's coat falls open as she leans forward to extinguish her cigarette, revealing the nightdress she still wears beneath it.

'You didn't hear the storm this morning?'

'It didn't rain again, did it? There was no sign on the landing.'

'No, no rain this time. Just wind. There's a tree in the boiler house.'

'What?'

'It smashed the boiler. Quite beyond repair.'

'Are you sure?'

'Darling, spare us your incredulity and go outside to look.'

Isla steps cautiously outside. Sure enough, an elderly elm protrudes from the smashed roof of the outhouse which shelters Marshwood's venerable boiler. Low sullen clouds begin to spit rain. Isla beats a hasty retreat.

'I can't believe it broke the boiler!'

'Did *you* have any hot water this morning?'

'No,' admits Isla. 'But it just seems so . . . extreme.'

'This whole situation is extreme,' says Nancy. 'I'm going to make some phone calls. Assuming the phone line is working. Oh, and by the way, you can't cook because there's no gas.'

'Why not?'

'Somebody forgot to pay the gas bill.'

'I didn't receive it.' Hunched in several cardigans beneath her coat, Bella appears abstracted and quite incapable of anything as earthly as actual speech, but the voice which floats disembodied from the general area around her carries an unmistakable ring of stubbornness.

Nancy points to a small pile of letters on the table, apparently only very recently opened.

'Not reading is not the same as not receiving,' she says sternly.

'Who are you going to call?' asks Isla.

'I don't know yet. Builders. Plumbers. Roofers. God, if he'll listen.'

'I'll come with you.'

'Stay with your grandmother.'

'Where are Kitty and Esther?' asks Isla once Nancy has left the room.

'They had to go. Did you read the diary?'

'Let's not talk about that now,' says Isla. The larder window looks onto the boiler house, and this is where she now stands to survey the destruction outside. 'It doesn't seem right. Not with all this going on.'

Bella ignores her, as only Bella can. 'Do you know why I gave it to you?'

Isla is not sure which is worse, talking about the diary or talking about the Armageddon which Marshwood is fast becoming. Bella seems to have little interest in her disintegrating house this morning. Isla gives up.

'Yes,' she says with a touch of impatience but really, who can blame her? 'I read it.'

'And?'

'I think I understand what he meant. About dying.'

Bella looks alarmed but also a little disappointed. 'Tell me,' she asks. 'Has your mother ever talked to you about her painting?'

'Excuse me?'

'The last time she came here – it must have been a couple of years ago – she spoke of paintings that were touched with grace. A spirit which breathes life into them, which transforms them from paint and canvas and pleasing compositions into something greater. The intangible energy that can turn even a poorly executed painting into something which sings.'

Isla remembers the sketches Callie showed her towards the end of her stay in San Rafael, of the children playing in the garden against the background of the Alpujarras.

'She has talked about it,' she admits. 'Though I'm really not sure how this is relevant.'

'She says that is how she "finds" your father. Did she tell you that?'

'No,' says Isla. 'She didn't.'

'He – Louis – he *was* that breath of life. And we, I suppose, were his materials. I think I told you Clement referred to him once as an angel, do you remember?'

'I think so.'

'Jack was the same.'

'*Jack?*' Isla lets out a sharp involuntary bark of laughter. 'You think *Jack* is an angel?'

'I don't mean in a religious sense!'

'Well obviously, but still . . .'

'He transformed you,' says Bella firmly. 'You glowed, all the time you were with him. I know you thought you were being discreet, but every night I heard you leave, and every morning I heard you return, and you never showed the slightest sign of being tired. He gave you wings, energy, life! It's what Louis writes about in his diary: what the encounter with that German pilot did for him. Moments of illumination. They're very rare. You have to hold onto them.'

'Of course, but . . .'

'No, *you* have to hold onto them, you, you, you. You and Jack. You mustn't let it slip away.'

'Slip away?'

'Like I did.'

'Oh Granna . . .' Isla looks helplessly at her grand-mother, who blinks a few times in quick succession before glaring back. 'Granna, he *died*. What could you have done?'

'More,' growls Bella. 'Much, much more.'

'And Jack reminded you of Louis . . .'

'You loved him!'

'Loved him . . .' Nancy has left her emergency cigarettes on the table. Isla takes one out of the packet, briefly considers taking up smoking, then puts it back, remembering she has not yet had breakfast. 'You talked about moments of illumination. Here are some of mine. My wedding day. The days my children were born. Moments – I can't even describe them, they'll seem so mundane – moments with the three of them, holidays, Christmas, the children bringing us cold tea in bed because they're not allowed to boil the kettle, Richard surprising us by leaving work early, the time we went to the sea for a picnic once and ended up eating fish and chips in the car in the pouring rain. Did Jack tell you why he was going back?'

Bella, still looking mutinous, shakes her head.

'Something terrible happened to him there. He was involved with a woman who was killed. He made her a promise before she died, but he didn't feel able to keep that promise until – well, until we talked about it.' She frowns. 'I think I always knew that what we had wasn't real life, even though I did love him – *do* love him, in a way. He said I was myself when I was with him, and I suppose that's true. But I was myself twenty years ago. Twenty years ago. That's the point. When I left him in the summer to go home, I knew what I was going back to – the good bits and the bad bits and the bits I wanted to change. I was going to make it work, Granna. Because Richard, me, Beth, Marcus – Jack may have been a shining light, like you say, but the four of us together, we were like gold. Not always very shiny gold, but precious.'

'But he hit you!'

'He's no angel either.'

'And you were so unhappy!'

'Believe me, this is worse.'

'Then you have to go back to him!' declares Bella.

'I'm not sure I believe in second chances,' says Isla. 'Not after all this.'

Far away – beyond the kitchen and the old breakfast room, the dusty dining-room and the gloomy passage – Marshwood's only telephone rings, its shrillness amplified to air raid loudness by a small device acquired by Nancy from a home shopping catalogue. Bella and Isla, lost in thought, ignore it. There is so much Isla has wanted to say to Bella – it's my prerogative to fuck up my own life but you have no business getting involved, don't use me to make sense of your mistakes – but what will it change? Instead she slips her hand across the table, beneath her grandmother's. Bella acknowledges the gesture with a brief pressure of her own fingertips. A new warmth enters the kitchen.

'I saw him, you know,' says Isla suddenly.

'Who?'

'Louis. I think it must have been him. Last night, in my room.'

Bella nods. 'I'm pleased.'

'The memoirs and everything . . . is that what you were building up to?'

'Not when I started. But it's a good way to end.'

'A very good way to end.'

Their smiles at each other across the table are tentatively conciliatory. And then Nancy crashes in.

'That was the estate agent!' She stops to catch her breath.

'The one who's depressed?' enquires Isla.

'He's had an offer for the house!'

'No!'

'Yes!' Nancy does a little dance. 'God *was* listening! He's had an offer, and he's bringing the buyer over this morning.'

Bella has gone very pale. Isla gets up and goes to stand behind her chair. She leans over to pick up one of her grandmother's hands. It is cold. She rubs it briskly, as she would one of her children's.

'We have to tidy up,' whispers Bella.

'Tidy up?' Nancy's wide-eyed cartoon incredulity lacks only a speech bubble of question marks. 'Darling, the *state* of the place . . .'

'The pans and so on.'

371

'We could, but the carpet and the dripping ceiling are a bit of a giveaway, don't you think? And anyway, it wouldn't make any difference. Allen said—'

'Allen?' interjects Isla.

'The agent. We got quite chummy, as a matter of fact. He didn't want to talk to me at first, but I made him. Anyway, Allen said this buyer's under no illusion about the state of the house.'

'Did you tell him about the tree and the boiler house?'

'Better not, I thought. Nor the gas. But these are all details.' Nancy, flying against her own advice, almost skips to the broom cupboard in the scullery and emerges with a cobweb-festooned vacuum cleaner. 'The point is, he isn't coming for a *viewing*. He's buying the place, and he's clearly disgustingly rich. He offered the asking price.'

'It must be the American,' says Bella decisively. She rises painfully from her chair. 'We'd better get ready for him. I think, since the rain has stopped, we *should* see about the pails. And perhaps get rid of all those towels. Isla dear, put them in the washing machine. We'll make coffee, it'll cover the smell of the damp. And light fires. Yes, lots of fires. I've had the chimneys swept.'

'When?' asks Isla.

'Recently.' Bella looks vague. 'Nancy, do you think you can manage the vacuuming? I think I will dust. There must be some polish somewhere. Beeswax! That's what we need. Isla, when you've finished with the water pails, will you look after outside?'

'Outside?'

'The terrace and so on.'

'But Granna, the wind—'

'Oh darling, just try. I want Marshwood to look her best for this man. Poor old lady, caught with her teeth out . . .' Bella raises a hand to her forehead and gathers herself with a visible effort. 'Just like the war,' she says brightly. 'Making the best of things.' She pretends not to see the look of concern exchanged by her old friend and her granddaughter. She *will* treat this extraordinary event as a piece of good fortune. She will *not* be seen to give in to maudlin tears. This is what she has decided. To entrust Marshwood, her home, the repository of all her adult life, to the care of this stranger, this American who will put his own stamp on it, who will turn Clement, Louis, Isla's haven into something all his own.

In order for the others to believe her, she has to leave the room. If she catches one more look of sympathy, if Isla touches her one more time, she will break down and cry, and where will *that* leave them all?

'I am going to dress,' she enunciates. 'Then I shall come back down for the dusting etc. No, it's all right, darling.' She stops Isla with a hand gesture. 'I don't need help. I can manage perfectly well on my own.'

*　　*　　*

373

'I can't bear this,' says Isla when Bella has left the room.

'Don't be silly,' says Nancy briskly. 'It's terrific news. You know it is. And frankly, darling, you've been lucky.'

The pans emptied, Isla tidies her own bedroom and the kitchen before going outside. It is her favourite kind of autumn day. A strong wind chases the ominous grey clouds which streak the newly washed sky, throwing a patchwork of sun and shadow onto the lush green of the hills. Isla goes the long way round the house to the barn that houses the gardening tools, making a detour through the orchard to inspect it for further damage. The jasmine curtain still hangs from the quince tree at the far side, but this season's unpicked fruit lies rotting on the ground. Obviously – she did not come this year as she usually does at the end of summer to make them into jelly. The apples and plums have suffered the same fate. Brown fruit ringed with mildew squelches beneath her feet and the uncut grass reaches almost to her knees, soaking her jeans and boots. From this angle, she can see where water from the roof of the house has spilled out of a leaking gutter and soaked into the deep honey of the stone, staining it a dark brown. She crosses over to the lower gate and out into the field beneath Marshwood, passing another victim of the storm, the Conference pear planted for her own first birthday in celebration of her favourite fruit. The grey and black

374

carcass of its broken trunk leans out of the hillside at a drunken angle. *How fitting*, she thinks. She is beginning to feel the weight of this first walk knowing that Marshwood will soon no longer be hers. The wind, picking up, whistles through the naked woods, shaking out the last droplets which cling to smaller branches. From where she stands she has a view straight down the valley to the village squatting damply beneath its ring of hills. She wishes, for Marshwood's sake, that the sun were shining. What had Bella said? *Poor old lady, caught with her teeth out.* On this day of days, before the odious, mad buyer stakes his claim, Marshwood should be radiant.

Well, if the sun won't oblige, she will do what she can. She gathers a stiff broom, a hessian sack and a pair of gloves from the gardening shed, then scans its hooks for other useful implements. She spots Clement's old apron and ties it round her waist, slipping secateurs and a roll of PVC coated wire into its pockets. The pegs by the door still sport a fine selection of his hats. Isla lifts one now, his favourite black and orange checked deerstalker, and rams it defiantly on her head. 'Right, Grampsy,' she says out loud. 'Let's show 'em.'

Marshwood's gutters and drainage holes are choked with fallen leaves, blown there by the snow. Isla works her way slowly around the house, clearing each one in turn. Her hessian sack grows bulkier with each pause, her knees more damp and her cheeks more pink. The final gutter cleared, she makes her way back to the terrace. Here, in the shady corners furthest from the house, she slips on a slick of leaves turning to mulch. Ridiculous to use more water after the rain, but now Isla is on a mission. She drags the hosepipe from where it is kept outside the kitchen door and connects it to the outside tap, turns on the water then covers the end of the hose with her left thumb to create a stronger jet while she scratches at the stones with the broom she holds in her right hand. She works with a kind of vengeance, the angry desire to reclaim Marshwood for her own, a sob-choked rage against herself for having stayed away so long. Her scrubbing done, she turns off the hose and her work acquires a more regular pattern as she sweeps leaves into small piles which must be gathered immediately into her sack before the wind blows them apart. She is calmer now. Elements of her conversation with Bella come back to her. *No second chances.* What did this say about the possibilities thrown up by life, the temptations? Were they always to be ignored? What if you wanted more than the hand you were dealt? Was it better, always, to walk away rather than risk damage to the fabric of everyday life? *If I had not strayed with Jack, would I still be with Richard? Surely it happened for a reason. Even though I don't see it yet, perhaps this way we will all be happier. We will be able to move on, as Jack himself has moved on. Yes, perhaps it has all happened for the best.* Even as she thinks this she is shaken by the realization that she does not mean it, because the truth is that she would give anything now to go back and make her marriage work.

Kee-kee-kee! Isla pauses and looks up, leaning against her broomstick. The pile of leaves at her feet dances unattended in the wind, but she no longer sees it. High above the valley, on a level with Marshwood, a kestrel rides the buffeting thermals, head still, wings beating a gentle hover, grey tail feathers fanned out. She scrunches up her eyes for a better view.

'All summer,' she tells the kestrel. 'All summer, my little boy waited to see you, and you never showed your face. And now here you are. I'm taking it as a sign. I'm not sure of what yet, but it has to mean something.'

The kestrel dips his head and swoops. She holds her breath, hoping – poor prey – for a kill, but he catches a lower current and hovers again before appearing to lose interest and returning to the woods with a few lazy beats of his wings. Isla breathes out and returns to reality, a reality which involves wet clothes, a cold wind, runaway leaves and the sound of a car pulling into the drive. *Of course*, she remembers. *The lunatic American who is taking this on.* Well, the terrace is almost swept, and the passing of vacuum cleaner and dusters has hopefully given Marshwood's interior a semblance of superficial respectability. From where she stands, she sees valiant puffs of smoke emerge from its many chimneys. It is not *entirely* unappealing, this crumbling house she loves.

From the drive on the other side of the house she hears the sound of a car door slamming, the doorbell ringing. Male voices float towards her then pause, presumably to accommodate female voices which do not reach her. Isla backs into the shadow of an old yew tree. She knows she should go in but somewhere in amongst the many Islas who reside side by side, or superimposed, or in some configuration or other within her, the rebellious child is alive and well, declaring that surely, as the youngest person here, she is not needed for this meeting. Surely Bella, owner-in-residence, will do the honours supported by Nancy and nobody will miss her if she kicks around a little longer in the garden. The voices have stopped. Isla hugs herself with her many-sweatered arms and feels misery engulf her again. This, then, is it. The American, whom she imagines as rotund, badly dressed and unabashedly cheerful, will be stalking Marshwood's corridors making inappropriate remarks about improvements. Probably he will have a wife in tow, or a secretary, or even – the irony is not lost on her – an architect.

'Isla!'

Bella is calling her. She should go in. She knows she should go in. She wipes away her gathering tears with the palm of her hand, aware as she does so that she is streaking mud across her cheeks.

'Isla!' Her grandmother appears on the edge of the terrace, gesticulating wildly. 'The buyer!'

'I know,' calls Isla. 'I'm coming. I was just finishing up.'

'You know? You can't possibly know! The buyer, oh Isla, I don't know what to say . . .'

She tails off. She can see from Isla's face that it is too late to say anything. She took the circuitous but more discreet route through the kitchen to get here, leaving the estate agent and his mystery buyer with a stunned Nancy in the drawing-room. She had hoped to reach her granddaughter first to warn her of what was coming, but the man has taken matters into his own hands. The unusually nervous man who barely spoke to them when he came in but demanded in a hoarse whisper to talk to Isla, and who when pressed for explanations muttered something about grand gestures and medieval contests. The thin, exhausted man who knows her granddaughter well enough to come looking for her outside. The man who at this precise moment is walking towards them down the steps from the French windows while Isla, in her grandfather's unspeakable hat, watches with an expression of incredulity which Bella hopes – she really, really hopes – is about to turn to joy.

The man who is Richard and who stands on the edge of the terrace, holding out his hand.

Natasha Farrant on *Some Other Eden*

I am thrilled that *Some Other Eden* has been chosen by Tesco Book Club as its choice for October, and delighted to have the opportunity to write a few more words about it. It is the characters which make *Some Other Eden* for me, and so it is the characters I have chosen to focus on here. I love them all: Bella for her fierce independence, the Coven for their gallantry, the children for their liveliness, Jack for being so sexy, Clement such a darling. I'm not sure I love Richard, though I do feel sorry for him and rather admire him for his final absurd, romantic gesture . . . Space is short, however, so I will focus on two – Isla and Louis, my own favourites – and draw in the others as I go along.

Isla

If she were American, she would be just a 'regular mom', a busy homemaker who has given up work to look after her children. Her early childhood aside, there is nothing dramatic or tragic about her. Her life (and this of course is the problem) is perfectly ordinary. Who doesn't know an Isla? And yet, for an author, she represents a considerable challenge. How to portray this deeply dissatisfied woman, who appears to have everything she could possibly wish for, without making her seem selfish and spoilt? And how to make her *interesting*?

Isla is a mass of contradictions: wilful and submissive, hot-tempered and tender, she loves her children fiercely, but family life both makes her blossom and withers her. She is naturally impulsive, as her relationship with Jack and her whirlwind romance with Richard demonstrate, but over the years she has become muted and restrained. I don't think it is possible to pin Isla down in a few words, but if I had to define her most salient characteristic I would say that it was her yearning to love and to be loved. Which, to me and I hope to my readers, is ultimately what makes her so loveable.

Her unhappiness is a quiet, everyday affair. It stems to an extent from her childhood and the loss, one way or another, of her parents. She is stubbornly determined to give her own children the stable, ideal upbringing she missed out on, and this determination makes the gradual atrophy of her marriage all the harder to bear. But, unorthodox childhood aside, Isla's state of being remains a commonplace affair. She isn't really unhappy so much as extinguished – what the French call *éteinte*. And then along comes Jack – brooding, selfish Jack, with his own wealth of trouble, his need for comfort and reassurance – who reawakens in her all the intensity of adolescent emotion. Do Isla and Jack love each other? It almost doesn't matter. In time, she and Richard will come back to each other with a more mature understanding of marriage – an equal pact, a long-term adventure in which passion ebbs and flows but love hopefully remains. Jack will understand that his life is not with Isla. But for now, both are lost, and both turn to the past for answers. He hankers for the innocence and promise of their childhood love. She remembers what it was to feel really alive.

Should we judge her for the way she behaves? All I can say is that writing their summer idyll at Marshwood was a joyous experience, one of those precious times when characters return in spades all the energy their author puts into their creation. Given the circumstances – Isla's unhappiness, her history with Jack, his presence, Richard's absence, the yearning for love I have already written about – I don't know what else she could have done. She could of course have been strong and ignored the vital impulse which brought her to Jack's bed. But then she and Richard would have carried on just as before, with one more sacrifice for Isla to hold against him, and their relationship would have continued to degenerate. Crises, however painful, force us to re-evaluate our state of affairs. I know that other people – the book's early readers, editors and so on – have drawn different conclusions about Isla's behaviour, but I can't find it in myself to condemn her.

Louis

Family history plays a role in the genesis of *Some Other Eden*. Louis, the young Free French pilot who makes his way to Marshwood, was inspired by tales of my own father's godfather, himself a Free French pilot who spent a lot of time in England during the Second World War and who sadly disappeared in a sortie over France. He features in *Diving Into Light* as Mimi's absent brother. This is not, however, an account of a real man's life or character: if Isla was a difficult character to flesh out, Louis sprang from my keyboard fully formed and entirely, wholeheartedly himself.

An author friend of mine claims that there are only two plots: the one in which the main character goes on a journey, and the one in which a stranger comes to town. I'm not sure I agree with the general principle, but *Some Other Eden* does fall into the second category. Louis, like Jack, is the outsider whose presence precipitates change.

Louis loves laughter, music, dancing, the thrill of flying, France, tennis, gardening, cards, good food. This love of life, which transcends everything he has been through, is like manna from heaven for Bella and Clement, each lost in their own private misery. And he of course gleans solace from Marshwood – his own Eden. Yet there is a lack of balance about the relationship between these three. When all is said and done, one can't help feeling that Bella and Clement have taken more than they have given. They give little thought to Louis's traumas, perhaps because he disguises them so well, more likely because, for all their charm and outward generosity, they remain wrapped up in themselves and the little universe they have created for themselves at Marshwood. Bella, in refusing Louis, does the right thing by her husband. Clement, in telling Louis there is no longer any room for guests at Marshwood, speaks only the truth. And yet both have betrayed him. They know that Louis, despite his exile, the bitterness of his military experiences and his love for a married woman, is still and will forever remain an innocent, and that as such, he is deserving of more care.

There are people like Jack who stampede through our lives like rampaging bulls, wreaking chaos and turning everything upside-down. But isn't it often the case that, once the china has been replaced and the shop put back in order, these whirlwinds vanish as suddenly as they appeared? Whereas people like Louis linger longer, touching us with their gentle presence and getting under our skin in a way that makes them impossible to forget. Their legacy is one not of chaos but of light, of tenderness and grace and the glimpse they offer of something 'greater', beyond our everyday lives. Clement refers to Louis as an angel, and the more I think of it the more I agree. Despite the sadness of his parting from Bella, despite his untimely death, I smile every time I think of him.

It is impossible to write about *Some Other Eden* without lingering for a moment on Marshwood itself. It is based, of course, on a real house, though not one I have ever set foot inside, and I have taken huge liberties with its description (just as I have changed its name, and the names of all the surrounding places). But it does back on to an old fort, with magnificent views over the valley, and I used to walk past it regularly on country walks and dream of living there. If I owned such a place as this, I felt, I would never want to leave. I would fill it up with books and friends, I would write and bring up children and be eternally, blissfully happy. There are places which make you believe that this is possible, and it is very hard to give up the idea of them, even as you very sensibly tell yourself that happiness should and does not depend on bricks and mortar and splendid views. This is what Marshwood is to Clement and Bella, to Louis and to Isla, to Jack, ultimately even to Richard, whose extravagant purchase shows his wife that he has bought into the Marshwood myth. Richard parts with hard-earned cash to buy Marshwood. You could argue that the price Clement and Bella pay is Louis. In the end, Marshwood and its promise of happiness supersedes all else, and with their subtle sacrifice of Louis it becomes more than ever their *raison d'être*.

There are obvious, indeed deliberate similarities between Bella's and Isla's stories. Both fall for the 'stranger from out of town'. Though their responses are very different, with Isla living the relationship to the full where Bella holds back, both in a sense reclaim Marshwood through their actions: Bella by refusing Louis, Isla by giving in to Jack.

'What is your book about?' The question every author dreads, because how do you summarize months, even years of work in a few words? Sacrifice, compromise, passion, boredom, loyalty, betrayal, love consumed, love denied, love lost, love as something that grows, disappoints, changes, evades and reignites . . . Eyes soon glaze over, and succinct answers have their uses. If I had to give a one-word answer to the question for *Some Other Eden*, that word would be this: marriage. Because although it might seem more obviously to be a book about its counterpart, adultery, for me *Some Other Eden* celebrates the patient, battered, dogged qualities of that enduring institution. Bella and Louis, Isla and Jack: these are the glamorous, exciting lovers. But Bella and Clement, and Isla and Richard – these are the real couples, if only because they live together in the real world.

London, 24 August 2009